More praise for The Book of Jeremiah

"With scope, depth, and feeling, this novel in stories examines pivotal experiences in the long life of a single character: Jeremiah Gerstler, the son of Jewish immigrants, a loving husband and father, and an accomplished professor of political science. Zuckerman explores how these experiences shape Gerstler, change his perceptions of himself and others, and reverberate across time. The result is a moving, multifaceted portrait of a life, in all its dimensions."
—*Small Press Picks*

"In 13 skillfully crafted stories, Julie Zuckerman introduces us to Jeremiah Gerstler—the son, the father, the husband, the political science professor and the Jew . . . There is something familiar about Jeremiah, as if he is someone you know—perhaps a cousin, uncle, or friend. Each story can be read as a separate entity [but] bound together they form a moving and delightful novel that not only tells Jeremiah's story but also paints a picture of the Jewish experience across the decades . . . *The Book of Jeremiah* is Julie Zuckerman's debut collection of stories and it is a winner."
—*The Jerusalem Post*

"*The Book of Jeremiah* is a novel of stories full of rich imagery"
—*The New York Jewish Week*

"Zuckerman has carefully crafted a novel out of her stories, and one that repeats an echo throughout. It reads almost like a prophecy: something happens in the past and we know it will affect the future, we just don't know how. Again and again, themes and objects and people reappear in different stories and each time, we see them in a different light. Love and loss, courage and fear, religion and passion all take on new meaning as we move through the novel. Similarly, we vacillate between both sympathizing with and rooting against Jeremiah as we come to know him more truly. We love him and we hate him. We feel for him and we are annoyed by him. Zuckerman tastefully compiles her stories to give just the right effect."
—*Centered on Books*

THE BOOK OF
JEREMIAH

A NOVEL IN STORIES

JULIE ZUCKERMAN

Press 53
Winston-Salem

Press 53, LLC
PO Box 30314
Winston-Salem, NC 27130

First Edition

Cover image and design by Claire V. Foxx

Author photograph by Oz Schechter

Library of Congress Control Number
2019934221

Printed on acid-free paper
ISBN 978-1-941209-98-1

For my family

The author gratefully acknowledges the following journals in which these stories first appeared:

34th Parallel, Issue 16, 2011, "MixMaster"

American Athenaeum, Fall 2013, "Three Strikes"

Bryant Literary Review, Volume 16, 2015, "Gerstler's Triumphant Return"

The Dalhousie Review, Winter, 2013, "Transcendental"

The MacGuffin, Fall 2012, "Clandestiny"

Red Wheelbarrow, Volume 13, 2012, "Signals"

Salt Hill, Volume 38, Spring 2017, "A Strong Hand and an Outstretched Arm"

Sixfold, Winter 2013, "Birthday Bash," Winter 2015, "Tough Day for LBJ," Summer 2015 "The Book of Jeremiah"

Contents

A STRONG HAND AND AN OUTSTRETCHED ARM

(1938)

Rikki's son keeps the live chicken tucked under his arm, giving it a little *zetz* every time the wicked Haman's name is chanted. Rikki flinches with each squawk, but Jeremiah seems unconcerned by his mother's squeamishness. "Relax, what's to be afraid of?" says Rikki's husband. Leave it to Abe to dream up the Purim costume of a ritual slaughterer for their eleven-year-old, arranging with the fowl market in East Bridgeport to borrow the bird for the night. Mottled, tea-colored feathers drift to the floor, and Rikki collects them in tissues so the synagogue won't look like a chicken coop. Looped around Jeremiah's belt is a six-inch-long fake knife made out of plastic, a straight blade with no point at the end. Abe, son of a kosher butcher himself, has declared the imitation to be "very close" to what a real *shochet* would use, though the chicken does not seem worried.

When the reading is over, everyone shuffles into the social hall for the festive Purim activities. A few ladies shrink back at Jeremiah's chicken, but most people commend the Gerstlers for their creativity. Even the synagogue's Hebrew teacher is bemused, shedding his customary exasperation. "A better costume for him, you couldn't pick!" Rikki offers a tight, uncomfortable smile. She detects an underhanded compliment; the man is not in the habit of heaping praise on her middle child. "A firm hand at home, some discipline, is what he needs," the teacher had said only a few weeks ago, following Jeremiah's second or third prank in class. *Oy vey is mir.* Abe's many good qualities do not include toughness in the discipline department.

Now, waiting for the magician and costume contest to begin, Rikki chats with her girlfriends while keeping an eye on her children. Lenny stands off to the side with another gangly fourteen-year-old, and Ruthie plays clapping games with two friends, all three little girls dressed as Queen Esther, the heroine of tonight's story. Jeremiah is surrounded by a circle of boys waving their hands in his face. He bounces up and down, organizing the group into a line. An older boy fumbles with something in his pocket and procures two coins in exchange for a turn with the chicken. *What in the world?* Her son checks his wristwatch, and after a minute signals to the boy that his time is up. With one hand he reclaims the bird, extending his other palm to the next boy in line.

"No!" Rikki arrives as the second boy fishes two pennies out of his pocket. "We've got to give this chicken back tomorrow and we can't pass him around. Put your money away."

"Ma. . ." Jeremiah starts, but his disappointment seems mild. He points to the older boy. "I'm not giving Howie back his money. He already got his turn."

She doesn't have to look far to see where he comes up with these cockamamie ideas. Abe, over in the corner with a group of men, seems barely older than a boy himself, a baseball cap in place of his yarmulke. Her husband chuckles whenever she conveys the Hebrew teacher's reports of Jeremiah's mischief-making and his recent insistence their son is becoming a big troublemaker. *So, nu, he put a caterpillar inside his teacher's yarmulke?* Abe asks. *That's a good one!*

"Poor dear! He's going to give you a heart condition," says her friend Toby, who looks pale and gaunt herself.

There's a magician entertaining the younger children, but Jeremiah amuses himself by sneaking up on unsuspecting girls and making the bird squawk. They squeal, run to their parents, but again Abe says, "What's to be afraid of? That scrawny thing couldn't feed a family of two!"

During the costume fashion show, the audience gives hefty applause to a boy dressed as Haman and a girl dressed as the Scroll of Esther. To Rikki's surprise, the clapping intensifies when Jeremiah takes his turn. "Terrific get-up," she hears. The chicken twists and strains, as if wanting to escape, and her son makes a show of it, screwing his face into funny expressions.

"A regular performer," Abe's pals say, patting him on the back. Rikki would like to scurry after Jeremiah to collect the shedding feathers, but Abe holds her back. "See how he carries himself in a crowd," Abe whispers, admiring. She wishes her affectionate feelings for Jeremiah would come more naturally; she is nagged by guilt that they don't. She knows she shouldn't compare her boys, but from Lenny she gets *nachas,* pride in his accomplishments; from Jeremiah only *tsorres.* Troubles and more troubles. Thank goodness for Ruthie, still sweet and huggable at five.

A hush falls over the crowd as the rabbi announces the results of the costume contest. He proclaims Jeremiah as the overall winner, and the little *shochet* beams as if he's just eaten a month's worth of brisket. He bounds up to the stage to collect his prize, holding the chicken over his head in a victory pose. Even at a distance, Rikki recognizes the mischievous gleam in her son's eye. All her alarm bells go off. Jeremiah holds the bird by its neck and raises it above his head. She recites a silent prayer that he won't begin swinging it or fling the poor creature into the crowd. Frowning, the rabbi leans over to whisper something to Jeremiah. At once, the impish grin recedes, and Jeremiah tucks the chicken back under his arm. Rikki is faint with relief, but mortified, her cheeks scarlet: the rabbi obviously senses her son is a troublemaker, and his parents, failures.

The rabbi laughs. "Wrong holiday!" Never wasting an educational opportunity, he explains: waving a chicken over the head to atone for sins is performed before Yom Kippur, not Purim.

"You see?" Abe whispers. "He knows he hasn't behaved well lately, so he's repenting."

Rikki's throat is dry. She's never heard her son express remorse for his mischief. "Repent?" she asks. "I should live so long."

◆ ◆ ◆

Passover follows quickly on the heels of Purim; no sooner is one holiday finished than Rikki must start preparing for the next. She's sitting in Abe's easy chair in their wood-paneled den, compiling lists of cleaning schedules and menus when a loud rapping at the front door startles her. Her hand flies to her chest and she takes a deep breath, trying to steady the hammering in her ribcage. Seventeen years in America and still she associates the sound with angry mobs, the pogroms that raged throughout Poland before they'd left, the sneers of local bullies who made a sport of humiliating Jewish boys by pulling down their pants or shoving them into the bushes. Her brother, one of the few who stood up to them and returned their taunts, paid for his wisecracks with blood and bruises. Through the window, she sees it's just an errand boy. Her momentary relief evaporates when she rips open the envelope he's given her: she's been summoned for a meeting with Mr. Pennyford, the headmaster at Jeremiah's elementary school. Her son is a few months away from graduating from the sixth grade. *Vey is mir.*

An hour later she is in Mr. Pennyford's office, file cabinets lining the walls, diplomas on display, a dim photograph of an army regiment from the Great War on his desk. Though he's ushered her in and indicated for her to sit, he doesn't speak for several long moments. Rikki's hands shake, her stomach clenches. Mr. Pennyford flips through a yellow pad filled with notes, his lips cheerless and pursed.

The headmaster clears his throat and begins reciting a litany of problems. Today's incident: Jeremiah leaving a dead mouse wrapped up in a fancy box on his teacher's desk. Thinking it a gift, she'd opened it and ran screaming out of the classroom.

Rikki covers her eyes with her hand, shaking her head in consternation. Mr. Pennyford is not finished. *Jeremiah displays no respect for his teacher or any authority. He's becoming a wise-mouth.* As he reads from his list, her heart sinks with each accusation.

"He's clever," Mr. Pennyford says. "Always does well on his tests. But he's become a problem. A few weeks ago, someone 'borrowed' tools from the janitor's cart and used them to 'fix' the radiators in Jeremiah's classroom, so it was too hot to sit inside. It's taken some investigating, but your son was definitely the main perpetrator." His tone is angry, threatening. "That's called vandalism, Mrs. Gerstler. I could have gotten the police involved, you know!"

"What?" The floor should open up to swallow her.

"The police! Destruction of school property is unacceptable. A crime, in fact!"

She is speechless, shaking her head, afraid to ask: *what now?* A queasy sensation travels from her gut to her throat; she swallows and prays she will not be sick in his office.

Mr. Pennyford continues: she should not be surprised to know that he's been forced to whip the boy from time to time. "Most boys try to keep this from their parents, because they'll get worse beatings at home."

She nods at this logic. "I guess. . . .I'm sure you do what you have to do." Immediately she is stricken with guilt. *Some kind of mother she is, encouraging the whipping of her own son.*

"Consider this a warning. If he doesn't quit this behavior, or if there is any more vandalism, he's out. Should I so much as find his name drawn on a desk with a pencil, I'll send him to Stratford!"

Tears form in Rikki's eyes and she tries to blink them back. Underneath her pocketbook, her hands crumple and uncrumple a tissue. "Stratford?" she asks, her voice a whisper.

"A special school for delinquents." Mr. Pennyford makes a clucking sound.

Delinquents! She doesn't like this harsh, English word, which makes her think of junior gangsters. Rikki forces down a mixture of dread and anger at Mr. Pennyford's insinuation. Jeremiah is a bit like her brother Leibish, afraid of no one, always getting into trouble. But a criminal? Impossible. And yet she feels a chill, a speck of doubt. This is what they've struggled for, all these years in America, that their son should be a no-goodnik?

"It would be a real shame for a smart boy like him to have to go to that place," he says.

"He's a boy, is all," she mumbles in protest. She wants to tell Mr. Pennyford that her son is kindhearted and easygoing like his father.

How, during the worst of the Depression, Jeremiah befriended the out-of-work tramps on East Main Street and insisted on bringing them holiday leftovers. But her English fails her. Her eyes are blurry; she can no longer hold back her tears. She wipes at her face, apologizing.

"I see this is quite a shock, especially as Leonard never causes any trouble."

She nods and wishes for the thousandth time that Jeremiah would be more like his older brother. Mr. Pennyford offers her a fresh tissue. Her Zeyde Wolf was a schoolmaster; how would he have reacted to such behavior from his American-born great-grandson? But he could no more imagine Rikki's life in America than she could know what it had been like to be smuggled out of Russia dressed as a woman to escape the Czar's army. And would he even recognize her, his own granddaughter, who, soon after she arrived in the country, changed the "v" in Rivki to a "k" because it sounded more American?

She pictures her little boy in the school for delinquents and remembers that Stratford is where one of the Schlossberg boys had been sent; instead of mending his ways, the toughs there only pushed him further down a ruinous path of gambling debts, brawls, and who knows what else? The family fled back to Brooklyn in shame. The last she heard, someone had taken up a collection to help the poor parents with legal fees after the boy had been arrested.

She gathers her courage. "I've just remembered some things about that school. Isn't it a bit extreme, what you're proposing, based on his offenses? Has he been violent?"

Mr. Pennyford stands, flipping his legal pad to the front, signaling an end to their meeting. "No, but we often see behaviors like this as the first step. See that your husband has a talk with him."

Rikki nods at Mr. Pennyford's suggestion, despite her internal skepticism, the voice in her head saying, *you should only know*. She's beginning to understand—seventeen years into her marriage—that Abe's tendency to shy away from conflict is a disastrous flaw in child-rearing. She shakes Mr. Pennyford's hand, thanking him for his time. "You should live and be well, Mr. Pennyford, but I hope we don't meet again until sixth-grade graduation."

◆ ◆ ◆

Abe's late hours—his liquor store open until 11:00 p.m. most nights—
make it difficult for Rikki to have a long discussion with her husband
on any matter. And she's heard enough about Abe's own shenanigans as
a young boy to know that she has no choice but to handle this herself.

"It's very serious, what you did, breaking that radiator," she tells
Jeremiah. "Do you understand that?"

"Aw, that was just a prank," he says. "All the fellows were jazzed
up when we had our lessons on the playground."

She pictures the scene: sixth-grade boys whooping with joy,
celebrating her son's sabotage. "You can't do that. You just can't! Do
you want to go to a school with horrible boys? Criminals? Because
that's where you're headed, according to Mr. Pennyford."

He shrugs and mumbles, "Fine."

Next, Rikki insists he write an apology to his teacher for the dead
mouse, but when he hands it to her for examination, the note is so
sloppy and insincere she crumples it in disgust. The boy must be taught
some respect, be made to feel the consequences of his actions. She
marches into his room and scoops up his marbles.

"Noooo! You can't take 'em!"

"I can and I will. Start behaving, mister, and then we'll see."

"But that's my special Akro set. Lenny gave them to me!"

"Well, they're mine for now." She remembers how proud he'd been
when his older brother deemed him a crack marble player, worthy of
such a gift, but she announces her conquest with childish triumph.

Rikki plans to seek advice from her girlfriends at their weekly card
game that evening, but when she arrives they are preoccupied with
more troublesome news: their friend Toby Solomon has been diagnosed
with the dread disease, a horrible fate for Toby, Max, and their three
children. They form a rotation to prepare meals for the family. They
will sit with Toby when she's up for visitors. Toby shouldn't fuss with
Passover, they agree, so Rikki will host the Solomons for one seder
and someone else will have them at the other. What's five more guests
when she's cooking for twenty? An extra potato *kugel*, a few more
kneidelach, a larger brisket.

Rikki is glad she hasn't mentioned her summons to the headmaster; she loves her friends but can easily picture raised eyebrows at her son's behavior. Better she shouldn't give them fodder for tittle-tattle.

Later in the week, Lenny reports seeing Jeremiah shove another boy, and Rikki worries that Mr. Pennyford is right—the kind of impulsive behavior her son is exhibiting is only one step away from more aggressive acts. Each time she tries to mend something, her stitches come out uneven and she rips them out. She snaps at Ruthie for spilling juice on her dress. The lilac bushes in their small yard bud and flower but bring her little comfort this year. On Abe's one early night at home, she starts an argument with him when he insists he doesn't need to hire extra help in the store. "I think you *like* working long hours. This way you don't have to deal with your family responsibilities."

"That's enough, Rikki."

"You want our son should be a no-goodnik? Like Harry Schlossberg?"

"*Genug*!" he yells, banging his hand on the table to make his point: enough.

"Me, you're angry at?" She tells him he's not doing Jeremiah any favors by slapping him on the back in approval of his pranks, or all his talk of the things *he and his friends* used to pull on their teacher. The Stratford school is serious business. And she can't shake the comparison with her brother the wise guy, coming home with bloodstained shirts and once a broken nose.

"He's a boy, is all," says Abe. "Try not to let all the little things bother you so much."

"Little things?" she says, bristling.

Listening from the next room, Lenny calls out that he's heard Jeremiah has been running around school halls with an arithmetic book on his head and singing racy songs.

"Downstairs, Jeremiah! Right now!" She asks Lenny to join them; Jeremiah adores his older brother, and she hopes he'll be able to talk some sense into him.

"Mr. Pennyford was very clear," Rikki says when the four of them are gathered around the table. She rests her hands on the gleaming red enamel. "If you keep messing around, he'll kick you out. Or call the police, if you vandalize anything again."

"That was a prank, I told you." Jeremiah turns to his father. "A pretty good one, too!"

Abe is trying to suppress a smile; she darts him a look.

"Yes, no more vandalism!" Abe says. "And where did you learn racy songs?" Is that a wink he gives his son? Are they smirking?

"Abe!" She waits a beat to see if he has anything to say.

"And what's this about a fistfight. . ." she starts.

"Listen here, Jeremiah." Lenny chimes in, trying to take on the role Abe won't, but his inflection is patronizing. "You've got to knock it off. Do you want to be known as a screwball? That's what the boys call you. I know you're trying to be funny. But quit it."

"Hardy-har-har," says Jeremiah. "Poor Lenny. Your brother is a screwball." His voice drips with insolence. "Maybe you should try to joke around a little more." Rikki closes her eyes, fearful of what will come next. She understands, too late, that she shouldn't have included Lenny in the meeting. Jeremiah's idolization of his brother is long dead. "Maybe then you'd have a couple more pals yourself. Be less of a crumb."

She gasps. Lenny does not lunge at him, as Rikki would have in his place. Lenny clamps down his jaw and pinches his lips together, his face seems to crumple. Whether Jeremiah belittles his brother to spite his parents or out of real ill will towards Lenny, she doesn't know.

"Apologize to your brother," she says. Rikki is certain Abe will demand the same.

"Son, I hate to do this, but you're leaving me no choice. One more incident and I'll confiscate your comic books *and* baseball card collection."

That's it? Rikki wants to scream. Jeremiah shrugs, as if to say, *so what?*

"Apologize right now," she repeats. Jeremiah smirks again. Her anger white hot, she reaches across the table and smacks him across the face, toppling over Abe's glass of juice. Sticky orange pulp spills over the enamel surface and streams onto the floor.

"Rikki!" Abe's eyes widen in surprise.

"What's the matter with you?" she yells at her son. Her hand smarts, and rings of pain reverberate up her arm. Jeremiah rubs the raw red mark on his cheek, blinking back tears. "How can you talk like this? Go to your room!"

Jeremiah runs from the table, but what leaves her cold is Abe's condemnation. He's frowning, working his jaw. She grabs a rag, wets it, and begins to mop up her mess. Has she gone too far? She tosses the rag in the sink and beckons Lenny for a hug before excusing him. "Just ignore him," she whispers.

"Are you finished now?" Abe asks when they're alone. "You think this is the right way?"

"Finished? I don't know the right way. But I can't tolerate his behavior!" She's at the sink, rinsing the rag and wringing out the extra water with force. Her hand burns.

"So you smack him?"

She faces him, seething. "You never discipline him. Always I have to be the bad guy! If you wouldn't be such a weak example of a father, he wouldn't pull this *shtick*."

Abe's mouth opens in disbelief. Vehemence in his eyes instead of the usual merry sparkle. Her words are jagged pieces of glass, piercing his blown up sense of Abe-the-all-around-good-guy.

"My father didn't appease. A few times with the belt buckle and that was enough. A firm hand from his father is what he needs. Everyone says so. And if you won't do it, I'll have to!"

"You want that I should hit him, too? Hmm?" Abe's eyes flash with anger but his voice remains steady.

"You're poisoning my relationship with him!"

"No, Rikki. It's not me." He sounds weary, almost sad. But then: "Maybe what he needs is a mother who reaches out to him! Who doesn't lavish praise on one son and not the other!"

Abe doesn't hurl retaliations often; his words lacerate. For a few moments they glower at each other and then Abe stomps off, slamming the back door. Her heart beats wildly, but she forces herself not to give into the tears stinging the corners of her eyes. She rests her head in her hands.

In a moment, she will rise. Passover is coming and there is much to be done; twenty-five people counting on her. Her thoughts dart to the Solomons and what will become of Toby's children; Rikki was eight years old when her own mother died. Her life's most enduring sadness has only grown with the years; could Rikki have been a different kind of mother if she'd had one on which to model herself? She wipes her hands on her apron and surveys her kitchen. The glare from the sunlight is harsh, illuminating the dust and crumbs in the hard-to-reach corners.

She chips off a piece of ice from the bottom of the icebox and wraps it in a rag. She finds Jeremiah lying on his bed, his eyes puffy. "Here," she says, placing it gingerly on his face. "I brought you this." She is ready to stay and explain herself, but Jeremiah squeezes his eyes shut, refusing to look at her.

"Go away," he says. "Just go!"

Five days before the holiday, the kitchen is fully *kashered*, rid of flour and bread and other items that are not permissible on Passover. The everyday and Shabbos dishes are in boxes in the basement and in their place are the special cookware and plates Rikki will need to prepare the seder meal. She has wiped down every cabinet and scoured the counters. Sunlight streams into the kitchen at an angle that adds to its shine, and though her arms ache from scrubbing she takes pride in the accomplishment.

"A floor you could eat off of," Abe says. Thank goodness his anger is never long-lived.

She beams. Jeremiah's behavior has improved since the family conference last week, and she's cautiously optimistic. Her son has stopped snickering when Mr. Pennyford's name is mentioned. Though Abe maintains it's the threat of losing his baseball cards or comic books, Rikki thinks she may have slapped some sense into him. Baby steps towards maturity, she hopes.

In the last two days before the holiday, she cooks from morning to night. There are never fewer than three dishes being prepared simultaneously. Rikki schools Ruthie in peeling vegetables and has her mix the batters for the wine and sponge cakes. The air is thick with the smell of cooked carrots soaking in a honey and raisin sauce and with the rich, meaty aroma of three batches of chicken soup. Rikki ticks off the menu items in her mind and tries to quiet constant worries: *will she have enough food?* Her eyes are raw and red from chopping onions, and every so often she must shake out the palm of her hand, numb from grating potatoes. But these tasks she does lovingly: despite the backbreaking work, Passover is her favorite holiday. Plus, the preparations are a diversion from Toby, who looked awful when Rikki last visited her. Max, who had dark circles under his eyes, told her what she already suspected: Toby is not responding to the treatments.

Now, fully ensconced in her cooking and unable to leave the house, Rikki dispatches Jeremiah to the fishmonger. He is to purchase the carp needed for her *gefilte* fish—one of her most-loved dishes, widely praised at family events. She gives him specific instructions on the size, approximate weight, and color of scales.

Within an hour, he's back. Rikki unties the bundle, her nose alerting her before her eyes.

"I said a carp, not a pike!"

"Ma, I swear I thought that's what he gave me!"

"I gave you specific instructions."

"I know. Sorry, Ma," he says, before adding, "but can't you use a pike instead?"

This is true, but she and Abe both prefer the oily-tasting carp to the milder pike, and the thought of enduring a lecture by her sister-in-law on the topic is unbearable. "Yes, but I *needed* a carp. Now the fish will have no taste!"

"I'll tell you why he got the pike, Ma," Lenny says, appearing at the door of the kitchen. "Because it costs two pennies less per pound. I'll bet you a dime he took the change and bought himself some licorice at Finkle's." He looks his brother up and down, nodding. "That's about your size."

Jeremiah lunges at his brother, shoving him out of the room. "Hey!" Lenny cries. He shoves back and stands with his fists clenched.

"Jeremiah!" She notices a thin black line around his lips, confirming Lenny's accusation. "Is this true?"

Jeremiah says nothing.

"Come here," she commands, but he stays rooted to the floor. "Don't you know how lucky you are to have a Papa who provides for you? This is how you thank us, with lies and stealing?"

He looks at the ground, his cheeks flushed.

"Don't you ever think of other people? Look how helpful Ruthie is being. And look how Lenny studies! We're scrimping and saving for him to go to college. And you, selfishly wasting money on candy! Come here."

She reaches into his pocket and pulls out a candy wrapper. Soon, she won't be able to do this; he'll be too big and strong. She thinks of her father and of Leibish. If she doesn't start teaching Jeremiah lessons now, it will be too late. She grabs his arm and turns him around, her right hand raised. *Smack!* Four smacks across his *tuchus*. She heaves with exertion, shots of pain radiating from her hand up to her shoulder. She is about to get the belt strap when she sees Ruthie whimpering in the corner. Her mixing spoon has clattered to the floor, tears are streaming down her face, and she is calling *Mama, Mama, stop.*

"I said I was sorry," he says, sputtering before he sprints out of the room. He returns a few seconds later and throws down four pennies on the kitchen floor. "There's your change!"

"I didn't raise you to be a liar or a *gonif*, mister!"

"I wish you were dying," he yells, running out. "Like Mrs. Solomon."

He doesn't mean it. He can't mean it. She quivers for a moment, but steels herself, blinking several times. No tears. She closes her ears and pretends not to hear a thing.

By four o'clock on the evening of the holiday, the furniture is rearranged; two extra tables extend from the end of the dining room table and into the living room. Twenty-five place settings and wine glasses line the table, along with makeshift paper place cards decorated in crayon by Ruthie. With the cooking complete and Ruthie down for a nap, Rikki sinks into her bed for a few blessed minutes. The aches in her feet and back are immediately soothed. Her mind still races.

Tonight they will read the *haggadah,* recounting how God redeemed the Children of Israel from slavery in Egypt with a strong hand and an outstretched arm. Rikki and Abe have their own Exodus story, leaving the old country for a better life here. *Her* children will never be forced to hide in a barn for three days during a pogrom. They've been in America almost half their lives, and her appreciation for the country has not waned, though for the first time she wonders if her children are too soft. Perhaps a double dose of determination and gratitude would do Jeremiah some good. The boys know the stories from the *shtetl,* and here in Bridgeport they've witnessed men panhandling on the sidewalks and hobos lining up for soup kitchens—surely Jeremiah knows how fortunate he is. He apologized for his outburst the other day, and she doesn't think he'll make problems tonight, with the whole family gathered and Abe running the seder with his usual jollity. ("In every generation," states the *haggadah*, each person must act as if he or she was personally redeemed out of slavery, but Abe always tries to make the seder fun and memorable for the children).

Seders by the Gerstlers start late, only after Abe returns home from the liquor store. The guests begin arriving at 10:00 p.m., everyone in their holiday best, and the kitchen bustles with activity. Though Max Solomon and his children are in quiet, somber moods, Toby has put on a bit of rouge and insists she's feeling well enough to help. Rikki's not sure she believes this, but she seats her in the kitchen and tasks her with shelling the hard-boiled eggs.

Bowls of saltwater are prepared, matzah is placed on the table, and finally at eleven after Abe is home and changed, they sit down to read the haggadah. The aroma of chicken soup emanates from the kitchen, hearty and nourishing, and Rikki thinks it might be the best smell in the world, though they will not arrive at the festive Passover meal until page seventeen. She sits at one end of the long table, closest to the kitchen, with Abe and the boys all the way at the opposite end. She is filled with the warmth of her holiday table. She loves their new Maxwell House Haggadahs, the traditional Hebrew text on one side, an English translation on the other. A coffee company distributing free Jewish books—only in America! They take turns reciting the passages. Ruthie and the other small children chant the Four Questions beautifully.

It's after midnight, but the children are wide awake and engaged in the rituals. Abe asks various guests to get up out of their seats and act out different parts of the story. Those playing Israelites pantomime hauling boulders while others act as their Egyptian taskmasters, standing over them with hands on hips, demanding they work faster, faster. The three Gerstler children are Moses, Aaron, and Miriam, leading a group of guests through the parting of the Red Sea. Others are designated to play the roles of the four sons—wise, rebellious, simple, and the one who does not know how to ask—and must then answer questions about the Passover story in character. Abe's creativity is a gift; these are the moments Rikki feels blessed.

They begin reciting the Ten Plagues, dipping their pinkies into their wine glasses and spilling drops of red wine on their plates for each plague. *Dam, tzfardea, kinim, arov.* Blood, frogs, lice, wild beasts, and so on. Each affliction meant to soften Pharaoh's hard heart and convince him to free the slaves. They chant the list by rote.

At Abe's end of the table, a sudden commotion. Rikki hears tiny shrieks, then a clapping of hands, then exclamations of "oh my god!" People are scrambling up from their chairs and away from the table, and it takes Rikki several seconds to understand. Several live frogs have been let loose on the seder table. Frogs! Jumping from plate to plate, on Rikki's good Passover dishes! She glowers at Abe—this is too much—but his mouth is dropped open in surprise. A shoebox sits on Jeremiah's plate; he is trying to coax the last one out.

"Jeremiah!" Rikki screams. Blood is rushing to her head and she thinks she might pass out. The nerve, to unleash vermin in her spotless house. On her *dishes*! "Get them out of here!"

Her son grins his *who, me?* look. But then he hops around the table, making a show of catching the frogs. The dark brown spots running down the creatures' backs in two neat columns seem almost hand-drawn, and when Rikki catches sight of a fleshy orange underside she feels a wave of nausea.

"Abe! Do something!"

But he doesn't hear her, not over the shrieks coming from her sisters-in-law and nieces. Rikki knocks over her chair, her face is aflame, scrambling to collect dishes. She tries to hurry down to the other end of the table to implore Jeremiah, to grab hold of her boy and shake him, but so many people are out of their seats that she can't move quickly. Jeremiah ducks underneath and around the table and chairs, trying to catch the last frog; he is oblivious to her fury, or perhaps, he's anticipated it in advance and is avoiding looking at her. With a sickening feeling she wonders if he pulled the stunt for the sole purpose of baiting her.

The speckled critter jumps in and out of the saltwater and proves adept at evading human hands. It lands on Cousin Sussie's neck, causing her to faint and slump against her husband. The men and boys join in the effort to catch the frog. Two glasses of wine are knocked over, red liquid spatters onto the table; thank goodness she'd put a thick clear plastic covering over the tablecloths. Rikki grabs the bowl of *charoset*, lest the frog jump in the "mortar" of apples, wine, walnuts and cinnamon. Several other women grab the matzah plates and small dishes of horseradish and celery to protect the ritual items from being spoiled. Rikki feels as if she is floating, detached, watching the scene from above. "A few frogs, what's to be afraid of?" Did her husband really just say this? *Vey is mir.*

Sussie comes to just as Jeremiah catches the last frog. His breaths come in rapid, heavy gasps, but he is looking to his father, triumphant with his mischief-making. The whole thing may have only taken a few minutes, but Rikki's holiday is ruined. She feels split: she imagines the whipping she will give, pain reverberating in her arm, already palpable. The other part of her propels into action, grabbing every plate touched by a frog. She must scrub every surface. She calls for people to hand her their plates, their glasses—anything that the filthy creatures may have touched. Where had he gotten them from, her little devil?

Rikki works mechanically, but through her fog she hears someone— no, a number of people—clapping and laughing. She doesn't understand how this can be, until she sees that her husband is leading the applause, the look on his face one of pure pride. "Atta boy, Jeremiah. That's the way to make the plagues come alive!" Abe turns to his cousin. "Come, come now, Sussie, you're fine!" Sussie nods though her face is peaked. Abe says to Rikki, "You see, she's fine. Maybe a glass of water."

Though some of the men and boys are heaving with exertion, Rikki can't escape their grins. Max and his kids are smiling for the first time this evening, and even Toby's cheeks are red with merriment. "Terrific stunt!" they say. "Did you see that last guy, with the big eyes? He hopped right out of the saltwater—I guess he's a freshwater frog!"

Abe motions for her to sit, but with a sharp shake of the head she indicates no. "If four frogs caused such a disruption to our seder," he says, "imagine what those hundreds of frogs would have been like for Pharoah!" Max and Abe laugh so hard, tears roll down their cheeks.

"I sincerely hope you haven't unleashed lice on us, or locusts!" someone says.

Sussie's cheeks return to their normal hue. The sisters-in-law sit down. Toby's eyes are glistening and gay and she thanks Jeremiah for the chuckle.

"Rikki, sit!" Her arms are full of plates and she is making her way back to the kitchen.

"Abe!" With one word she silences him; he won't try to interfere with her mission to free the dishes from amphibian germs. But when she returns to collect more things he seems to be looking at her with great sadness. He's always urging her to lighten up, to not worry so much, to relax, to enjoy life. But how could he think that live frogs in their house, in front of their guests—even *on* one of their guests—is acceptable?

And yet the guests have survived. Lenny is studying his brother with admiration. This will be a seder to remember, one that is talked about in the family lore: *remember the year Jeremiah brought the frogs?*

"You should keep going," Rikki says to Abe now, indicating the haggadah, "otherwise we'll never get to the meal." Her breathing has steadied, and she takes a long look at her son, whose face is flushed with triumph. She can almost see his mind turning and planning stunts for future seders.

"Go help your mother," Abe says to Jeremiah. "And bring another rag for the wine."

Jeremiah scampers in and out of the kitchen, doing her bidding. She's sent the other women who've offered to help back to their seats.

"It was a joke," he says when they're alone.

She holds up her hand to stop him. "I know." Her voice is firm. The swinging door between the kitchen and the dining room is shut but she can hear her family and friends carrying on with the seder.

Jeremiah's eyes cloud over, as if he knows what's coming. It is loud in the other room. The whimpers of a boy might not be heard. His expression is despondent, similar to the sad look Abe cast her way a few minutes ago. Her son is no longer glowing in triumph or shiny with childish excitement. Because of her. No one else—sisters-in-law excepted, perhaps—has taken her son for a no-goodnik, an emerging scoundrel. Only Rikki, his own mother.

Jeremiah looks at the floor. "Sorry, Ma," he says, mumbling to his shoelaces. "I thought it would be fun. Sorry if I wrecked your seder."

But it is I who have squelched your delight, she thinks. Was Abe any different as a child? And hadn't she been elated to leave the austerity of her father's house and make her life with someone who knew how to be jovial and make others happy? Early in the marriage, she'd get tearful if she overcooked a brisket or if her cookies came out hard as rocks, but Abe would eat every bite, making funny quips instead of reprimanding for the waste.

She grasps his shoulders and he tenses. What does he see in her face? She pulls him to her in an embrace, surprising them both. In reaction, he squeezes her hard, as if he's holding on before parting forever, asking forgiveness for every time he's hurt her.

"Well, you made Toby and Max laugh," she says into his hair. That's worth something, she knows. She wants so much to protect him, to mold his character into what she thinks is proper. *Relax, what's to worry?* Abe's voice reverberates in her mind. *He's a boy, is all.*

"Please God," she prays silently, still holding her son, "may my arms always be outstretched to my children." She does not want to be cast off in the desert, like the older generation of Israelite slaves who lived to see their freedom but not the Promised Land. Her son loosens his hold, but she draws him in and clutches him a bit longer.

THE BOOK OF JEREMIAH

(2006)

Jeremiah rips the packaging, hands quaking and breath drawn. His fingers feel nimble, like those of a child tearing open a gift. The brown paper lies in shreds on the floor and he clasps the thick volume, holding it at arm's length for the initial assessment. His eyes take a few seconds to focus on the title: *Globalization and Crisis: Essays on the International Political Economy in Honor of Professor Jeremiah Gerstler's 80th Birthday*. Eighteen essays—six of his own and twelve of his colleagues and former students—reflecting a lifetime of scholarship. A faint smell of glue springs from the spine, and he inhales with gusto. He fingers the crisp, sharp pages. As soon as he clears the lump in his throat, he'll phone his editor to commend him on the final product.

Jeremiah has read and commented on all the articles, seen the galleys, and had one of his grad students proof them three times. The one thing he hasn't seen—Peter wouldn't let him—are the introductory dedications. "Trust me, you'll be pleased," his editor said.

"A Festschrift," Peter said, proposing the idea a little over a year ago.

"Get outta here," Jeremiah replied, swatting away the suggestion with a flick of his wrist. Secretly he was thrilled, and wanted to run home to tell Molly. A book written in one's honor symbolized the pinnacle of an illustrious career, and he truly did not know the appropriate reaction. "Is this the University's way of telling me to retire?"

They bantered back and forth, Jeremiah insisting he didn't want anyone fussing over him, Peter rolling his eyes and ticking off a list of potential contributors. Ten minutes of weak protestations before he acquiesced. *The Book of Jeremiah*, Peter took to calling it. ("Oh, I hope not," Molly said of the nickname. "That's all doom and gloom.")

Now, Jeremiah brews a cup of tea and parks himself in his reading chair, deliberately not extending the footrest. He wants to be fully awake to examine the volume, to savor its freshness. Sunlight streams into his study. The rays dance on the spines of his books and on the framed photo hanging on the wall: he and Molly surrounded by their five grandchildren. Pity his parents aren't alive to see this moment. He could guess, though, what his father might say: *Never mind the fancy honors.* Abe Gerstler's accented English rings inside his head. *I just want my boy should be a mensch.*

There are four dedications in the volume: from the poli-sci department chair, two former students, and Hannah Gerstler, Ph.D., Assistant Professor of International Affairs at Williams College. He swells with pride every time he sees Hannah's name. Her piece is lovely, a testament to his influence on her and on his field, but as he reads the other dedications he gets a clammy, sour taste in his mouth. *Feh!* They extol his research, mention the four times in his career he's foreseen events or trends, but nary a one mentions his devotion to students, family, community, or anything remotely personal. A goldfish could have written more inspiring tributes. Perhaps in his excitement, he's missed the gratifying phrases. He skims the pages, seeking words and anecdotes to make him sound more likeable, not just someone with a "quick analytical mind" or "sharp intellect that's transformed the field."

Again he hears his father's voice: *What's to expect? Es libt zich alain shemt zich alain.* He who praises himself will be humiliated. Though Abe, when he was alive, often boasted to his friends about "my son, the professor," Jeremiah is skeptical as to whether his father— a simple but generous, convivial soul who performed quiet acts of charity—truly valued his chosen profession. A life in medicine, or some other helping vocation, would have made his parents prouder.

"Professor Gerstler is deeply committed to a correct reading of the sources. Woe to the student who comes to class unprepared or attempts a less-than-airtight analysis," reads one dedication. "He demands rigorous standards of his students and does not tolerate academic laziness." *These you call dedications?* He wants to scream. *Woe to the student?* The underlying message is that Professor Jeremiah Gerstler, despite his academic achievements, is mercurial, volatile, and impulsive.

Jeremiah heaves himself out of the recliner and hides the book in his desk, slamming the drawer shut. He wanders into the kitchen in search of some chocolate or a piece of his wife's blueberry pie as a temporary assuagement. Hanging on the fridge is the invitation to the reception in honor of the book's publication. Molly will try to drag him. "Forget it," he says aloud to no one. "Not on your life!"

Molly takes her time reading the dedications, every so often glancing up to mention a nice phrase. "They're not bad at all! I don't understand why you're so upset."

Jeremiah grunts. He could have predicted she would say he's being too sensitive, too touchy. "You don't get it. I've seen other Festschriften in my day. The dedications are much nicer. Trust me." He hates that she won't admit to an honest reading of the text.

"But can't you see the bigger picture? This whole thing is a testament to you. A huge honor!" She adjusts her reading glasses and points. "Here, in Jim Blackwell's dedication, it says that the university's been able to attract top students because of your reputation. That's gratifying, isn't it?"

"Forget it!" He snaps, frustration growing. They've been together more than fifty years, and she's always trying to whitewash slights against him. He'd feel better if she would just grant his indignation some legitimacy. "I'm sick of talking about this with someone who can't understand!" Not that he has anyone else to talk to. He doesn't want to be around anyone right now, even her—especially her. He grabs his car keys and bangs out the front door.

"Where are you going?" Molly calls. He trudges down the driveway, waving her off. The oppressive August humidity gives the Berkshires air a stiff, suffocating quality. "Fine. Be that way!"

He slams the car door and turns on the A/C at full blast, starting to drive without any destination in mind. His favorite spot on campus or the library? He can't face Peter yet. Or Marcella, that obtuse grad student, who'd seen the dedications and failed to mention anything. He drives along Route 7 for a few minutes with half a mind to drive all the way up to Williamstown to see his grandson, or just sit in a shady spot, gazing up at Mount Greylock, but it's too damn hot. His navy and white gym bag lies on the floor of the passenger side; he'd forgotten to bring it inside yesterday. His bathing trunks and towel will be a bit damp, but a swim will do him good.

The façade of the Jewish Community Center is a diamond lattice grid meant to look like a repeating Star of David, though in Jeremiah's mind it resembles an egg carton. Six- and seven-year-olds from Camp JCC race past Jeremiah, their counselors trailing behind and admonishing them not to run in the halls. The building buzzes with activity; the walls are decorated with pictures from nursery school graduation and recent swim team meets. A photography exhibit of Buddy Glantz's recent charity mission to Eritrea is on display in the main foyer. The bulletin board features upcoming activities and events: a Holocaust film screening, a volunteer trip to New Orleans to help rebuild after Hurricane Katrina, the usual flyers advertising tours to Israel.

The tiles in the men's locker room are lizard-like, pukish green and scaly, but Jeremiah doesn't mind. He welcomes the familiar, comforting odors of mildew and body sweat. He lets out an animal-like yelp, and changes into his trunks. A younger man, post-workout, casts a questioning glance in his direction, as if to ask after Jeremiah's welfare, but he waves him off. "Fine, I'm fine. Terrific, in fact."

This is not strictly true. On any given day Jeremiah experiences at least three or more minor physical annoyances, some causes for concern and others mildly irritating. Today's aggravations include pain in the back of his knee and water stuck in his ear since yesterday's swim. He'd tried to extract it with a Q-tip, but no matter how much he stretched his neck to one side and thumped the opposite ear, the water remained, sloshing around, taunting him. *Enough already with the self-pity,* some inner voice tells him. *You swim fifty laps, several times a week. Not bad for an old man.* Is this his father talking, or himself? He's never sure.

Thank goodness for the water, some laps in the pool. As he strokes, images of the black faces from Buddy's pictures surface in his mind. He's always donated to Buddy's causes, but he's never himself taken off a full week to donate his time to a charity mission. When his thoughts swirl to the Festschrift somewhere along his ninth lap, he rationalizes to himself that the dedications don't matter, and by lap thirty-two his attitude is "screw 'em!"

He'd like to believe Molly—that he's just being too sensitive—but he's not sure he can trust her instincts on this. She's never fully grasped the pressures and politics of academia. Despite her failings, though, Molly is his rock. A gem, he boasted all those years ago when he was first married, and still true today. And wasn't his family—two children and five grandchildren—some kind of accomplishment? Most credit to Molly, of course, but he'd had a hand in raising them. Hours spent reading to them, discussing current events, trying to shape them into thoughtful, independent people. Indulging his grandchildren, like the time he took his then baseball-obsessed grandson to Cooperstown. Benjamin had wanted to read every sign under every exhibit. Six hours to go through two floors, God help him, though now Jeremiah cherishes the memory.

Jeremiah emerges from the pool transformed and makes a short stop in the locker room before heading to the *schvitz*. He loves sweating out his toxins in the wet sauna, shaving cream dripping down his face. He takes a seat and senses pressure in his ear; terrific, he's now got two waterlogged ears. He bends his neck to one side and thumps his ear, much to the amusement of Herb Cohen and Buddy Glantz. They are ten years his junior, schvitzing after their weekly squash game. They've been best friends since childhood, and Jeremiah's never seen one without the other. He wonders what it would be like to have a best friend for sixty years, or even twenty. When he had a regular racquetball partner, they rarely socialized off the court.

"Q-tips, Jeremiah," Herb says.

"Never mind!" Jeremiah waves them off. "Nice pictures, by the way. I mean from your trip to Ethiopia."

"Eritrea," Buddy corrects.

He hopes they can't see the flush creeping up his neck; a professor of international political economy should remember his countries! "Right, that's what I meant."

"A fantastic experience." Buddy reports that he and his wife are headed to New Orleans soon. A regular *tzadik,* this Buddy. Again, the thought niggles at Jeremiah; yes, he gives to a number of worthy causes every year, but what of other good deeds? He resolves to take a closer look at those flyers in the foyer of the JCC. Of course, as a retired dentist, Buddy has a lot to offer some communities. What use can an old political science professor be to an area ravaged by war, natural disasters, and poverty?

"Power to you, Buddy," he says, getting up to leave.

He tilts his head in one last effort to rid his ear of the water, and again they say, in unison, "Q-tips!"

On the day of the book reception—Molly doesn't give him a choice—Jeremiah grits his teeth and dons a lightweight sports jacket and slacks. He combs the thinning strands of white hair on the top of his head as well as the thicker curls in the back. "It's a bad idea," he says, warning his wife. "No one's going to come."

Molly takes his hand and kisses it. She wears a pale yellow summer sweater and floral skirt. Her hair is newly dyed for the occasion, the burnt carrot shade unbecoming for a woman of seventy-four—or a woman of any age, for that matter—but he's learned not to reveal his true thoughts on her hair.

"Come on, this is going to be nice. They're honoring you, and your book." She speaks as if he's an unpopular teenager, a mother encouraging her son to make more of an effort in social situations. "You can do this."

His gut tells him otherwise, but somehow, he allows her to take his arm and lead him out of the house to the car. His mind is numb for the ten-minute drive to campus. Save four or five cars, the parking lot behind Dalton Faculty House is empty. He winces. "Let's get this over with."

Molly rummages in her oversized handbag and produces a boutonniere.

"Oh, for god's sake!"

"Shhh. You'll be fine." She pins it to his jacket.

Inside the Faculty House, he's vindicated: no one attends book receptions. Certainly not one planned with the spectacularly bad timing of a Sunday afternoon in mid-August, when people are on vacation. But here is Jim, his department chair, along with the department assistant and two younger faculty members, not yet tenured. Peter and another editor from the university press munch on canapés and mini-cucumber sandwiches. Two waiters from the dining service stand with their hands folded behind their backs, ready to serve.

They've invited a dozen couples, but as Jeremiah glances around the room he sees only four friends: three of Molly's, plus the on-again, off-again companion of one of them, a man Jeremiah's only met in passing. The other husbands—the ones who are still alive—are probably out playing golf. A notion previously skimmed over and ignored hits him with terrific force: "their" friends are Molly's. Jeremiah files through the names of men he's been close with at one time or another: some have died or moved away, but he can't blame everything on death or distance. His former friends include Phil and Sam Cohen, brothers whom he genuinely likes but whose wives he's managed to offend on separate occasions. Raleigh Fox, his old colleague from D.C., but he messed that up in his typical, blundering way decades prior.

A wave of exhaustion sweeps over Jeremiah, and he scans the room for a comfortable chair. When was the last time he had a conversation of personal significance? Sure, he can bluster about politics and the economy, boast about children and grandchildren, and talk baseball, but he can't recall the last time anyone sought out his advice on a personal matter. His son, perhaps. One or two of his graduate students over the years, but those troubles pertained to research complications or a structural problem in a thesis.

Molly chats with each person, thanking them for coming, though the slight crease in her forehead indicates that she, too, is anxious. She brings him a plate from the dessert table with mint brownies and a cinnamon pastry. The gooey sweetness of the sticky bun does nothing to alleviate his dejection. There is food for fifty but he counts a dozen people. "Whose brilliant idea was this?" he whispers to her. "To have a book reception in the middle of August?"

"Think positive!" She shushes him again—he hates when she does this—but her voice has an urgent pitch to it, a restrained hysteria.

When Hannah arrives with her husband and son, Jeremiah brightens a bit. He greets his daughter with an embrace, shakes Tom's hand, and cups Benjamin's face between his hands, planting a kiss on both cheeks. At sixteen, Ben towers over him. A good boy, his grandson, despite his unhealthy obsession with video games.

"Well," Hannah says, biting into a mini sandwich and looking around. "These are tasty."

"I *told* your mother we should cancel the whole thing," he whispers. "Can I just get up there and say, 'Thanks for coming, enjoy the food, I've got to run now?'"

"No, you cannot. Smile and try to be gracious."

He grunts. A few more people file in—colleagues from the history and economics departments, the dean of academic affairs. The room is a third full.

Sunlight filters through the large bay window. Jeremiah can see a few summer students—orientation leaders who'd moved in mid-August—lounging on the grassy mound called College Hill. They wear tank tops and flip-flops, reading books or fiddling with their phones. Ah, the relaxed, carefree youth of today.

Jim Blackwell clanks his fork on a glass. He welcomes everyone and congratulates Jeremiah and the university press on the book's publication. Peter speaks next, saying what a pleasure it's been to recruit and edit the essays in the volume, how he's enjoyed learning new facets of the international political economy, and how working on a Festschrift is always a privilege. Jeremiah is no longer listening; all he hears is *"wah, wah, wah,"* like the teacher's voice in the after-school *Peanuts* specials.

Someone nudges Jeremiah towards the front of the room. Despite a sickening sensation in his stomach, his legs obey. His mouth is dry, and he motions for Hannah to bring him water. He glances at the small crowd, now close to twenty. "I kind of figured nobody would show up, so I didn't really prepare any remarks." A complete lie; inside his jacket pocket are five single-spaced pages of musing on the international political economy. "Thank you all for coming. Thanks to Peter, my editor, and to Marcella, my research assistant. Where are you, Marcella?" He doesn't see her. "I guess she had other plans." One of Molly's friends emits a nervous titter. He clears his throat. "It's funny to see a thing like this out in print. I mean, who's going to read it?"

Peter's face pales. Molly's eyes are urging him to do something, to say something, but he can't understand her meaning.

"Sorry. I really am. . ." Jeremiah searches for words, coughing into his hand. "I am very honored. And I probably could give a synopsis of some of the conclusions in the book. But if you want to know what they are, you'll have to buy it." He looks at Peter triumphantly. "That way we'll have at least a few sales. Ha, ha."

His forehead is slick with sweat and his mind goes blank. He can't seem to form a single intelligent thought. "I think the only one who wants to be here less than me is my grandson." At hearing his name, Ben goes wide-eyed, his face flushes red. "Ben, whadya say we skip out of here and head over to O'Sullivan's? Whoops. I forgot, you're not allowed in there." His attempts at humor fall flat; he can't control his mouth, it seems. "Sorry, I guess I'm just a little *faklempt*. That's Yiddish for 'overcome.' I actually haven't had a thing to drink, though I probably should have."

Molly is at his side, whispering in his ear, and he holds up a finger to the crowd. "Just say thank you and how much this means to you, and then goodbye," she says. "That's it."

He ignores her. "My wife is reminding me that no one wants to hear from a has-been professor. Anyway, when I decided to go into this field, something like fifty years ago, it wasn't even really a field. I was helped along the way by many scholars. Triffin, for example. I hope we've made a difference in people's understanding about the complexities of political and economic power and the way they interrelate." He pauses. "Of course, it's too bad the guys in Washington don't get it." He cringes at the futility. "Anyway, who gives a damn, right?"

Nervous laughter, but he soldiers onward.

"To tell you the truth, lately I've been wondering if we political economists make one bit of difference." His voice wavers. His entire career dedicated to the field. And now he sees his wasted potential. Has he saved a life? Alleviated anyone's suffering or done one bit of good? He thinks of Buddy the dentist, going off to provide care wherever he can. He feels faint and glances around for something to hold on to. There is no podium. Molly stands by his side, and he thrusts his arm around her for support. She nearly stumbles as he leans his weight on hers. Out of the corner of his eye, he sees her blinking, the way she does when she's trying to hold back tears.

"Anyway, I could go on, but never mind. Thank you to my lovely wife and family for putting up with me. Thank you all for coming. And now I think I really could use a drink." Everyone is silent. "Dismissed," he says, a bit too aggressively, like his old grammar school principal. "Dismissed! Scram! Enjoy the food."

Molly takes him by the arm and leads him over to a sofa with floral cushions. She's taking shallow breaths. He feels bad he's put her through this.

"Tell your friends I'm sorry," Jeremiah mumbles. She and Hannah huddle around him, with his son-in-law and Ben a step behind.

"*Our* friends," Molly corrects. "Maybe you were right—this was a bad idea."

"Don't say I didn't tell you so."

"I made him come," Molly says, close to tears again.

"Mom," Hannah says softly. "Keep it together. He's just having a bad day."

Isn't he entitled to a bad day sometimes? He has a ready list of gripes about his life. *No*, the rational side of his brain fights back. *You weren't abused as a child. You have a dedicated wife. A daughter, smart and accomplished, and a son, though far away in California, who's turned out all right.* What's the matter with him? His father's voice again: *A life with more blessings, you couldn't have asked! He wants more, yet!* He hangs his head in shame, listening to this battle, his intellect on one side and his jumble of emotions on the other. To be in the spotlight brings to the surface all the old fears, the anxiety of being called out as a fraud, like the prophet in the real Book of Jeremiah.

Molly whispers something to Hannah and Tom about helping Jeremiah to the car, but at that moment the waiter wheels out a triple-decker chocolate cake with pink buttercream roses along the edges. Everyone starts singing "Happy Birthday." He's forgotten that Molly planned this as a belated birthday celebration. He draws a deep breath, forcing a smile. The room by now is half full, and he glances around at the people who've come to honor him. An image flashes in his mind and for a second he sees everyone holding paper cutouts of his own face in front of their own. Like that John Malkovich movie. A comical notion. Being Jeremiah Gerstler. His days have not been the stuff of high action, supreme sacrifices, or major tragedy.

"Oh, brother," he says. "Ben, come over here." He leans on Ben's arm, hoisting himself off the sofa, and blows out the candles. Thankfully there are not eighty of them. In the slight lightheadedness that results from his exhalation, a thought crystalizes. He closes his eyes and tries to recall the details of the flyer from the JCC. He hopes his family won't dismiss him as foolish. He's now reached an age his father never saw, long past the time he should have done something to truly honor his memory.

"Dad?" Hannah asks. "Do you want to go?"

Jeremiah shakes his head. He's beginning to feel more like himself, the heavy mood lifting. "I'm okay." He sits back down and gathers his family to him. "I just had an idea. A revelation, if you will, of something I need to do. Or maybe not *need,* that's not the right word. Something I should do, or at least try." He explains about the trip to rebuild New

Orleans. Volunteers of all ages needed for tasks both physical and non-physical. "There's library work, cataloging, mending books. Stuff like that. And I was thinking maybe Ben could come with me."

Hannah's mouth drops open, and Ben says with excitement, "Are you serious?" His grandson has never been to New Orleans. "Nice!" He looks to his parents for approval. "Can I go?"

"Um. We'll talk about it." For once, his daughter is at a loss for words.

Molly shakes her head and gives a little laugh. "If that's what you really want, dear." He can see from the look on her face, and Hannah's too, that they're thinking, *there he goes again, Mr. Impulsive.* But this is the flip side of impulsive, the sunny quality. Madcap decisions turning out well. As a boy during the Depression, he'd convinced his mother to bake cakes for the local slop house. Today it would be called a soup kitchen. If he delves into the far corners of his memory, he is sure he can come up with a few more examples. He feels his father standing behind him, proud and beaming, ready to place a kiss on his forehead.

"Maybe you'll come with us, Mol."

"I'll have to think about it."

"Good. Then it's settled." Even though he knows, of course, that it isn't. He'll need to coax Hannah into the idea of letting Ben come with him. He'll take the family out to dinner, equipped with the full details, and try to listen to her concerns. And he knows that one week of volunteering does not make up for a lifetime of not. But for the moment, he feels youthful again, energized by his idea. Excited for another trip with Ben, to watch him engaged with something meaningful. He rises from the couch, this time without the assistance of his grandson's strong hand, and ambles over to the waiters serving the cake.

The chocolate icing doesn't hold a candle to Molly's, but Jeremiah savors the rush of sweetness in his mouth. He gulps down two cups of water, finds a napkin, and wipes his face clean of crumbs. He joins a group of colleagues standing in a small circle, and they each take a step back to make room.

"Actually I did prepare a little speech, but I decided not to bore you." They smile politely, as though they haven't all just witnessed his near breakdown. He knows they think he's a relic, with his bowties and brown leather briefcase and lunches his wife still packs in compartmentalized Tupperware. But he's not quite finished yet. To those standing nearby, he announces the trip with his grandson as if it's been planned for months. If Hannah hears, he can count on his daughter—even in her annoyance—to give a private reprimand, not a public one. "You!" he calls to Ben, motioning him over and cuffing his shoulder playfully.

Intelligent thoughts and speech return. Jeremiah begins expounding on the domestic political economy; he might make this trip into something of a research project! He speaks with the feverish excitement of an adolescent about to embark on a journey. Perhaps the Festschrift is a testament to his career, but the Book of Jeremiah is still a work-in-progress. Can they see that? He keeps talking, even as the circle around him dwindles and people drift toward the dessert table and out of the room.

CLANDESTINY

(1952)

The interviewer's flattop, stiff with wax, announced he was A Person of Authority. Not to be messed with. Jeremiah was trying not to stare at the jagged white scar running from the nail bed on the man's right thumb to his wrist. *Tell me again why you want to work for us.* His tone was confrontational. Jeremiah's thick file sat on the table between them, and he wondered if this would be the same recruiter who would be visiting his parents, provided he made it that far in the process. What kind of impression would his mother make, he wondered, in the face of such intimidation? He gathered that Agent Morehouse was the type of man who disliked people with foreign accents. Jeremiah measured his words. "I want to serve my country. First of all. Second of all, I think I might be good at it."

Morehouse dropped his pen and snickered. "What makes you think that? We see a lot of fellows like you, you know, who've watched *The 39 Steps* or a couple of other Hitchcock flicks and then come in here and think they can be heroes."

This was part of the game, Jeremiah understood—the man looked as if he was following stage directions for playing a menacing mobster or a bully. Jeremiah swore to himself that he would not be baited. The first interview had been nothing like this. This second meeting was meant to ratchet up the pressure on potential recruits. More of an interrogation than an interview. The man's scar—for such a thing, could not, in Jeremiah's limited medical knowledge, have been the product of a childhood accident—suggested a knifing.

"I'm good with languages: fluent in German. Yiddish, of course, and a bit of French and Hebrew," Jeremiah said. "And I've studied the service extensively. As you know, since it says so in my letter of recommendation from Professor Finch."

"Professor Finch." Agent Morehouse spat the words out. "That old geezer. What did he do during the war except sit on his rear end and give lectures about out-of-date tactics?"

"Well, sir, the man is nearing seventy! And, with all due respect, in the first war, he fought in the Battle of the Marne and came out with a Medal of Honor, so I don't think you can call his patriotism into question." Professor Finch was the one who put the idea in his head in the first place. The OSS had morphed into a new organization, signed into law by President Truman, and there were opportunities for physically fit, bright young college graduates to continue to serve their country. It was a heck of a lot more glamorous than trudging through mud laying wire cables, which is what Jeremiah did in the war. And it held more appeal than his current activity: slogging through volumes of political treaties and declassified information to write a master's thesis.

"Fair enough, Gerstler. I'll leave Finch aside for a moment. It's nothing personal. His briefings were just boring as hell."

Jeremiah was cautiously optimistic; there seemed to be a slight yielding on Morehouse's part. If Jeremiah passed the interview, he'd be invited to spend three days in Washington with other potential recruits for the next level of screening. They'd be given practice missions, written exams, and physical challenges, so that the Agency could select only the very best, the men who could be trusted with the nation's security. Until the middle of his senior year, Jeremiah had entertained various career ideas—journalism, law—before settling on academia. Taking complex geopolitical situations and developing original theories invigorated him. His master's thesis dealt with the role of the clandestine services and how intelligence affected U.S. foreign policy decisions. He was moving along steadily in his M.A./Ph.D. track at Columbia when suddenly Finch made an offhand comment about Jeremiah doing well in a career in intelligence. The new Agency, Finch had said, could use bright, ambitious young men like him.

The idea had taken root: why should the clandestine services remain just an academic interest? The more he thought about it, the more ardent his desire to be accepted into the CIA.

Unfortunately the process—Finch's connections helped but were no guarantee—could take several months. Several sleepless months. The fifteen-page questionnaire had covered every conceivable topic, from his family ancestry to a list of his past girlfriends, "lessons" he had learned while in the service in Europe, his feelings on Communism, and his thoughts on the massive amounts of foreign aid the U.S. was pouring into Western Europe. He had been advised not to tell anyone he was applying, so other than Finch and his parents, no one knew.

Morehouse fired question after question, probing Jeremiah's loyalty to America from every angle. "When did your parents come to this country? What language do you speak at home? What happened to your relatives in Europe? Do you have any close relations living overseas? In the Soviet Union? In Israel?"

Most of the Gerstlers had come to America in the 1920s or earlier, Jeremiah answered, and the few who hadn't were murdered by Hitler. He had one close relative living in Israel. It was impossible to know Morehouse's views on the young Jewish State, so Jeremiah didn't elaborate. His first cousin Jackie had been an air force engineer with U.S. troops in North Africa and then a volunteer in '48, helping the nascent Israeli Air Force, but this didn't seem relevant. After all, dozens of young Jewish American pilots had done the same. Ben-Gurion himself had commended Jackie for his efforts; the family had a picture of the Prime Minister shaking his cousin's hand and presenting him with a plaque.

Morehouse nodded—surely this fact was already known and in his file—and picked up a new line of questioning. Had Jeremiah, or any of his family members, ever been a member of the Communist Party?

"What about the Rosenbergs?" Here the venom in the agent's voice returned. Certainly Jeremiah, he intimated, must have had some contact with the traitor, since they shared the same "antecedents" and both Jeremiah and Julius Rosenberg had served in the Signal Corps.

"That's ridiculous," Jeremiah snapped. His stomach burned with anger at the suggestion and its underlying anti-Semitism, but he forced himself to stay in control. "I only know about the man from what I've read in the newspapers. Same as everybody. Personally, I think he's a disgrace to the Signal Corps. And to my people."

The interviewer let it go; apparently this was the correct answer. He switched topics again: how had Jeremiah developed his research interest in the OSS in the first place?

"Oh, I was always a sucker for spy stories when I was a kid." A complete lie. The real answer was that he'd met a gal right after the war, and from some of the fishy questions she asked, he'd gotten all charged up, thinking she was a double agent. His suspicions turned out to be unfounded, and there was no reason to implicate the woman now, who, as far as he knew, had gotten married and was living an ordinary life in the Midwest.

Morehouse jotted something in his notebook and then moved to a new topic: how *did* intelligence gathering affect policy decisions, he wanted to know. At last, comfortable subject matter, Jeremiah's forte. He expounded on a series of covert actions in the shadow war against Germany, the merits of psychological operations such as Radio Free Europe, and which Congressional avenues were more effective than others. In the second half of the interview, Morehouse's tone turned friendlier, encouraging, as if he was starting to recognize the value of having a policy wonk like Jeremiah in the Agency.

"Okay, Gerstler. You'll be hearing from us." They shook hands, Jeremiah imagining the scar transposing itself onto his thumb. The thought of having such a dangerous-looking mark made him shiver with anticipation.

Each time the phone rang in the hall of his graduate dormitory, Jeremiah worried it would be Morehouse on the other end of the line. Or worse, some secretary calling to inform him that his candidacy was being terminated. But the times the phone was for him, it was usually one of his parents. Anxious. They weren't in favor of this spy business. After the war, when Jeremiah had come back and told them he wouldn't be going into the family liquor business, it had taken his father some time to get used to the idea. But by now, Abe had become a strong supporter, crowing to his friends about his son's being in the Ivy League. On his way to becoming a big-time professor. "With me, not going past the eighth grade!" He spoke about the glorious educational opportunities in America. So this aspiration, this sudden veering towards a possible new career, had his father worried.

Meanwhile, Jeremiah needed to get back to his thesis writing. He had done most of the research, but there were several books he needed to consult again. It had been weeks, he realized guiltily, since he had visited the stacks in Butler Library. There was a new girl working behind the desk, a Barnard coed, most likely. Her thick black hair was braided down her back, reminding him of Hedy Lamarr in *Tortilla Flat*. Maybe the real reason he was interested in the service was that his mind was never far from the beauties who had contributed to the intelligence efforts. He handed the girl his list of books, and she sent the request up through one of the dumbwaiters. It was a quiet day in the library—most Columbians were congregating outside on the Low Library steps, buzzing about whether Eisenhower, their very own university president, would win the upcoming primary in New Hampshire. Jeremiah watched the girl behind the desk finish cataloging a stack of returned books and start flipping through a student activities circular.

Student activities. It had been ages since he had done anything other than work on his CIA application or his thesis. Here he was, living in New York City, and when was the last time he'd been to a museum, seen a show, or taken a stroll through Central Park? He didn't have time for such diversions, he reminded himself, though now he remembered the words of Karen Fisher, a girl he'd taken to a few dances in his final year of college. They had met in a political science seminar and he'd been fired up that such a pretty, clever Jewish girl was interested in the same subjects he was. "You're too single-minded, Jeremiah," she had said on their fourth and last date. "Sure, I like politics, but it doesn't have to be the only thing you talk about. It's dragsville, to tell you the truth." He winced, recalling it now. If he was going to be a good spook, he decided, he would have to make an effort to get to know other disciplines: chemistry and technology (this, if he made into the Agency, would be taught), as well as the classics, music, and art. Who knew what he would have to pretend to be—an art dealer? an opera aficionado?—while gathering important intelligence on a mission.

Jeremiah handed his library card to the Barnard student behind the desk when his books arrived. "Anything worth going to in there?" he asked, pointing to the circular. "What do you recommend?"

She examined him, a quizzical look on her face. "I guess that would depend on what interests you."

"As you can see," he said, gesturing to the stack of books, "I've got my main interest covered. So I'm looking for something. . ." He hesitated. He wasn't really sure what he was looking for, and he was afraid of sounding stupid. "Something new."

She peered at him, squinting as if trying to draw a conclusion. "All right." She hesitated. "But are you really interested in the arts or are you just trying to become a hep cat?"

"Hey!" Her words stung. Was he so obviously a wet rag? "Never mind." He collected his books and started for the exit.

"Wait, come back a second," she called. "Sorry, I didn't mean to. . ." She flushed. "I didn't mean to be rude." She pulled out a pen and circled two events in the activity calendar. "I don't know if you like music, but here are two events I think look interesting."

She had circled a flamenco guitar concert at the Cathedral of St. John the Divine as well as the unveiling of a new electronic music composition by a Professor Ussachevsky, who, according to the handout, was the chairman of the department. Jeremiah had an inkling of what flamenco guitar music was, and he thought he'd rather work on his footnotes—a task he dreaded if there ever was one—than subject himself to a concert, even if the setting was grand. And electronic music? What the devil was that? It sounded painful to the ears.

"Yeah, well, thanks," he grunted. Who was he trying to fool?

◆ ◆ ◆

The news arrived that he'd made it to the next level of screening. Thrilled, Jeremiah headed to Washington for three days of intensive assessments. At first, he felt like the D.C. he'd landed in was in a foreign country, far from the security of home and the tri-state area. Everyone seemed to be blonde and from the South. Most had done time in the service. Many of the candidates were fluent in languages far more useful than his Yiddish and German: Russian, Chinese, Japanese, Arabic. Why had he not thought to study Russian? In the team-building missions, Jeremiah let others take charge when it seemed they knew more about a topic than he. In the leadership-testing exercises, he tried not to sound too pedantic when explaining a point of diplomacy to his teammates. He was curious as to what his psychiatric evaluation would reveal but was sure he'd never be granted access to it. The recruiters he met with—Morehouse and his flattop were nowhere in sight during the entire three days—were encouraging, welcoming. Jeremiah thought he had performed reasonably well, certainly compared to the bozo who hadn't found the room on the first day and started yelling at the receptionist for not placing proper signage. "Cool it," Jeremiah had whispered, but the man ignored him. The candidates wondered if the man was a plant by the Agency to see how they would react. How was the Agency going to whittle them down? He had heard that the final screening step was the security clearance: ninety-seven percent of candidates were weeded out due to something questionable in their backgrounds. Jeremiah couldn't think of anything remotely questionable in his, and he left D.C. on a note of optimism.

When he returned to campus, he attempted to turn his attention to his thesis, trying not to get distracted each time the hall phone rang. He was busy penning an opinion piece for the student-run *Spectator*—Eisenhower had now officially declared his candidacy—when there was a knock on his door. His heart lurched as he walked to the waiting telephone.

"Allo." His father's familiar voice came down the line, sounding worried. "I've got news." He switched into Yiddish. Cousin Jackie had moved back to America to work on a friend's political campaign and test the political waters for himself. He hadn't been back in his parents' house more than two hours when they came to arrest him. Jackie was being charged with gun-running and a host of other activities that were illegal according to the 1939 Neutrality Act.

"What?" Jeremiah shrieked into the phone. That certain influential American Jews had helped procure arms for Israel he had known, but he had been ignorant of Jackie's involvement. "And now, of all times, he's decided to come home?"

There was to be a hearing the day after tomorrow in Queens, his father continued. Abe himself could not leave his liquor stores, but he expected Jeremiah would want to attend to show his support and help his Uncle Martin and Aunt Leah.

"You know what this means, don't you?" Jeremiah said.

"Stop with the self-pity." If there was one thing Abe couldn't stand, it was someone feeling sorry for himself. "He's not a criminal. More like a hero, if you ask me." The picture of Jackie together with Ben-Gurion came back now, making sense. As well as the time Jeremiah— on a trip to the city back in early '48—had bumped into his cousin in the East 60s, near the Copacabana night club. Jackie was carrying a big package that had "Hadassah medical supplies" stamped on the box. Doing a favor for his mother, Jackie had lied. Now Jeremiah remembered a trickling of reports, something about a Hotel Fourteen in that same neighborhood, where a man named Teddy gave out false identities and recruited American Jews to the Haganah.

He would have liked to attend the hearing and the trial, if only to strangle Jackie for dealing a death blow to his Agency candidacy, but he decided, just in case there remained any hope of being accepted, to distance himself from his cousin. Instead, Jeremiah followed the trial in the papers. His father was annoyed with him for not attending. The Jewish Agency had gotten involved, and Mickey Kellman, the prominent New York lawyer, had been hired as Jackie's attorney. His cousin pleaded not guilty, on the grounds that the law was unjust, but the prosecutor's office had built a strong case. Apparently Jackie had not only organized shipments of guns, scrap metal, and spare parts but had also been instrumental in smuggling several B-17 Flying Fortresses out of the United States. He had purchased the surplus aircraft and then sent them to Israel via Mexico and Panama. Jackie himself had been on one of these flights, and his voice could be heard setting the flight course on a tape produced by the prosecution. Additional witnesses were brought in—Czechs and Panamanians and others who testified not only about the aircraft but about the entire ring. A sinking sensation filled Jeremiah as he read the reports. How was it that all of this had been going on and he hadn't known a thing about it? He felt cheated. Where had he been in the spring of 1948? What had so occupied his thoughts that he hadn't realized what his own cousin was up to?

Midway through Jackie's trial, the rejection letter arrived. His Agency application was no longer under active consideration. Jeremiah had been expecting it, but he couldn't shake his feeling of the unfairness of it all. Why should he be held accountable for his cousin's actions? He wondered if Morehouse would be frank with him if he tried to follow up. He remembered the wax and the flattop, the sneer in the agent's voice as he tried to flap Jeremiah's patience. It wasn't worth asking, he decided. His destiny was a life among books, in academia. Perhaps, with time, his insights and theories would be recognized in the intelligence community, and just like Professor Finch, they'd call on him as an outside consultant.

Now that he had been officially rejected, Jeremiah was free to attend the trial. The prosecution had already laid out its evidence, and it was the defense's turn. He watched from the back, fascinated. The lawyer, Kellman, put on a dazzling show, making a big deal about the unjust law, the underdog Israel, and pulling out witness after witness in support of Jackie's actions. There was no denying one of Kellman's central arguments: millions of European Jews might still be alive had the State of Israel existed in 1933. A letter from Ben-Gurion was brought into evidence: the actions of Jackie and his fellow gun-runners represented the Diaspora's single most important contribution to the survival of Israel.

On his first day at the trial, Jeremiah noticed a familiar-looking young woman sitting a few rows in front of him. During a break in the proceedings, she walked up and whispered something to Kellman. When he saw her face, he remembered: it was the Barnard student who worked in the library. Was she in training to become some sort of paralegal? What was she doing here? She seemed to know his aunt and uncle as well, stopping to chat with them as she walked back to her seat. She looked older than she had at the library, her black hair long and loose against a blue-and-green-print dress. A classy chassis, his college buddies would have called her.

He waited for her in the hallway when the session adjourned for the day. She walked past him, chatting with another woman who'd been in the courtroom, though they parted at the exit. He rushed outside and caught up with her on the stone steps. "You go to Barnard, don't you?" She nodded, and her neck reddened, a sign she recalled their encounter. "Do you remember me?" he asked. "From the library?"

"Sure," she said. "I didn't see you at the electronic music opening, or the flamenco concert."

"Yeah, well, they weren't really my scene."

"But this is?" she asked, gesturing to the stone courthouse, the bailiffs patrolling, the reporters waiting in line at the payphones to call in their stories.

"Well, what are *you* doing here? Do you have some connection to the case?"

"I asked you the same question."

"The defendant is my cousin." *And I don't know if I should kill him or hug him*, he wanted to add. He was starting to come around to his father's point of view: maybe his cousin had done something heroic.

"Really? His lawyer is my father."

"You're Mickey Kellman's daughter?"

She extended her hand. "Molly Kellman."

Jeremiah introduced himself. "Do you always come to your father's trials or only the ones with a lot of media attention?"

This one was a case close to her heart, she confided. She had been too young to really participate in the operation, but she'd served as the lookout for her brother and his friends as they packed supplies and brought them to Queens for shipment.

"What kind of supplies?" he wanted to know.

"Whatever was needed. Machine gun parts, scrap iron, mess kits."

Jeremiah was stunned. He had heard bits and pieces throughout the trial, but he had no idea as to the extent of the Haganah's operations—that even Zionist-minded teenage girls were part of the effort. Suddenly his anger at his cousin took a new turn. Where had he been? Why hadn't Jackie thought to include him in this business? The whole course of his career might have been different. Kellman had been convincing: his cousin was no criminal. Had Jackie and the Sonneborns and Kolleks and Konskers of this world not intervened and sent arms to the young fighters, the Jews would have been crushed. Again.

Only a few more days of arguments remained, and since Jeremiah and Molly were both coming from the Upper West Side, they arranged to take the subway together. He learned that she was a sophomore, nineteen years old (though she seemed far more worldly than him at twenty-five), and contrary to his initial impression, had no desire to study law. She had, in fact—after some deliberation about going into nursing—just declared music as her major.

A week later, the verdict came back unanimous: guilty as charged. Jeremiah's aunt and uncle were concerned that this would mean jail time, and Jeremiah himself couldn't see how it wouldn't. "My aunt hasn't stopped crying since the verdict," he told Molly later. She scoffed. Having grown up with a prominent lawyer for a father, she seemed to know much more about the legal system than he did, though he had been reading up on similar cases.

"Jeremiah," she said, "I really ought to give you a lesson in the way things work around here. Don't you know that the judge is in the mayor's pocket? The mayor's brother is one of the ones who helped us—he told us which longshoremen would look the other way when shipments needed to get out. We've got a lot of support from the Irish and Italians. You know that, don't you?"

"Sure," he lied. "The family is just worried they'll give him a stiff sentence." The CIA, Jeremiah recognized with dismay, had been right to reject him. What kind of clandestine officer could he have made if he didn't even know the basics of how things worked in New York City politics? He had focused too much on national politics and foreign policy—he didn't know a thing about government on the local level. And he hadn't been trusted enough, or his abilities hadn't even been considered by Jackie, as someone who could have helped. His whole life was headed to nowheresville.

Kellman called a family conference before the sentencing. The lawyer explained there would almost certainly be a fine, though he had it on good authority that the Jewish Agency would pay the bill. But the judge would want more: something that would send a message. If Jackie wanted to avoid prison, he would have to give something in return.

"Community service?" Jackie asked hopefully.

Kellman waved his hand. "No way is that judge going to let you off with community service."

No one spoke for a few minutes. During the silence, an exquisite idea crept into Jeremiah's mind: "Offer to give up your civil rights."

"What?" his cousin asked, his voice rising.

"It's been done before, hasn't it?" Jeremiah asked.

Kellman nodded, thinking over the idea. "I like it," he said finally. "By god, I like it." It would mean, the lawyer explained, that Jackie could no longer vote, run for public office, or serve in the U.S. military. None of these things, Kellman said looking to Jackie, would be a particular problem for him, would they?

"You mean it's that easy?" his aunt asked. "That's all it would take to keep him out of jail?"

"Ma, wait a minute. . ." Jackie had moved back to the States to explore running for office.

"What's the big deal, mister?" his uncle asked. "So you won't go into politics, so what?" One by one, everyone except Jackie was agreeing. A good idea, a fair deal, they murmured.

Kellman nodded at Jeremiah in approval. He had no doubt seen Molly and Jeremiah congregating outside the courthouse, and now he came over and rested his hands on Jeremiah's shoulders. "This is just the type of gesture I think the judge will go for." Jackie was glaring at his cousin, but the rest of the family, and more importantly Kellman and Molly, were beaming at him.

And so it went: a $10,000 fine (indeed paid by the Jewish Agency), and an abrogation of Jackie's civil rights. It was juvenile, Jeremiah knew, to be smirking inwardly as the sentence was announced, but he couldn't help it. Now Jackie, too, would have to rethink his career, saying goodbye to any political aspirations. Congratulations were exchanged, hands shaken in every direction and praise bestowed on Mickey Kellman. Jackie begrudgingly thanked him for coming to the trial. Jeremiah didn't intend to tell Jackie anything about his foiled candidacy. It didn't seem to matter. It had been folly to think he would have made a good clandestine officer. He knew now that his course in life was set: he'd stick with his original plan and continue in his Ph.D. program.

"Come on," Molly said to him as they left the courthouse for the final time. "Stop looking so glum. It's good news. We should have a drink and celebrate."

Jeremiah thought about the books waiting for him back in his dormitory. A quiet life of research in the library and teaching was a far cry from a prison sentence, but it would take some time to let go of his dream. "Yes," he told Molly, "let's get a drink."

BIRTHDAY BASH

(1992)

Three weeks before turning sixty, Molly Gerstler strode into Ace of Bass and came out an hour later with a sparkling new electric guitar. The Gibson Les Paul, in skyburst blue, was a gift to herself, something she'd wanted ever since her music teacher introduced her to classic compositions for the electric. The arrangements for Bach and Paganini, with their clean plucked lines, had sounded wonderfully modern. Molly had fended off suggestions of a big birthday celebration; now that she had her guitar, her only request was to spend the weekend at home in the Berkshires. "Just quiet, intimate family time," she explained to her husband Jeremiah and the kids, both of whom promised to come up from New York for the occasion. "No parties, no surprises, no fireworks."

"Quiet she wants," Jeremiah said, turning his face upward to converse with the ceiling as if she wasn't right there in the same room. "Yet she brings home an electric guitar!"

Jeremiah's tone was playful, but Molly felt the need to remind him that the hobby was a natural step in her musical progression, following a lifetime of teaching piano and several years of playing classic guitar.

"I know, I know!" he said, cutting her off. "You don't have to explain it to me. I'm happy for you, sweetheart. Really. Use it in good health."

Molly didn't tell him that the first few times she'd taken the guitar out of its case, she felt giddy, like a child unwrapping a fancy present with bows and curlicue ribbons. But also the opposite: strapping on the Les Paul allowed her to strip off the Molly who was the family's always-dependable domestic core, and turned her into someone edgier.

"Are you sure you don't want to just go away somewhere to celebrate?" They didn't have to do anything ambitious, Jeremiah said, a weekend in New York City with a show or two, a B&B on the Cape. Wouldn't she prefer that to hosting and cooking for the whole family?

"It's not hosting when it's our own kids and grandchildren," she insisted. The whole family was only five people: Hannah and her husband and their two small children, and Stuart, who at twenty-seven had yet to settle down. "I'll have everything I want right here." She was eager to play for Stuart, who'd sounded excited about her purchase. *Mom, you rock!* "Stu says he's going to dust off his drum set and we'll have a jam session."

"Terrific. I can't wait. Maybe he wants to dust off his resume." Jeremiah took it as a personal affront that their college-educated son was working as a bartender in Greenwich Village and seemed devoid of any inner drive or ambition. They hoped that Stuart would find a wife or a girlfriend to serve as a positive influence and help him grow up.

"I'm talking about doing something nice with him—making music—and you have to bring everything back to your frustrations." Her husband couldn't—or wouldn't—stop himself from making remarks that oozed with disappointment, no matter how many times she told him not to. She worried that Jeremiah and Stuart would be incapable of refraining from arguing for an entire weekend. Every time, she ended up as the referee.

"All right, all right," Jeremiah said, throwing up his hands in mock surrender. "Sorry. Go form a rock band for all I care. Go jam or jim to your heart's content. Just remind me to get some earplugs."

Molly sighed. Such a grouch, her husband could be, though even after four decades together there were still times when she wasn't sure if he was kidding or just being grumpy. Now Jeremiah came over from behind and drew her towards him, his arms resting lightly on her stomach. "I'm just teasing, you know that! I think it's sexy that my wife is taking up the electric guitar."

He tried to nuzzle her neck and make hubba-hubba noises, but she swatted him away and unclasped his hands.

"Just don't take up with Luis!" he said. He loved to rib her about her thirty-something guitar teacher, who wore tight black jeans and resembled a young Desi Arnaz Jr. *Luis is just trying to get in your pants!* Somehow these comments were meant to be taken as a compliment. *I want to sleep with you, so why wouldn't he?*

"Well, he is awfully cute. I just might!"

He froze, alarm on his face, until she rolled her eyes. "Oh, really now, Jeremiah! You're such a kidder yourself, you can't even see that I can be too, when I want to."

Molly laughed, leaving him standing there with his mouth open and feeling just a little bit mean as she headed for the practice room. Long ago, they'd converted the detached garage into her studio, where she'd taught local youngsters to play the piano for over a quarter of a century. Now *she* was the student, practicing power chords and experimenting with how tightly to hold the fret board on the Les Paul. She was having fun with it, delighted with how easy it was for her aging fingers to achieve the resonance and complex overtones she'd hoped for. Even her barre chords sounded punchy and alive. She was a girl again, fantasizing about being a famous stage performer. A rock star every time she picked up the instrument.

The first twinges of regret came when Jeremiah unloaded the groceries a few days before the birthday weekend. The piles of raw ingredients stared up at Molly like a long, dreary to-do list. Why had she chosen dishes that required so much *potchkying*? Though baking and cooking were her second and third loves, the preparations would not allow much time to practice her music.

"I'm not complaining, of course," said Jeremiah, as he caught Molly's halfhearted expression. "I love your veal and risotto and those peanut butter chocolate thingies, but maybe it's too much?"

"I'm fine." She swallowed a sigh, unable to admit to Jeremiah that perhaps he was right. She'd made the elaborate menu, so she had no one to blame but herself. She tied on her apron, telling herself she'd feel better once her fingers began chopping and mixing and the aromas from her oven filled the kitchen. "I'll get it all done."

"Well, you're predictable, that's for sure," Jeremiah said with a faint grin. "Too stubborn to admit maybe I was right." He put his hand on her shoulder. "Can I help with something? You know. Be your right-hand man, what's the culinary term for that?"

"Sous chef," she answered, smiling, her mood starting to lighten. She would tamp down her frazzled feeling. "That's sweet of you, thanks. But no." Jeremiah had two left hands in the kitchen. He could make himself a scrambled egg and put up water to boil, but that was the extent of his cooking abilities. "You can be the taster, how about that?"

"Sounds good to me."

"We'll have a nice weekend, won't we?" she asked. She shut her eyes and pictured her instruments: the Steinway Baby Grand, the Taylor acoustic guitar, and the Gibson Les Paul, with its gleaming finish, the shade of crystal blue water at a Bermuda beach. They weren't going anywhere, she told herself.

"Of course," he said. "I'll be on my best behavior."

She nodded, shooed him away, and put on her favorite Alex de Grassi recording. If she couldn't practice at least she could listen while she cooked.

Molly was bushed by the time Hannah and Tom arrived on Friday afternoon, but seeing her grandchildren brought out a deep, innate joy. Two-and-a-half-year-old Ben was still asleep, but five-year-old Pamela ran up and started chattering about the tea party she wanted to have with Molly. She swept Pam into her arms and onto her lap, swaddling her with kisses. She told her granddaughter that she still had too much to do to get dinner ready, but that they could have the tea party tomorrow. And perhaps, she added, they could hold the tea

party in the music studio and she would entertain them with songs on
the piano and maybe even on her new guitar.

Pam wrinkled her nose, not excited by the prospect, but then ran
off to play. Hannah deposited Ben on the family room couch, refusing
to put a towel down underneath him, though he'd only been toilet-
trained for a month. "It's fine, Mom. He *never* has accidents when
he's just napping."

Molly frowned but didn't feel like arguing.

Jeremiah checked his watch every five minutes. "Why can't Stu
ever get here when he says he will?"

She could tell by the scowl that his mood was cantankerous. She
wished Jeremiah had some hobby that she could send him off to do.
Something to calm him down and smooth out his rough edges, just as
practicing music did for her.

"Finally!" Jeremiah said, a while later.

Molly went to the window and waved in welcome. Stuart's car was
in the driveway, but she spotted another figure in the front seat. Her
smile evaporated. A heavily made-up girl emerged from the front seat,
wearing a black T-shirt, black miniskirt, and black boots.

"Who in God's name is *that*?" Molly said. "Did you know he was
bringing a friend?" Hannah and Jeremiah both shook their heads no.
This was so like Stuart, she thought, not to mention he was bringing
someone. She didn't like to pry, never wanted to be one of those mothers
who would say in a false voice, *Anyone special in your life these days,
dear?* but inside, a small candle of resentment ignited. Was this Stuart's
idea of a happy surprise? Hadn't she made it clear that she wanted
this weekend to be just for family?

She marched outside, letting the screen door slam behind her.

"Hi!" Stuart pecked her on the cheek. "This is Tess."

The girl looked to be no more than twenty. She extended her hand
to shake Molly's. Even her nail polish was black. Good god.

"Hello," Molly said, taking Tess's hand and smiling wanly. She
darted her eyes to her son. "Stuart's told us all about you." Tess seemed
to catch the haughtiness in Molly's tone, and she looked back and
forth from mother to son.

"Yeah, sorry," Stuart said. "I should have told you she was coming. But I wasn't sure she could make it until yesterday. Hey, and it's kind of like, 'surprise!'"

"That it is," Molly said.

He shrugged, carefree, unaware of her attempt to ask him, telepathically, if Tess was a girlfriend, a friend, or just someone he was babysitting for the weekend.

"Well, come on inside." She could hear the ice in her tone and wondered if Stuart noticed. Molly felt like throwing a temper tantrum right there on the driveway. *This is not what I wanted! Who is this trampy-looking girl and why did you bring her home, Stuart?* She turned back towards the house without offering to carry any of their bags. "I've got stuff on the stove. You'll excuse me, Tess. Stuart will show you to the guest room. I guess the kids will have to go in the same room as Hannah and Tom."

Molly strode back to the house, only to find her grandson wailing. Hannah was peeling off his wet clothes and running a bath. Her son-in-law offered to wipe down the couch with soap and water, but Molly insisted that he call the Ethan Allen furniture hotline, which, at 6:05 on a Friday evening, was closed for the weekend.

The howling from the bathroom continued, and Molly chided herself for forgetting to keep her expectations in check. She should try to remember how stretched she often felt by family gatherings. Of course she wanted everyone together, but it didn't mean that her nerves didn't fray.

At dinner, Molly was irritable. Tess was a literal black blemish against the backdrop of the dining room, the table set with their good china and silver dinnerware used on special occasions. An extra-large bouquet of purple irises and baby's breath from Jeremiah sat on the server. *Why was Hannah so stubborn? Why hadn't Stuart told her about Tess in advance? Common courtesy,* she kept thinking, though she was having difficulty displaying some common courtesy of her own. It was as if the words coming out of her mouth were not hers but had been placed there by a ventriloquist. Trying to get her to relax, Jeremiah poured copious glasses of red wine. Molly drank hers as if she'd just emerged from a two-day hike in the desert. "So how did you two meet?. . . Oh, not at your bar, Stuart, at a club?. . . Do you frequent clubs often, Tess?. . . How old are you, dear?. . . Oh, really. And let me see, that makes you, what, a junior in college? Entering junior?" Molly expected Tess to say, no, I'm not in college, but instead the girl told her she was studying at Barnard.

A thin layer of mistrust fell away, and she said, "Isn't that funny, I also went to Barnard!" After a pause, she added, "Of course, in my day, they didn't let us girls dress like that."

"Women."

"Excuse me?"

"We're women, not girls," Tess said.

"Oh, right."

Tess gave tight, one-word answers, as if she was afraid that any extra verbiage would become an arrow that would find its way to Molly's bow. What a dull girl. Molly was going to need some more wine to make it through the meal.

When she brought out the main course, both Tess and Stuart held up their hands to stop her from serving them. "I guess I should have told you," her son said. "I don't eat veal anymore. Tess doesn't either. It's not humane, the way they treat the animals."

She frowned and rolled her eyes. "More for us, then," she said, letting the serving spoon make a loud scraping noise as she placed a helping on Jeremiah's plate.

Now Jeremiah piped in, asking Tess if she'd taken poli-sci classes (no), if she knew his colleagues Professor Della-Caprisi and Professor Weinbrenner at Columbia (no), what she was majoring in (chemistry), what she was planning to do after graduation, and so on.

"Med school, I hope," she said simply, and went on chewing on a piece of broccoli.

"Very nice!" cried Jeremiah. "Excellent!" He clapped his hands in that same son-of-a-gun style he'd become fond of. A quick glance at her husband and Molly could tell that he didn't seem bothered by this girl's appearance or age in the least. She could read his mind: he was hoping Tess would exert some positive influence on Stuart. Molly polished off her second glass of wine and poured herself a third. She was aware of the looks of alarm passing between her daughter and her husband, but she didn't care.

Molly peppered Tess with more questions. "How did you get interested in medicine?. . . Is one of your parents a doctor?. . . Really, a beautician? Does she own her own salon?. . . No?. . . And your father?. . . Oh dear, that's terrible. And you've got no contact with him whatsoever?. . . That's quite an accomplishment for your mother, sending you to Barnard on a beautician's salary, and a single parent, no less."

"Mom!" She felt someone kicking her under the table and looked up to see Hannah scowling at her. Hannah's tone was sharp, warning.

"I meant it as a compliment to Tess's mother!"

Tess's face turned a dark shade of purple, and she seemed to shrink a bit.

Stuart jumped in, eager to sway the subject. "Ma—here's the coolest thing: Tess is an awesome bass player."

"Is that right?" she trailed off.

"I was telling her about you, and she was telling me how much she wanted to get out of the city for the weekend, so I figured, hey, might as well bring her, right? She brought her guitar with her. We can all jam together."

Molly raised her eyebrows, her mouth twisting into a pucker as she considered this new piece of information. But just because the girl was a musician didn't mean Molly had to like her. "So—you're not. . . together?" Her confusion gave way to a slow relief, but then she saw her son exchange a look with Tess.

"You're right," she said quickly. "It's none of my business." Stuart inhaled and took hold of Tess's hand, glaring at his mother defiantly, and Molly knew that whatever their relationship might be, they were certainly sleeping together. She felt nauseous. "Tess, have you told your mother about Stuart? And she doesn't have a problem with the fact that he's twenty-seven?"

Stuart's fork fell to his plate with a clang. "Jesus Christ, Ma! Enough already! We're adults! What's the matter with you?"

Molly was unused to fighting with her son. Later she would blame what she said next on the wine, on the state of her emotional turmoil. "I was very clear, Stuart. I really just wanted this to be an intimate weekend with the family. No offense, dear."

Stuart was on his feet. "C'mon," he said to Tess. "Let's go."

The girl was trying, Molly could see, to hold her head up high, to decide how to best react. Her jaw set, Tess followed Stuart without a word; Molly guessed she was about to cry.

"Don't mind her," Jeremiah called to Tess, trying to intervene. "She's just a little wound up. . ." The screen door slammed before Jeremiah could finish his sentence.

"Happy fucking birthday, Ma!"

"Stuart!" Molly cried. "Wait!"

But she couldn't bring herself to get up from the table. Jeremiah went after them. For a few moments Molly sat transfixed, as if someone was blowing up a balloon in her chest cavity. She didn't know anything about medicine, but she imagined a thousand little synapses going off in her brain. Pop, pop, pop, pop, the sound of irrevocable bursting.

A sinking, desperate feeling came over her, though she also felt strangely detached from the outburst. She could hear Jeremiah speaking to Stuart on the driveway. Now here was a role reversal, she thought, almost amused. *I've been the mean, bitchy one and Jeremiah has to apologize for my behavior.* "What the fuck?" her son was yelling.

Hannah's voice reconnected her to the scene. "Mom! You can't treat people like that! I don't care how much she looks like a witch!"

"Vampire, I was thinking." But she was in no mood to be reprimanded by her daughter. Molly got up, stacked a few plates and sulked into the kitchen. She was furious at herself for losing control. Furious at Stuart for bringing this girl home. Even furious at Jeremiah for taking the girl's side. All of a sudden Molly felt a strong sense of déjà vu, and she covered her face with her hands. She saw it now with horrifying clarity: the ventriloquist controlling her mouth was her mother! Sarah Kellman had never made Jeremiah feel welcome in the family. Growing up, Molly had not known her mother to be unwelcoming, but when she met Jeremiah, a new side of her mother had been revealed. The one that seemed to care only about social stature, expensive dinners, *appearances*. But even as the epiphany passed, Molly knew genetics were no excuse; she'd have to own up, sooner or later, to the fact that she'd been terribly rude to this girl.

Hannah came into the kitchen to check on her. "You can't treat people like that, Ma!" she said again.

"I don't know what came over me."

"You were so passive-aggressive. No, actually just aggressive."

"Thanks Han, you're really making me feel better."

"Is something bothering you? Is it too much for you to have all of us up here at the same time?"

"No! I mean, I don't know. He just threw me for a loop when he brought her home, unannounced. Plus, she's half his age!"

"And how old were you when you met Dad? Hmm? Nineteen, right? And he was twenty-five?"

"That was different. We were both serious about our studies and our future. We were both more mature than Stuart is today."

Hannah rolled her eyes. "Whatever, Ma. It's not that different. You should really apologize. To her and to Stu."

Molly wanted to climb under the covers and stay in bed for a long time, but with Hannah standing sentinel, she forced herself to contend with the situation.

Jeremiah had not come back inside yet, nor had she heard a car driving off. Perhaps Stuart and Tess were still outside. They were in the car, she saw, talking to Jeremiah through the window, but the engine was off. Molly held her head high and stepped outside. When he saw her approaching, Stuart started the car. She motioned for him to wait, and though her voice was stiff and the words bitter, she forced them out. "I want to apologize for my behavior. I'm sorry, Tess. If I'd known you were coming I would have been a bit more prepared. I guess I just. . .I hope we can start over."

Stuart glared ahead, refusing to look at her.

"Will you come back inside? Please?"

"No. We're leaving." He shifted the car into reverse and started backing out of the driveway.

Molly nodded. Behind the angry look in Stuart's eyes she could still see his shock, the pain she'd caused. She wanted to crumple herself up into a little ball and stay that way. For as long as she could remember, *she* had been the one to protect her son from Jeremiah's disappointment and sarcastic vitriol.

"He'll be back," Jeremiah said. "Not sure about Tess, though."

"Did they take their stuff?"

"I think so. They didn't have much. Couple backpacks. A guitar."

"I don't know what came over me. Maybe I'm having a breakdown."

He chortled. "Not my Molly." He put his arm around her and started walking her back into the house. Jeremiah had such a blind spot when it came to her faults. He was never as forgiving or patient with anyone else, except maybe Hannah. But faults she had. Starting with the way she'd just treated Tess. Now she started to fret. What if Stuart and this girl actually stayed together? Tess, her future daughter-in-law. It was unlikely—who in their right mind would stick around after such treatment? Molly had driven her away. If Stuart stayed away too, she'd only have herself to blame. She began babbling to Jeremiah, worries spilling out.

"Mol. Mol! Stop it. They'll be fine. He's not going to disown you over this. Everyone snaps sometimes. Even you."

Tears sprang to her eyes. Molly Gerstler didn't snap. Some stable domestic core, she was.

Against the darkening sky Jeremiah was smiling.

"I see you're enjoying this," she accused.

"No, not enjoying. Well, maybe a little. Maybe now Stuart will see that I'm not always the bad guy. He called you 'unhinged.' Ha! Usually that's what he calls me." Jeremiah's smile turned into a broad grin. "So you're in good company."

"Great." She did not feel like being in anyone's company. "I think I need to be alone for a bit. I'm going to the music room, okay?"

"Okay, Bon Jovi."

"He'll be back, right?" She'd wiped the tears from her eyes, but the knot in her stomach remained.

"Stop worrying. I've said much worse to him—and vice versa, I might add—and we haven't turned our backs on each other yet. He's a good kid at heart. I know that."

Molly nodded. Maybe that was their problem: that they both still looked at Stuart as a kid. Someone who'd never grown up. Or maybe that, too, was only in her mind, and she needed to acknowledge his waning dependence.

Molly let herself into the music room. Which instrument to play? She looked at her acoustic guitar, sitting lonely in the corner. She'd neglected it these last few weeks, in her attempt to become more proficient in the electric. What had she been trying to prove with this new hobby? That she was still young and carefree and cool? What a joke! Tomorrow she'd be sixty. Back in the house she had two grandchildren. Stuart was no longer a baby or even a boy, but a young man who had to be left to make his own decisions, his own mistakes.

The piano beckoned. In Molly's mind, there was nothing more soothing than Chopin. She sat down to play Nocturne in C-sharp minor. Her fingers flowed over the keyboard. Despite the wine, the complicated trills gave her no trouble at all. She played another Chopin and tried to put the ruined weekend out of her thoughts.

She felt calmer, but still restive. She stood and ran her hands over the piano in apology before strapping on the Les Paul. She knew her Chopin would not sound nearly as good on the electric; she needed to keep working on her chromatic exercises and the left-handed fingering to get it right. She no longer felt like a rock star, but damn it, a woman her age could still improve at the guitar.

Tomorrow she'd do the tea party with her granddaughter. If Stuart didn't return, she'd find out where he was and apologize again for her adolescent behavior. She didn't want to be sixty going on sixteen. The couch against the back wall of the music room had never looked as comfortable, and Molly lay down to rest, falling into a deep sleep.

Jeremiah came in just past midnight, nudging her awake. "The kids are back," he said. "Thought you'd want to know."

He squeezed her hand and led her back to the house. "Happy birthday," he whispered. "Welcome to the sixties."

SIGNALS

(1945)

Jeremiah peered up at the long-legged blonde standing by his table and nearly spit out his chicory-laced coffee. He hadn't known what to expect from Mary McDonald, RN, Second Lt. of the 107th Evacuation Hospital, but even if his brother had described her allure in a letter, Jeremiah could not have conjured the looker who now stood before him. She wore a navy blue skirt that did not quite cover her splendid knees, and a white blouse with ruffles, inviting attention to a nice set of bazooms. Her hair was pinned up, but a strand had broken free and dangled near her face. Only when she cleared her throat did Jeremiah jump to his feet, flushing, and pull out the chair for her.

The café on Rue Madeleine was full of elegant French *dames* wearing printed crepe fabrics and feathered hats; other than a few midshipmen Jeremiah spotted sitting in the back, he and Mary were the only Americans. Despite the sticky heat of July and the short supply of sugar and real coffee, the mood was festive. Paris had been liberated nearly a year before, and with the end of the war, there was talk of France abandoning the ration system.

Jeremiah felt no part of their *joie de vivre*.

"Did I startle you?" Mary asked, a slight smile on her lips, her voice smooth as cream.

"No. I mean, yes," he stuttered. The last several months had passed in a stupor, but now his skin prickled with nervousness, as if he'd jolted awake from a bad dream. "I guess I figured you'd be in uniform." He looked down at his own olive drab issue; it hadn't occurred to him to don civvies for his five-day furlough. He had two more days before he'd have to make his way back to the 45th Signal Corps Company and continue the task of rebuilding the civilian radio infrastructure destroyed by the Krauts. Although the war in Europe was over, he'd only earned twenty-nine points according to Uncle Sam's rating system—not nearly enough to go home. In three weeks, he was being redeployed to the Pacific, where the fighting raged on.

A flurry of thoughts swirled through his brain as he attempted to make polite conversation. *Hubba hubba*, for one. *Holy mackerel*, for another. He was trying to calculate how old she was, wrestling to work out the whole picture he'd imagined after reading and rereading her letter. A beautiful blonde falling for his bookish, serious older brother? It didn't square at all with his image of Lenny, who'd never had much luck with girls before the war. A point of ridicule, one which Jeremiah was ashamed to think of now. Perhaps Lenny had become a different man since he'd last seen him.

He swallowed hard and shook his head. "I'm sorry. This is all very strange for me."

Mary pursed her lips and nodded kindly. "It's difficult for me, too," she said softly, and he felt his unease receding. Her eyes were hazel with specs of black. She scrutinized his face—and then, a flash of recognition. "Ah. Your forehead and eyes. It took me a few minutes, but now I can see the resemblance."

From his wallet, Jeremiah pulled out a snapshot of his brother taken in 1942, just after he had completed the medic's course. Lenny was grinning wildly, cap askew, one of the youngest cadets in the 114th Medical Battalion. How proud Abe and Rikki Gerstler had been of their firstborn. Studious, industrious, obedient—these were the words that came to mind when people mentioned Lenny. These were the words repeated in his obituary, along with "patriotic," "heroic," and "magnanimous."

He passed the photo to Mary and watched as she brought it to her lips for a kiss. He felt his chest swell up. The same searing pain he had felt for himself, he now felt for her, too. And Lenny. It was rotten.

Jeremiah was trying desperately not to cry in front of Mary McDonald. He knew nothing of her until two months ago, and as far as he knew, his parents still didn't know anything. If Lenny had been alive, Rikki would have been in hysterics over his taking up with a midwestern *shiksha*, with her blonde hair, perfect skin, and all-American farm girl looks. Jeremiah understood with perfect clarity why Lenny had never mentioned her to anyone in the family. But the reality of Mary gave Jeremiah pause and widened the gaping hole he'd felt since Lenny's death: how well had he really known his brother? Her existence filled him with turmoil. He couldn't suppress the childish thought that had his parents known about Mary, they would have been sorely disappointed in his brother, for once.

They ordered a second round of coffees. It was easier to talk about the war than to talk about Lenny. As a combat nurse, Mary had seen every kind of human misery. She told him about the Battle of the Bulge, how in the first horrible days she and her fellow nurses, medical officers, and wardmen had been forced to move their field hospital three times within the week, leaving everything but their patients behind. In one seventy-two-hour period, her hospital, built for 650 beds, had taken in over 2,500 soldiers.

"I don't know how you do it—all those shrapnel wounds and amputations." He shuddered, feeling lily-livered. Jeremiah didn't tell her he'd thrown up the first two times he'd seen a dead body.

Last fall, Jeremiah had been terrified to be sent to the Continent, but the knowledge that his big brother was nearby, helping to fix the wounded, taking care of people as he always had, lulled him into a false sense of security. Who would take care of him now? For a few minutes he and Mary sat in silence, lost in their thoughts. The brothers had never been particularly close—three years apart and wildly different in personality—but the war had brought them together, if not physically than emotionally. They'd written letters back and forth. Lenny's last v-mail predicted the war would be over in months and suggested they visit Paris together once victory was declared. Now here Jeremiah was in Paris, alone.

The conversation circled and kept coming back to Lenny. Jeremiah found himself relating to Mary the story of how Lenny had saved him from drowning when he was thirteen. A decade before, a boy named Marvin Greenberg had drowned in a local pond, and the Jewish mothers of the neighborhood concluded that if they didn't teach their boys to swim, they wouldn't be tempted to go near dangerous water. Jeremiah was playing with his friends near the creek when he fell in and started flailing. He shivered now, recalling the shock of the icy water, the fetid mouthful he swallowed, his panic. The younger boys started shouting and Lenny came running, jumping in and dragging his brother to safety. Unbeknownst to Jeremiah, Lenny had secretly learned to swim, ignoring the mothers' injunction. The brothers waited until close to nightfall before returning home to give their clothes time to dry. They'd mostly outgrown playing marbles by then, but that afternoon they enjoyed many games. Back at home, a hysterical Rikki hugged them both, but then, smelling the river on them, gave them each a spank.

"The funny thing is, I don't know if I ever thanked him for it," Jeremiah said, as he recounted the story. "There are so many things I would have done differently, wouldn't you?" How he'd bargained with God in those first horrible days after he'd heard the news. He would take it all back, every single mean, ungrateful, annoying younger brother thing he'd ever done, if only Lenny could be alive.

Mary nodded sympathetically. "We didn't have that much time together." Her eyes were diaphanous, misted over, and he thought he could see straight through to her pain.

"Do you think the Japs will surrender soon?" he asked, again trying to redirect. As much as he was looking forward to going home, though, he didn't like to think of his mother and father and little sister, Ruthie. He had seen news reports of the scenes in the States on V-E Day: people piling out into the streets, children dressed in costumes holding balloons, waiting, now, for good news from the Pacific. There would have been no celebration in the Gerstler house. He could imagine his mother locking herself inside their home on Norman Street, scrubbing the floors and the bathtub until her fingers were raw. And still the reports from Europe could get worse: the whereabouts of two of his father's sisters and their children, last seen in Budapest over a year ago, were unknown. He shuddered to think of what any more devastating news would do to the family.

He'd moved along a path of grief in fits and starts: shock, denial, bargaining, more denial, depression, numbness, and isolation. Jeremiah told Mary that he found himself dwelling on the day and the manner in which he'd been informed of Lenny's death, rather than on the news itself. He'd been called out of central mess by his CO and when he saw the Jewish chaplain waiting for him, his stomach clenched. He stood frozen in place, waiting to hear the worst. He could still taste the residue of C-rations in his mouth, the last bits of beef he'd ever enjoy; he hadn't been able to eat that particular ration since. The telegram the chaplain read to him provided no details, only that Lenny had fallen in Belgium on the 10th of January, 1945.

"Tell me more about him," Jeremiah asked, desperate for information. "I mean, what was he like in the army? Anything!"

Mary sighed and blew out ringlets of smoke for a few seconds, as if she was at a loss for words, and Jeremiah wondered if he'd said the wrong thing.

"He was smitten with me from the start," she began. "From the first time he brought in a wounded GI to my field hospital. When I got off duty that night, he was there, waiting for me, holding out a bouquet of wildflowers and saying he wanted to thank me for taking good care of his guy."

"That's nice," he said. He could understand how Lenny would have fallen for Mary, but—and this was a question he couldn't ask—what had she seen in him?

She studied her fingernails. "He was earnest, young. Wanted to do everything he could to save lives." She described Lenny's valor, his willingness to run from a covered position to rescue injured soldiers and his gentle way of helping the frightened, wounded men, so far from home. She wouldn't be surprised if he got a posthumous Purple Heart.

"I had no idea."

"We talked about getting married, you know," Mary said, and for the first time, he heard a bitter tone to her voice, as if she was chiding herself for becoming soft and romantic during a period that was anything but. "He was worried about how your parents would take it. Mine wouldn't have been too thrilled either, I guess." She told him, then, of her girlhood, of growing up the oldest of six in a small town in Ohio. She had gone to nursing school, and then volunteered after Pearl Harbor. She was twenty-six, she confided, her voice low and throaty. Jeremiah's eyes opened wide at this admission. Four years older than Lenny!

He felt a newfound admiration for his brother then. *Jeez, Len*, he wanted to say, *how did you snag this bombshell?* He remembered the time Lenny asked Susan Glassman to a dance and she rebuffed him. Lenny had stomped around the house for a few days—Jeremiah smirking in the background—until Abe told him to stop feeling sorry for himself. After this, Lenny had thrown himself into his schoolwork with greater vigor, finishing high school in three years and entering UConn before his 17th birthday. He'd taken two years of pre-med classes before the war caught up with him. The memory was like a cuff in the gut, and Jeremiah put his head in his hands. Why hadn't he been nicer? *Please forgive me, Len.*

Under the table, his knee was shaking. Mary pulled out a pack of Pall Malls and offered him one.

"Thanks," he said, accepting. "I don't usually go in much for cigarettes but I'll have one now."

"What *do* you go in much for?" Her voice was sultry, a distinct change in her tone, and he blinked in surprise. Was she making advances, or was he misreading the signals?

"Beg your pardon?"

"Relax, Jeremiah," she said, sighing. She fiddled with the matchbook. "I just mean, what kinds of things do you like? What have you done in Paris these last few days, for example?"

He told her then how he had wandered around the city. With his army-issued Kodak PH324, he'd shot footage of postwar Paris: the

Eiffel Tower, the Arc d'Triomphe. Street scenes. The cigarette calmed his nerves, and once he got past his initial awkwardness, Jeremiah found Mary remarkably easy to talk to. Her eyes seemed to sway back and forth, from him to the other patrons and back to him, but never in a way that made him feel he was boring her. They signaled a waiter and ordered more drinks—tea for Jeremiah and cognac for Mary.

She asked of his plans once he got back to the States and he said he supposed he'd go to college.

"I think my father would like me to go into the family business," he said. "That's what everybody always figured: Lenny, the smart one, will be the doctor, and Jeremiah, the screwball, will work in the business." The "business" was three liquor stores in Bridgeport that kept Abe slaving most days until midnight. Once Ruthie was old enough for school, his mother worked the till, and Jeremiah had spent many an hour stocking the shelves and sweeping floors.

"Don't be so hard on yourself," she said. "Leonard said you can be a whiz when you want to be."

He flinched at the name "Leonard." At home, and for his whole life, his short twenty-two-year life, his brother had never been anything but "Lenny." But secretly, Jeremiah was pleased Lenny had recognized that he, too, had intelligence. "He said that?" Jeremiah did not have any great desire to go into the liquor business. He'd become a bit of a news junkie during the war; perhaps he'd become a newspaper man.

Hours had gone by since Mary stepped into the café. He'd done most of the talking that afternoon. Kind of a pseudo-*shiva*, the first time since Lenny's death that he'd met someone who seemed interested in all he had to say about his brother. The regular Jewish week of mourning was not possible for soldiers during wartime, the chaplain had explained; instead, he'd taken out his switchblade and made a small tear in Jeremiah's uniform as an outward sign of his loss.

Mary yawned, and Jeremiah worried he was boring her. "I suppose you've got to be going," he said, a bit glumly, and signaled for the check.

◆   ◆   ◆

The afternoon had turned to evening, and outside the passersby had thrown shawls over their shoulders. Nearby, a street band played a French tune, and they wandered in the direction of the music. Jeremiah didn't want Mary to take her leave just yet and suggested they take a walk down the Champs-Élysées. He'd been there the day before to take a small film of the Eiffel Tower. She seemed interested in the camera, so he went on to tell her about rolls of film he'd taken during the war, and then about how his company had often been forced to improvise with radio links to make sure messages could get through to headquarters. As he talked, he moved back and forwards in time, from basic training at Camp Crowder to the special equipment the Signal Corps had developed. Mary nodded eagerly; she had seen some of these special radios, she said, and had always been curious about how they worked. He explained the technology to her as best he could.

"My, you're sharp!" she said. He felt a tingling go up his body. "You're, what? Nineteen?"

"As of today, yes."

"Today's your birthday? And you didn't mention it until now?"

"I haven't felt much like celebrating, as you can imagine."

"Oh, but you must!" she cried. "The living must carry on. Let's go dancing. I know a good place over in the next *arrondissement.*"

He shook his head no. Had she heard a word he'd said the entire day? She seemed to accept his refusal, and as they walked down the boulevard she chatted about the French fashions. If he closed his eyes, her voice reminded him of butter, soft and creamy. She linked arms with him, as if this were the most natural thing in the world. He stopped dead in his tracks.

"Oh, sweetheart, relax," she said. "Haven't you walked arm and arm with a gal before?"

Sure, he wanted to say. Sure I've held hands with girls before. But not my dead brother's girl. "It's been a while," he said, feeling the color rush up his neck. He realized, with a start, that his face was not the only part of his body that was heating up. He dropped her hand. "Sorry. I just feel a bit funny about it is all."

To anyone walking past them, Jeremiah thought they must have cut an interesting pair: a tall blond walking with a medium-height, round-cheeked Jewish boy. That's how he was starting to feel around her. A boy, unnerved by her sophistication. Unsure of everything he thought he knew.

"Of course. I'm sorry," she said. "But listen to me: Leonard would want you to keep going with your life. I know he would. To have fun sometimes. Lighten up. Like this." She spun to face him and before he knew what was happening, her lips were upon his, planting a hot, wet kiss. "Happy birthday," she said, breaking into a smile.

"Oh!" was all Jeremiah could stammer out, his eyes wide in disbelief. Who was this woman? Where had Lenny found her? Maybe she was one of those good-time gals, some kind of floozy. Or maybe a femme fatale. He couldn't quite put his finger on it, but there was something dangerous about her. Why else would she take such an interest in him? It couldn't only be that she missed Lenny.

Her smile, which he'd found delightful in the café, now appeared serpentine. She started walking and he trotted to catch up. "Say," he blurted, without thinking, "you're not one of those Mata Haris are you?" He'd heard reports of all different types of women—a children's author, nurses, journalists—working for the OSS and the Allied intelligence efforts. The Germans surely had their own network of secret agents working within the American army.

He spotted, in her cheek muscles, a slight tensing. It lasted only a fraction of a second before she burst out laughing. "You certainly are a silly boy. Whatever in the world gave you that idea? I think you've seen too many moving pictures."

Reddening, he backtracked. "I'm just kidding with you. See, I'm trying to lighten up, like you said." Though he wasn't kidding, not entirely. Her laughter sounded practiced, false. Why had she asked him so many questions about the radio equipment? Why had he never heard of her from Lenny? At the same time, he recognized the absurdity of his suspicion: why would a double agent bother with a lowly Private from the Signal Corps? Not to mention the fact that the war in Europe was over.

To prove that he was joking, Jeremiah started repeating one-liners he had heard about the French and their lack of fighting heroes. Mary grimaced but then let out a tee-hee that again sounded false. "You remind me of Leonard. Both so funny."

"How?"

"Hmm?"

"How was Lenny funny?"

"Why, he told jokes just like you."

Again, he thought: *Imposter!* But no, she wasn't a spy. His brain, clearly, was not working properly. He sensed she wanted something from him, but he could not imagine what. This Lenny that she described sounded so different from the image of his older brother he'd carried; he felt desperate to know more, but not from her. He would write to his brother's army pals as soon as he could.

"You know," she said, "it's been so nice to meet you. I'd love to meet the rest of your family."

Her comment gave him pause. Had Lenny given her the impression that the Gerstlers were well-off? Why else could she possibly want to meet them? "I'm not sure what kind of welcome you'd get, to be honest with you."

She took a drag on her cigarette and puffed out a perfect circle of smoke. "I'm sure I can handle them."

Yes, he thought, but not the other way around. His mother would be beside herself. He might as well start sitting *shiva* for her, too, if she learned of Mary's existence. "I'm not sure my mother is ready to hear about you. Not yet."

Mary sighed and looked at him as if he were a simpleton. "You don't understand a thing about women, do you?" she snapped. "Any mother would be happy to hear a report about her son. She's dying for information. Trust me."

And you, Mary, don't know a thing about Jews, he thought. At least not the old-world, immigrant Jews like Abe and Rikki. No, he resolved. He'd have to do everything in his power to make sure that Mary did not contact his parents. He sensed that the more he insisted, the more persistent she'd become.

"You know what," he said. "Can I ask you just to wait, a bit? Let me see how they are when I get back. Assuming I get back. Then I'll be in touch." He knew, as he said it, that he would never follow through. "Maybe you're right," he said, for effect. "Maybe my mother *does* want to hear more details about Lenny. But please, not yet."

For a moment, she was silent, studying him, and he was sure she could tell he was lying. "All right. I'll wait."

Jeremiah didn't trust her, but for now her word would have to do. His mind started racing—who could he write to in Bridgeport to intercept his parents' mail? What did she want from them? He couldn't shake the thought that it had to do with money or—God forbid—was she pregnant? A quick glance at her midriff confirmed that she was not. Suddenly he was furious with Lenny for leaving him. Angry at the goddamn Nazis and angry at the rest of the world for not stopping them before this could happen. Angry at Mary for pushing him, playing with him. Even angry at his parents, for all those years they'd given Lenny favorable treatment.

Jeremiah needed to get away from her. Run far away, his mind screamed. Fast. Back to his hostel, to his unit. He couldn't decide if the whole thing had been a mistake. At some point, he'd have to sort through the entire tangle of his emotions, the signals his brain and body had been sending him. "Listen," he said, trying to contain his anger at the unfairness of life. Lenny dead at twenty-two. Jeremiah left to fill his shoes, knowing he'd never be adequate. "Thanks for meeting me today, but I need to go now." He tipped his cap and left her standing there without any further explanation.

Shiva for Lenny was over, but he still wanted to grieve for his brother, his poor brother whom, apparently, he'd barely known. Could you ever truly know another person? Staggering back to his hostel under the weight of this thought, he threw himself on his bed and cried for his lonely self.

THREE STRIKES

(1932)

In his whole nine years, Lenny can't remember feeling this mixed-up, even though he hasn't done anything wrong. He's sitting next to his father in the synagogue, listening as the congregation recites the special Rosh Hashanah prayer: *Avinu Malkenu, our Father, our King, we have sinned before You.* The adults around him chant the haunting, powerful melody, first in a murmur, then in a louder, unified plea for God to be gracious. If God is so great, Lenny wants to know, why—this year of all years, when his favorite team is playing—does the Jewish New Year fall on the same days as the World Series? The last time the Yanks were in the Series, Lenny had been too young to appreciate it. Later, after the festive lunch and the relatives have gone home, Lenny plans to slip out of the house and walk over to the Barnum Avenue drugstore, where the neighborhood men will be listening to today's game. He's not usually a sneaky boy, and he hopes God will forgive him this once.

Inside the synagogue, the service drags on, and Lenny is jealous of his younger brother Jeremiah who, at six, is allowed to play outside. Lenny isn't thinking about the prayers. His mind is on hits, runs, and strikeouts. The sweet crack of the bat connecting with the ball. The thunder of the crowd pulsing through the static of the radio. He tugs on his father's suit jacket and asks if he can go outside for a bit, but, no, he's benched: the elder Gerstler shushes him and tells him he must stay in for longer.

He shifts in his seat, daydreaming about the moment later today when the Yankees will sweep the Series. He's sure of it. Despite the prohibition of turning the radio on during Rosh Hashanah, he's learned from a non-Jewish neighbor that the Yanks beat the Cubs in yesterday's game, bringing the series to 3-0. He felt the agony of missing the game but was triumphant at the news. Today, even though he knows he should be praying for forgiveness and redemption, he's beseeching God for a Yankees win.

"Give heed to the clarion call of the shofar," the Rabbi bellows for the third time today. Some of the adults are bored; he can hear murmuring in the rows behind. Finally, towards the end of the service, his father relents and allows Lenny to go out and play.

Lenny makes his way to the empty lot next door, where other boys with fathers who are not as strict are playing: stickball for the older boys and marbles for the younger. His brother is kneeling in the dust, counting his pile of coveted bluish-green corkscrew marbles, his white holiday shirt and navy knickers smeared with dirt. Lenny smiles, thinking of his plan. After lunch, he's going to volunteer to look after Jeremiah so his parents can rest, but then they'll sneak to the drugstore to catch the game. He's even saved a Bit-O-Honey and a peanut chew, one to get Jeremiah out of the house and the other in exchange for a promise not to tell. The kid might not know much about baseball, at least not yet, but he'll do anything for candy. It's surefire.

Lenny leans against the wall and turns his attention to the stickball players, wishing they'd let him play and dreaming of being a better hitter. The boys are focused on their own game—arguing over who's batting next, yelling at the boy who just struck out—but Lenny wants to talk about the Series. "A better lineup, the Yanks couldn't have," he says, rattling off the batting order. "Lou Gehrig, batting fourth for the grand slam." He mimics an announcer's voice and assumes Gehrig's slugging stance. When no one picks up the conversation, he starts reciting batting averages for the Yankees lineup.

"Aren't you a real abercrombie?" says an older kid as he gets up to bat.

Lenny shrugs; it's not the first time he's been called a know-it-all. One of his father's friends calls him "Bridgeport's number-one baseball whiz," a title he wears proudly. He and Jonny Allen, the rookie pitcher, share a birthday. But the other boys don't seem interested in statistics, so after a bit Lenny wanders back over to the marble game, just in time to see Jeremiah flick a reddish-blue marble into the circle for a win. Secretly, he's looking forward to their afternoon together. He would like to tell Jeremiah about *the plan*, but he's afraid he'll tell Mother and Papa by accident. He knows it will work: with Johnny Allen as the starting pitcher, the Yanks can't lose.

The green clock on the kitchen wall reads 3:08 p.m. by the time lunch is over and the last relative says goodbye. Lenny watches his mother wash the dishes and his father dry and stack them in the cabinet. He is trying not to appear too anxious, but the game was scheduled to begin at 2:30 New York time. He'd known he would miss the first inning or two, but now he is getting nervous. His parents are slow in washing and drying. Instead, they gossip about their relatives: Cousin Mendy, out of a job for three months, is having a hard time feeding his family. Sussie has been forced to take in needle and button work for nine cents an hour, instead of having a better-paying factory job that might pay double.

Papa says, "We're lucky that selling eggs and butter will never go out of business." He hopes to have his own store one day.

When the dishes are done, Lenny jumps out of the chair, eager to volunteer to watch Jeremiah. But his mother beats him to it. "Play quietly in the den," she instructs, "so we can rest. If Jeremiah gets too jumpy, take him over to the park on Noble Avenue. But no further than that." She is always cautioning him not to wander down East Main Street, where the tramps like to gather.

Lenny nods, trying to hide his smile. The park on Noble Avenue is three long blocks away from the pharmacy on Barnum Avenue, though he knows that to go further and get caught would mean a heavy punishment, like no baseball ever.

"What a responsible boy you're becoming," his father says. "A better son, I couldn't ask."

His mother leans over and kisses his forehead and calls to Jeremiah to mind his big brother. Lenny waits until his parents have climbed the stairs to their bedroom and shut the door. If they walk fast enough, they might make it by the fourth inning.

Lenny finds Jeremiah on the front porch playing with his marbles. With the Bit-O-Honey, he lures his brother down the steps, and onto the sidewalk, heading for Barnum Avenue. "Come!" he tells him. "We're going on an adventure." He doesn't say where they are going, or how they're about to be part of Yankee history. To tell him the truth would only raise questions, like why they can't just turn on their own Philco, Model #20.

As they cross over East Main, still two blocks from the pharmacy, Lenny takes Jeremiah's hand. They pass hobos sitting under the awnings of closed shops. One tramp is curled in an entryway and looks dead, but then Lenny notices that the man's brown hat covering his face is rising and falling as he snores.

"Look over there." Lenny points across the street to divert Jeremiah's attention, but his vision is drawn to a row of beggars slumped against the ledge of the church yard. The line extends all the way around to the back of the building. The men wear hats of all shapes and sizes, and some hold walking sticks. Their jackets are too tight, the sleeves torn, with filthy white shirts sticking out.

Despite Lenny's efforts to shield him, Jeremiah notices, and asks, "Why are their clothes so dirty? What are they doing?"

"They're waiting to get food, I think. Don't worry about them. We don't go there anyway, so mind your own business." Lenny tightens his grip on Jeremiah's hand.

"Ow! Let go of me," Jeremiah whines.

"Hurry up then."

They pick up the pace, passing Pearl's Bakery and Meyerson the fishmonger. Lenny worries he's missed the *whole* game. Surely he would've heard cheers if it was over?

"Where are we going?"

"You remember what I told you about the Yankees, right?"

Jeremiah looks up at him with wide eyes, a dribble of candy juice sliding down his chin. "Uh-huh."

"Today we're going to sweep the Series. Won't that be grand?"

"Sure." Jeremiah pulls his gray marble bag out of his pocket. "Can we play marbles when we get there?"

"Later!" The drugstore in view, he sees a thick cluster of men and boys congregating at the entrance. He starts to run, begging Jeremiah to keep up. "Come on, will you!"

Motioning for Jeremiah to sit on the bench just outside the store, Lenny pushes his head into the crowd, listening for some tidbit, some stat, some crack of the bat, to let him know his team is winning. Instead he hears a snigger, tongues clucking. Babe Ruth has just struck out. Before he can ask the score, he hears the official, tinny voice of the announcer coming over the radio: *Ground ball by Gehrig. . .and the Cubs retire the Yanks with an easy out at first. Another disappointing inning for the Bronx Bombers.* And after a pause: *If you're just tuning in, the Chicago Cubs are up, 4-3 at the bottom of the fourth.*

Lenny can hardly believe his ears. "What!" His voice rattles. "How's that possible?"

"Where you been, kid?" The fellow standing next to him frowns. "That damn rookie Allen gave up four runs in the first inning!"

A wave of disappointment washes over Lenny, but he tries to stay hopeful. *They can still turn it around,* he tells himself, and in the top of the sixth inning the Yankees pull ahead, only to have the Cubs catch up almost immediately. Every time a Chicago player is up at bat Lenny feels like he's holding his breath; judging by the strained looks on the faces of the other boys and men, they are too. Once in a while, Lenny pulls his head from the crowd to look for his brother, and each time he sees him waiting on the designated bench. *Good.* Jeremiah catches his eye and points at the soda fountain through the window, to which Lenny shakes his head, a firm no. Lenny didn't bring any money—their parents would never allow them to spend money on Rosh Hashanah, certainly not to buy such a luxury. He ignores his brother and goes back to listening to the game.

At long last, the Yankees take a strong lead in the seventh inning, scoring four runs off of back-to-back singles by Combs, Sewell, and Ruth. The crowd erupts with cheers, but Lenny doesn't have much time to celebrate, because Jeremiah is tugging on his sleeve and asking, "Is it over yet?" For reasons Lenny cannot understand, Jeremiah has not caught on to the enthusiasm or the team spirit surging through the store.

"No, ding-bat! It's only the seventh inning! How many innings are there in a baseball game?"

"Nine." Jeremiah looks down at his feet. "I want to go home."

Lenny fishes out the other piece of peanut chew, but it doesn't placate him this time. "Don't you want to listen? It's the World Series, game four, only the most important game of the year!"

Jeremiah frowns. "You said we were gonna play marbles." He holds up his bag.

"Later, I said. Not in the middle of the game, for Pete's sake!" Lenny's attention wavers as the glorious sound of the ball hitting the bat, followed by the crowd cheering, pulls him back to the game. "Just go back and sit on the bench. We'll go when it's over!"

Lenny half watches his brother sulk off, but he doesn't care. The Cubs have the bases loaded now, bottom of the eighth. Lenny bows his head and scrunches his eyes shut, hoping for easy outs, and again his prayers are rewarded. By the time the ninth inning draws to a close, Lenny's heroes have scored four more runs. The radio announcer's glorious voice makes the triumph complete. *Once again, ladies and gents, the New York Yankees are the world champions! Final score: 13-6. Joe McCarthy can be proud of his team today—what a comeback for the Yankees!*

A shout of joy erupts from the drugstore crowd. Lenny savors this moment of pure happiness and watches the men and boys around him hugging each other, whether they're strangers or not. "Babe! Lou! Champions!" he screams for all he's worth.

Someone starts singing the words, "Take me out to the ballgame." Lenny and the others join in.

"For its one, two, three strikes you're out, at the old—ball—game..."

For a moment, Lenny thinks back to the unified voices in the synagogue this morning, but he finds this song more beautiful, more uplifting. Even some of the poor hobos from East Main, with holes in their shoes and sooty faces, have joined the crowd and gather to sing along.

As the crowd starts to break up and head in different directions, Lenny pushes his way to the bench where Jeremiah is waiting—only his brother isn't there. He scans the immediate area, but doesn't see him; the flow of bodies moving and expanding around him makes it difficult to find a small boy.

"It was Lazzeri's two home runs that sealed the game," someone shouts in Lenny's face. He feels a surge of excitement, but the fear of losing his brother weighs him down, keeps him from enjoying the victory.

"Jeremiah!" he starts shouting. There are too many men walking on the sidewalk. He shouts louder now. "Jeremiah Gerstler!"

When his brother doesn't appear, panic takes over, his heart frantic in his chest. Lenny searches the faces going past him, and he tries to stop each one, asking if they've seen a six-year-old boy.

A few kind men stop to hear Lenny out. "Haven't seen him. Good luck."

"What's he look like?" asks another.

"Brown curly hair, white shirt, navy knickers. Holding a bag of marbles."

"Sorry kiddo," he says. "Gotta be careful with kids these days. Some sick people out there. My wife cried for a week over the poor Lindbergh baby."

At this, Lenny's eyes bulge with fright and his body goes cold with dread. He runs back and forth in front of the pharmacy, standing on the bench to see over the crowd. He begins to contemplate the unthinkable: how can he go home and face his parents?

The panic creeps down from his throat to his belly and settles like a heavy stone. If God doesn't strike him down for this, Mother and Papa will. *Atta boy, Lenny. Such a good son, we couldn't ask.* He'll never hear his parents utter those sweet words again, and only now does it dawn on him how much he likes to hear them.

Lenny circles the drugstore, canvassing the area in all directions, his eyes scanning the stoops of the shops and the dark corners under the awnings. He prays, this time not to the god of baseball but to the Almighty Himself, promising that if Jeremiah is found, he will never again break the rules of the holiday. Never go behind his parents' backs. He even promises to sit in *shul* for the whole service, every Shabbos.

At five-thirty, the drugstore owner shoos out the last men and starts to close up for the night, pulling down the shades and locking the cash register. Lenny sits on the bench where he last saw Jeremiah, shivering in the early October chill. The crowd has dispersed, and Lenny is hoping to see Jeremiah come around a corner. He prays his parents haven't left the bedroom and discovered them missing. Maybe they wouldn't worry at first, thinking the boys are at the park. But as evening comes, his mother would expect them home. She'd pace the kitchen, worried. Lenny's imagination turns to the Hardy Boys books he's so fond of, with their tales of little boys being tricked and kidnapped. He never thought such a thing could be possible in Bridgeport.

Lenny starts to sob, wiping his nose on the sleeve of his good Rosh Hashanah shirt. His arms prickle with a cold sweat, his chest feels heavy. Despite the sense of doom coursing through his veins, he starts down the street towards home.

"You there," comes a voice from the manicured lawn of the church they'd passed on their way. The line of hobos has disappeared. "Come with me." The man is slight, his beard the color of the grimy yellow chicken fat Lenny's mother skims from the top of the soup. The tramp takes Lenny by the arm, startling him.

"Let go of me, mister!" He tries to pull away, but the man's grip is too strong.

"I seen you up the road, and when I came back here, I got to thinking. . ." His abductor leads him through the side entrance of the church.

This is his punishment, Lenny thinks. In a flash he sees the bones of tricked, kidnapped boys. He's just about to call for help when he sees a sign over the door:

JUDGE NOT, AND YOU SHALL NOT BE JUDGED.
CONDEMN NOT, AND YOU SHALL NOT BE CONDEMNED.
FORGIVE, AND YOU WILL BE FORGIVEN.

"Oh, I'm not. . .I'm not a Christian," Lenny stammers. "My mother is expecting me."

The man grunts and yanks him inside, where he comes face to face with a big cross hanging on a wall. Next to it is a painting of a woman with her arms spread, her head encircled by a glowing light. He's never been inside a church before and he begins sniveling again, his mind repeating one phrase over and over: *Mother! I'm sorry! I'm sorry!* He's dimly aware of men's voices coming from another room. His body feels rigid but the man jerks him forward, through another doorway.

The bright lights stun Lenny into silence. As his eyes adjust, he sees that he is in an assembly hall, with five long tables stretching the length of the room. Tramps sit at the tables, the remnants of leftover potatoes and stew on their plates and gravy stains on the tablecloths. A half-dozen church volunteers serve the men small pieces of chocolate cake and bruised yellow apples.

The man eases his grasp and points to a curly-haired boy sitting at the fourth table, his white shirt covered in greasy drippings.

"Len!" Jeremiah calls and waves. "Over here!"

It takes a few seconds for Lenny to understand. He is breathless by the time he reaches Jeremiah. "Oh, God. Oh, thank God. You're okay." His eyes water with relief, and he stops to wipe his nose. "How did you get here?"

Jeremiah shrugs, unaffected by Lenny's urgency. "I was hungry and I couldn't find you, so I walked back here. You said they were giving out food, remember?"

"And boy, can he eat," one of the men at the table says, chuckling.

Lenny sees a few bites of stew on Jeremiah's plate, and his eyes widen in shock; despite everything *he's* done today, he is appalled that his brother has eaten *treif*. Doesn't he know anything?

"He's an ace at marbles," another one of the tramps chimes in.

A volunteer approaches with several pieces of cake. Jeremiah is first to take one, but Lenny stops him. "We have to go now."

The man who grabbed him off the street says, "Sit down; what's the rush?" He reaches out with a grubby hand and Lenny takes two steps backward.

Lenny eyes Jeremiah, imploring him to get out of his seat and say goodbye. "We really have to go." When he makes no move to leave, Lenny takes Jeremiah by the hand and pulls him out of his chair. "We have to go," he hisses again.

"Come back and visit us any time, pal," a man missing two front teeth says to Jeremiah.

"So long, fellas." Jeremiah waves goodbye. They muss his hair as he passes, holding out their hands for him to give high-fives.

Jeremiah flashes a smile, and Lenny leads him toward the side door. They emerge into the dusky evening. The intermittent twittering of crickets follows them as they walk towards home. He's amazed at his brother for being so at ease with these men.

Lenny throws his arm around Jeremiah's shoulder. He has no words to express his deep relief. "I guess you weren't scared?" he asks, realizing he had come very close to striking out today, but was granted a last-minute save by the most unlikely group of relief pitchers.

Jeremiah doesn't answer, his nonchalance suggesting that he's not upset with Lenny. "They were nice. You said we were going to have an adventure."

An adventure was not quite how Lenny would've put it, but if that's what the kid wanted to think, it was swell by him. His mind spins. So many things have changed in the space of a few hours: dark possibilities he didn't even know existed, and even a newfound goodwill towards the beggars of East Main. "Stay away from those good-for-nothings," he remembers his father once saying. But maybe Abe was wrong about some things. Lenny walks a bit taller, feeling more mature, like a rookie who's gotten a taste of experience from the big leagues.

They are nearly home, the houses lit up with kerosene lamps, their soft glow illuminating the lilac bushes decorating the neighborhood yards. Lenny would have some explaining to do. He wasn't a good liar, and besides, Jeremiah could not be trusted to keep his mouth shut. As it is, on the short walk home, his brother has already mentioned—twice—that the fellas invited him back to play marbles, and that he'd sure like to.

Inside, Mother and Papa sit at the kitchen table playing cards, waiting for them. They seem relieved, but not overly worried. "Were you playing in the park? Did you lose track of the time?"

Lenny can't help himself; he starts to cry. He wishes he could be braver.

"What is it, Len?" His mother wraps him in an embrace. Faint aromas of chicken soup, carrot *tsimmes,* and apple cake—foods for a sweet new year—linger in her dress.

He buries his head in his mother's bosom.

"Speak up."

When Lenny stops his tears, he'll tell them everything. He'll tell them how he prayed for the wrong things, and that the tramps aren't such bad people. He'll explain and explain until they can find a way to forgive him. He also has his promises to keep, and many games of marbles with Jeremiah to make up. He'll even try to save his money and buy his brother a present, maybe the set of Akro sparkler marbles he's been asking for. Maybe then God would forgive him, too. And maybe if they aren't too mad, he'll see if Papa can spare some butter and eggs, and if Mother can bake a cake to take to the hobos. It's a new year, after all.

GERSTLER'S TRIUMPHANT RETURN

(1972)

Sitting among the malodorous teenagers—boys ripe with day-old sweat, girls thick with jasmine scents—Jeremiah tried to check his mounting vexation. He never would have guessed these shaggy-haired kids were honors students. They wore fringed suede jackets, peasant blouses, and despite the season, short, short miniskirts. Hannah seemed to be the only normal one in the group, dressed in Levis and the argyle sweater they'd given her for Chanukah. The bus hurtled toward its destination, and Jeremiah was stuck, no way out of his commitment to spend the next five days shepherding his daughter's tenth grade class around D.C.

He tugged at his hat, pulling it down over his ears to block out the noise. Towards the back of the bus the weird-looking boy wearing lipstick and eye makeup (*he thinks he's David Bowie,* Hannah whispered), strummed on a guitar and took requests from classmates. Jeremiah didn't usually feel old—underneath the tan corduroy fedora was a full head of wavy brown hair, more than he could say for a lot of men in their late forties—but in this crowd he was as ancient as the Founding Fathers. His bowties were hopelessly out-of-date, according to his daughter, and for this trip he'd acceded to her request to leave them at home.

Mr. Bruno, the young history teacher sitting a row ahead, wore his long hair tied back. Standards for teachers in the liberal, artsy atmosphere of the Berkshires were a bit too relaxed for Jeremiah's taste, and he found Bruno's ponytail off-putting. The man's flannel shirt gave off a whiff of something close to marijuana. Incense? Pipe tobacco?

How the hell had Jeremiah's wife cajoled him into chaperoning this thing? *Who better than a political science professor and former NSC staffer to accompany the class,* she'd said, knowing exactly how to play to his ego. It wasn't Molly's fault entirely. He could never resist a trip to Washington, a chance to catch up with his old buddies, a chance to breathe in the panoramic view from the top of the Washington Monument. And he figured he could use the trip to prepare for his all-important return to the capital next month, when he was scheduled to testify before Congress.

"So, what are you going to say to our esteemed congressmen?" Bruno turned to ask him as they crossed into Delaware. "Hannah told the class about your testimony."

Jeremiah glanced up in surprise; a warm glow spread over him. His daughter was proud of him! On the other hand, something in Bruno's tone—the way he said "esteemed"—made Jeremiah wary. "I'm going to be talking about the aftereffects of going off the gold standard."

The teacher stared at him blankly. Jeremiah knew his topic wasn't a lightening-rod issue like Vietnam, but scholars and a few astute people on the Hill cared.

"You heard about that, last summer?" Ever since Nixon's big announcement a year and a half ago that he was taking the United States off the gold standard, Jeremiah's expertise was in demand: requests for book reviews and conference presentations, articles for the college's alumni magazine, interviews in the local Berkshires and Albany papers, and—most exciting—the call from Raleigh Fox, his old pal from the NSC, asking him to testify before a new joint House/Senate subcommittee.

"Sure," Bruno said. "So did Tricky Dick do the right thing?"

Again, the cynical tone. "Yes, definitely." Jeremiah tried to keep any sneer out of his voice. "We should have done it years ago. Nixon was smart to do it." He sensed the young man tensing.

"I see." The teacher's expression was skeptical. Clearly he knew nothing of the global monetary system.

"Anyway, forget it." Probably best not to talk politics with Bruno, who from the looks of it had attended multiple war protests in college, or worse yet, was a draft dodger. Then again, by this point, who didn't want an end to this war that had already claimed so many lives? Anthony Oliver, one of Jeremiah's most promising students, had been ambushed in Quang Tri, nine short months after graduation. Jeremiah had represented the university at the funeral and the loss—the goddamn waste of 58,000 young men—made him sick with grief.

He sighed and shifted in his seat, telling himself to stop fixating on something he couldn't change. Molly's voice rang in his head, enjoining him to relax. He'd try to appreciate seeing the D.C. sites through the eyes of a younger set, Hannah and her friends. He was under strict instructions from his daughter to cause no embarrassment. No doubt the scheduled briefings at their congressman's office and at State would be given by junior officers since it was the week before Christmas. Here, Jeremiah assumed, he'd jump in, helping to explain the finer points of diplomacy and international relations to the teenagers.

Maryland rolled by: the thoroughbred racetrack he and Raleigh used to visit, the rusting railway bridges and the mill towers that dotted the path to Washington. When they crossed Route 495, he was lightheaded, a bit nauseous and uneasy. But he also felt something of a rush, as if closing in on the Center of Power could restore his vigor, like a superhero refueled.

Monday morning, the first full day of the trip, the group stepped inside the Washington Monument, unzipping their heavy New England outerwear as they waited in small clusters for the elevators. The National Park Service had stopped allowing people to take the stairs a year ago, though Jeremiah could imagine the students galloping up the steps like racehorses. D.C. was a town for young people with boundless energy. When Jeremiah emerged on the observation deck, he stepped to the window and whistled. God, he loved the view here, though the branches of the cherry blossom trees were bare. In the distance, near the Lincoln Memorial, ice floated on the Reflecting Pool. The people on the ground looked tiny from this height. How excited he'd been in 1955 to arrive in D.C. with his new bride, thrilled to begin their adult life. He'd felt the capital's push and pull for twenty years, ever since his mentor at Columbia had encouraged him to put his academic training to practical use for the country. He sauntered around the deck, taking in the vista from every direction. To the east stood the Capitol Building, majestic and gleaming. The hearing at which Jeremiah was testifying next month would be held in one of the smaller congressional buildings, but now, seeing that white dome, his chest swelled, inspired by the accomplishments of this great nation. His profound patriotism came from his immigrant parents, forever grateful to the United States, despite their sacrifices.

Instead of eating lunch with the group, Jeremiah slipped out to meet Raleigh at the Farragut Square Inn, a far cry from the 19th Street Diner where they used to debate the issues over greasy grilled cheeses. The upscale restaurant made him slightly anxious, and Jeremiah wondered what his former colleague thought of his career switch, eight years prior, from government to academia. Teaching wasn't quite as glamorous as working in the Administration.

"Fancy shmancy," Jeremiah said as Raleigh strode up and thumped him on the back. "Moving up in the world, I see." He hoped he didn't sound envious; he felt genuinely pleased for his old buddy. Raleigh was now a hot shot, the number two guy in the newly created Joint Study Committee on Budget Control.

"You too, Professor. Congrats on getting tenure, by the way." Jeremiah smiled and nodded. He knew he could count on Raleigh to understand that academic work was meaningful.

Over orders of sirloin steak, Raleigh regaled him with Washington gossip. Jeremiah stirred with nostalgic regret. Though he'd never felt like an insider during his nine-year sojourn in D.C., he'd been privy to some basic goings-on. He missed that, off in his quiet college town in the Berkshires.

The biggest buzz right now, his friend relayed, was this business about the Watergate hotel; the episode "stunk to high heaven," with fingers pointing high up in the Administration. Jeremiah had seen the article in *The Washington Post* claiming Nixon aides were involved in sabotaging Democratic candidates, but it seemed so ludicrous he hadn't believed it. "A collection of absurdities," a White House spokesman called the accusations. They shook their heads, marveling at the folly, and Jeremiah wondered silently if he should have stuck to his loyalties. He'd never before voted Republican, but Nixon's bold monetary policy combined with what seemed like significant progress on ending the war in Vietnam convinced him to back Nixon in last month's election. He admitted his defection to no one, especially not his liberal wife or daughter.

"The war will be over soon one way or another," Raleigh predicted when they switched topics to the breakdown of the peace talks. "Either the talks will resume or Congress will cut off funding in January."

"Thank God." Despite Kissinger's "peace is at hand" statement just before the election, the Secretary was now saying the United States would not be stampeded into an agreement. The war was not yet over. More boys like his student Anthony would die. Every time Jeremiah thought about it, he became incensed.

"Well, that's one of the things we're hoping to do with this new committee," Raleigh continued. "Curb the President's ability to spend or cut at his discretion."

Jeremiah asked about his upcoming testimony: What he should expect during the session, how long would he have to speak, how each Senator and Representative on the committee leaned politically. Raleigh briefed him on the protocols and assured him everything would go smoothly.

"I wish I could invite Bob," he said, of their old boss. "Show the guy I knew what the heck I was talking about. Should I put that in my testimony? My old boss didn't want to hear a thing about it?"

"No!" Raleigh nearly choked on a piece of steak. "For god's sake, no need to accuse anyone of incompetence." He covered his mouth as he coughed, exposing a gold wristwatch with a black face and red numbers on display, the new kind Jeremiah had seen only in commercials. "Focus on the research," Raleigh said. "Just sound sensible, bipartisan, not like some hothead who's there for political purposes. That's the most important thing."

"Roger that." He pointed to Raleigh's wrist. "Nice watch. How much are they paying you?"

Raleigh raised his eyebrows. "Jesus, Gerstler, you're direct!" He started to chuckle. "You haven't changed a damn bit, have you?"

Jeremiah gave a sheepish smile. "Is that a compliment?"

"Tact was never your strong suit. Good thing you switched to academia. You wouldn't have made a good politician. Or diplomat."

This was an uncomfortable truth, but painful to hear. The way to respond was to make light. "Yeah, Molly says I don't have an internal filter. But now, thanks to you," Jeremiah grinned, "I've been invited to testify before Congress. I wonder if the press will take an interest. I can see the headline in the *Post* already: 'Prof. Says He Tried to Warn Three Administrations on Faulty Policy.'"

"Oh yeah, that's right. I'm sure the *Post*—hell, *The New York Times*—they'll all cover your testimony. You'll be on the cover of *Time* magazine." Raleigh raised his hands to frame an invisible headline. "'Professor Gerstler's triumphant return.'"

He laughed heartily at Raleigh's joke, and after a bit, bid his friend goodbye. Hurrying back to the hotel to meet the group, Jeremiah turned the words over in his head: Gerstler's triumphant return. A long-awaited triumph for Gerstler. Pres asks Gerstler to head up special committee.

In the thrall of his fantasy, Jeremiah was unprepared for the throng of students and other guests gathered around a television screen in the hotel lobby. Angling to get better a view of the set, he found the history teacher, who shook his head sadly. "So much for peace," Bruno said. "We just started bombing the crapola out of Hanoi and Haiphong."

"What a dickhead," said a student, referring to Kissinger or Nixon or Laird, Jeremiah wasn't sure which. "Murderer!" said another, her tone angry. Though he, too, felt dismay at the news, Jeremiah was irked to hear the kids referring to the nation's highest officials in these terms.

Such a difference between this generation and his. He frowned and was about to reprimand them when Hannah caught his eye with a pleading look. This was his life now: the predictable, mundane reactions of college and high school students. Meaningless in the face of history.

He sighed. His lunch with Raleigh offered a glimpse of discourse on a higher level, a gilded world of action and inside intelligence. Would things have been different if he'd stayed in Washington?

Over the next few days, Jeremiah squeezed in one more meeting with a former colleague, but most of the time he was marshaling kids on and off the bus. They did head counts at every stop: the Lincoln Memorial, the National Museum of American History, and Ford's Theater, where the class hoodlum (as Jeremiah had come to think of him) imitated John Wilkes Booth. Jeremiah tried not to hover near his daughter, though every once in a while she'd drift towards him for a chat. *Have I ever been here before?* She was seven when they'd left D.C. and didn't remember much.

News of the bombing campaign in Vietnam—dubbed Operation Linebacker II by the Administration—was sporadic, but on Wednesday they heard of the first American casualties, as well as reports of massive civilian deaths on the North Vietnamese side. Jeremiah's stomach clenched with each account, as it had when the full story of My Lai came out. What had happened to the honorable U.S. forces, men he'd been proud, thirty years ago, to call his brothers-in-arms? With each report, he felt more duped, angry at the Administration and its manipulation. He'd wanted to believe Kissinger's promises of peace, but now he understood that he'd simply been a chump, fallible in his raw human need for hope.

Jeremiah and the history teacher took to discussing the news. He admired the way Bruno engaged the kids in debate; his long hair no longer seemed important. "Know any Yiddish?" Jeremiah asked him.

Bruno shrugged. "Maybe a few words here or there."

"Well, here's what I think: bombing for peace is like *shtupping* for virginity."

Bruno laughed. "Yeah, I've heard that one. But when I was at Michigan, our language wasn't so quaint."

He imagined Bruno in college, leading protests in his wiry glasses and goatee. Jeremiah couldn't recall doing anything radical in his whole life, unless you counted participating in a teach-in at the college. But even then he wasn't an outspoken participant, he'd just taught. He never wanted to do anything to jeopardize his candidacy for tenure. And some of the anti-war protests—the ones bent on villainizing the enlisted men—bothered the World War II veteran in him.

At the State Department, the tour guide waxed long on the building's architectural features and artwork, and Bruno had to prompt her twice before she explained the Department's basic functions. She seemed to think the students were more interested in the ceremonious aspects of diplomacy than in the meat of policy-making. Today was the final day of their trip, and Jeremiah hoped they'd be treated to a thought-provoking speaker, but as they walked along the corridors, the guide ignored the copies of treaties hanging in their heavy frames, instead pointing out portraits of former Secretaries and telling anecdotes about visits from various heads of state. Jeremiah and Bruno rolled their eyes.

"Down there," the guide pointed to a room at the end of a hall, "is where Dr. Kissinger gives press conferences or Q&A sessions, like the one he gave last week on Vietnam. Of course, we have a press briefing daily, during which reporters ask our spokesman anything they'd like relating to affairs of State."

"What time is the daily briefing?" Jeremiah called out.

Her face brightened, happy to have a question. "At eleven o'clock, every morning. That way the reporters can go back to their offices and file their stories."

Jeremiah checked his watch: 10:40 a.m. He sidled over to her. "Would it be too much trouble to see if we can stay for the briefing? The kids would love it." He motioned to his daughter and a few other students. "We've got a bunch of student journalists in this group."

A few of them, as if on cue, produced reporters' notepads. The tour guide looked uncertainly at them, and back at Jeremiah. She deliberated for a few moments, glanced at her watch, back at the kids, and then down the empty hallway. "Usually school groups need to get permission ahead of time, but it's almost Christmas, so I guess it'll be all right. You can stand in the back, but please don't interrupt during the briefing. Once the press is finished, I'll see if a public relations officer can answer your questions."

The students buzzed with excitement, and Jeremiah gave her a genuine smile in thanks. As they filed into the press room, lining the yellow walls, Bruno held back a smaller group of students before directing them to different locations around the room. Jeremiah stood along a side wall, scrutinizing the reporters. The press was not sympathetic to this latest bombing campaign; he wondered how tough their questions would be.

After the spokesman's brief statement, the reporters fired question after question, like a tennis ball launcher. Thomp, thomp, thomp. Jeremiah marveled at their ability to grab onto the slightest of hints in the spokesman's body language or the particular way he phrased a point. "Has the Administration considered that the bombings will only harden Hanoi's stance?" Thomp. "Sources say the President ordered the B-52 attacks on civilians as a mauling operation, to show Hanoi his determination. Comment?" Thomp.

"That's a ridiculous, libelous statement. We don't target civilians. Next."

"So, you may *strike* civilians, even though you don't *target* them. Is that correct?"

"No comment."

"Is it your position that you don't discuss civilian casualties?" Thomp.

Patiently, the spokesman lobbed the answers back at the journalists, reiterating earlier statements. The man could not be rattled, even as the questions grew more urgent. Jeremiah was both impressed with the spokesman's composure and frustrated by it. He would have liked the man to show some sensitivity, a little regret for civilian casualties and the massive destruction the U.S. was causing in Hanoi. Sorrow for the thirty-five Air Force men downed since the operation began.

At that moment, Bruno raised his right hand to his forehead and lifted one, two, three fingers.

The sound started as a buzz, almost imperceptible, but soon the entire room could hear the undeniable chorus of "Give Peace a Chance." The hum grew louder, into a mantra, a few students, Hannah included, singing the words under their breaths as reporters turned in their seats, mirthful grins on their faces. Jeremiah himself could not suppress a chortle. Terrific!

The spokesman scowled at the tour guide, now cowering against a back wall, hands at her cheeks. Jeremiah felt a little guilty: the woman would probably lose her job. The spokesman waited for the students to finish their song so he could resume his answers, but one song flowed into the next, from "Fortunate Son" to "Blowing in the Wind" to "Bring them Home." Jeremiah sang along as best he could; he didn't know all the words.

After initial attempts to restore the quiet—"thank you for that musical interlude"—the spokesman shrugged his shoulders and shouted to the reporters, "I guess that's it for now, folks. Merry Christmas!"

Just then, the class hoodlum and three other students raced to block the spokesman's exit. The reporters sprang into action, snapping pictures, asking for details—names, school, ages—and the students' opinions of the bombing.

Jeremiah felt his chest expanding with delight over his daughter and her classmates. He loved these kids. He'd be crushed if *any* of them were sent over there, yet he realized they were two short years away from compulsory service. Given recent events, he no longer trusted Nixon would keep his word and end the draft. Images of bodies flooded his memory: scattered corpses on frozen ground in France and Belgium almost thirty years before, the snow bloodied and crimson. A picture of his brother's inert body, a figment carried in his imagination since Lenny had fallen in the Battle of the Bulge, now mixed with visions of his student, Anthony, and the snapshots coming out of Hanoi. U.S. servicemen and Vietnamese soldiers and civilians alike, all lifeless. Tens of thousands of families broken by a son's death in battle, just as his own had been. Each life an entire universe.

Rationally he knew the two conflicts were vastly different, and he brooked no regret over U.S. involvement in World War II, or any war that was just. But this felt different.

"What happened to Kissinger's 'peace is at hand' statement?" Jeremiah yelled, directing his anger over the bombing campaign at the spokesman. "'Peace, peace,' he promised. But there's no peace!" He'd nearly choked up a moment ago thinking of Lenny, but now, looking at these kids, so *young*, he fumed. The thought of sending them to the jungles of Vietnam sickened him. His brother and Anthony were worth ten of this guy.

He was through being quaint and rational. He didn't care for discourse now. "One, two, three, four, we don't want your fucking war!" Jeremiah chanted, fist in the air. Within seconds, the entire 10th grade class was stomping their feet and bellowing with him. Their voices thrummed with passion. The room felt ablaze with their heat and the glare from the photographers' flashes.

They kept it going for almost a quarter of an hour, until security pried the students loose and snapped handcuffs on Jeremiah and Bruno, leaving only the other parent chaperone with the kids. Jeremiah heard the snap, snap of the photographers' cameras and students calling out bits of information to the reporters. Cold metal cuffs cut into his flesh, but his hands seemed detached from his body. His whole being coursed with energy, a sense of vigor and righteousness he hadn't felt in years, if ever.

After several hours in police detention, Jeremiah and Bruno were released with stern warnings to take their hippie views back to Massachusetts. The fact that he supported the President's monetary policies and wore bowties made no difference to them; throwing his lot in with the nation's youth made him a hippie. Jeremiah felt a little wild.

Hannah threw her arms around her father, and he squeezed her tight, relieved she wasn't furious with him over escalating the protest. "We had a bit of fun, didn't we, Hannah Banana?"

She held him out at arms' length, still stupefied over what he'd done. Then she laughed. "I can't believe they took you away in handcuffs. Those pigs!" She wanted to sit with him on the bus to hear all about the lockup. She examined the red marks on his wrists and kept exclaiming, "Oh my god! You're such a rebel!"

He beamed at her praise, though he had a niggling sense that something was out of balance. He'd telephoned Molly from the police station. She'd always identified with the anti-war protestors, and over the phone she sounded proud of him. He solicited reactions from the other students, wanting the feeling of vitality to linger for as long as possible.

They boarded the bus for the long trip home, a few hours behind schedule. Jeremiah kept up his verve while Hannah sat with him, but by Baltimore she'd moved to sit with friends. They traveled farther and farther away from D.C., and he was not sorry to be saying goodbye. All week, the question of whether he belonged in this city had dogged him, and he was fairly sure he had his answer now. The reality of his situation unraveled; his mind was like a jammed cassette tape, spiraling out of control.

He was finished here. There would be no return trip—triumphant or otherwise—no feted coverage of his academic contributions. In the morning, there'd be a small article in the *Post* about the protest. Perhaps all the way back on page five. Then a phone call. Raleigh, having a fit, would un-invite him from testifying. *Bastards*. His chest constricted, like something was squeezing his ribcage. He couldn't take a deep breath; the more he tried, the more he panicked. His hands and arms were sweaty, despite the chill coming through the bus window. Was this a heart attack? He struggled to remember the symptoms. After a few minutes the sensation passed and his breathing returned to normal, but a dark hole of regret had settled in his stomach. Why, why, why had he done it?

As the bus wound its way up the east coast, the students' wisecracks and squawking gave way to isolated whispers. A collective drowsiness descended, but Jeremiah was too wound up to sleep. He'd gotten worked up—was that such a big deal? It wasn't the first time he'd acted on impulse, for god's sake. He reached back, trying to analyze the moment he began chanting. He couldn't identify the rationale, only the emotion. He didn't ascribe to the political theory that nation-states always act in a rational manner, so why should individuals? What he knew was that the protest felt pretty wonderful and gratifying, perhaps even cathartic.

Arriving back at the high school parking lot in the middle of the night, the kids said their goodbyes. Several students hovered near Hannah and Jeremiah. A few polite ones thanked him for chaperoning. In their sleepy eyes he could see their newfound admiration, and this gave him a lift.

At home he found a neat stack of the week's newspapers on his desk, and despite the hour, he ruffled through them, reading reports of other impromptu demonstrations around the country. One editorial after another criticized the bombings, further validation that what he'd done was moral and right.

Climbing into bed at last, he inhaled the familiar, welcome scent of his sleeping wife. He restrained himself from waking her, though his mind was still swirling with thoughts of the protest. In the morning he'd tell her how it felt to be standing among the teenagers, their hope and optimism contagious. What was the inflection point in politics and economics, when a million micro-lives could cause a change in the macro, like pointillism in art? Maybe he'd ask Bruno how to get involved in the movement. He pictured the reporters, silently cheering from the sidelines, offering him encouraging winks and smiles.

TRANSCENDENTAL

(1983)

H e's in complete denial," Stuart said to his mother as he
watched Jeremiah inflate a long yellow balloon and twist it
into a giraffe, his third balloon animal of the evening. "He
does realize Hannah's getting married, not turning five, right?" His
sister, busy with her bridesmaids, didn't notice the mini pump their father
was carrying around in his pocket to supply the guests with balloons,
but to Stuart they were clear signs of his father's mental deterioration.

Molly agreed with him. But with so many wedding details to worry
about, she said, she didn't want to make an issue out of it. "You know
your father. He thinks he's helping, and the children seem to be enjoying
it. Besides," she said, lowering her voice, "he's not great with transitions,
and this is a big one, so if he wants to deal with it by making balloon
animals, does it really matter?"

"Okay, but it's not even like there are that many kids here," Stuart
continued. With only two or three children on the Gerstler side and a
couple more on Tom's, each child had received at least four balloon
animals by Friday night. On a sofa in the lobby of the Prospero Inn,
where many of the guests were staying, a red balloon dog had come
undone, and a green elephant was starting to shrivel. Stuart, home
from his first year at film school and self-appointed videographer,

panned the scene and did close-ups of the depleted balloons, wondering how long he would have to film them to show a time lapse of a balloon animal's entire lifespan. Through the lens of his BetaCam, his father's features looked clownish, his gray hair puffing out in unnatural places and his red, white, and blue polo shirt ("in honor of Flag Day" he'd explained that morning) too bright.

After a year away at school, no longer living under the same roof as his father, Stuart felt his relationship with Jeremiah improving. Provided his father could start relating to him as an adult, they could transcend their earlier patterns and a mutual respect between them might evolve, he hoped. But watching his family now, Stuart affirmed his decision to stay in New York for the summer. His father was a kook, his mother was in her drill sergeant mode (understandable, given the stress of organizing a wedding, but unpleasant), and his sister, well, who knew what was going through her mind? The thought of tethering himself to one person for the rest of his life held no appeal for him. He felt nauseous contemplating it. College and life in the city had finally given Stuart his independence, and he was not interested in ending his partying any time soon. He could handle his parents for a weekend, a week at most, but after that, anything was liable to set things off. Thank goodness he'd brought a stash of weed home with him.

"In wilderness is the preservation of the world," quoted Tom, one of the first times Stuart met him. Hannah and Tom were introduced at an inter-department wine and cheese gathering two years before, she a second-year grad student in political science and he a fourth-year in comparative literature, writing his dissertation on the New England transcendentalists. The rest of the Gerstlers found his penchant for quoting Henry David Thoreau a little irritating.

The Gerstlers couldn't object to Tom's credentials: smart (BA from Williams, M.A. and now Ph.D. from Penn), hardworking (holding down two jobs while studying), thoughtful (bringing Molly flowers each time he visited), and liberal (from working-class Democrat stock). Stuart could imagine Hannah and Tom's parenting debates and pitied his future nieces and nephews. If their professorial father was any indication, everything would be turned into an academic exercise: requiring reading, analysis, an immersion in "the literature." Stuart was not like that at all—other than a few physical traits, he and Hannah were no more similar as brother and sister than any two random people. She was a voracious reader, her grades revoltingly stellar. Basically she was a stable, dependable person who rarely showed her emotions, whereas Stuart liked to think of himself as a deep feeler, a sensitive soul. The seven-year age gap between them meant they weren't particularly close, though this did not preclude occasional venting to one another about their parents.

When Hannah and Tom's relationship had started to look serious, Stuart thought their religious incompatibility might be an issue for his parents. But while his father teased them about it—"You going to have a Chanukah bush or something?"—Jeremiah had surprised Stuart with how much he'd taken the fact that his future son-in-law was not Jewish in stride.

"What are you going to raise your kids as? Have you given any thought to that?" Jeremiah asked last summer, just after the engagement. They were watching the Red Sox lose to the Yankees, making Tom and Stuart groan and Jeremiah gloat. Despite living in Massachusetts for nearly twenty years, his father refused to switch loyalties.

"We're going to raise them as people. Little people," Tom said, grinning. "As mensches."

"Huh! Listen to him," Jeremiah said, gesturing to Hannah. "You've been coaching him, I see. You got any plans in that department? I mean, I'm not getting any younger over here. I'd like to be able to bounce a grandson on my knee a couple times before I die."

His sister sighed and reminded their father that she was in no rush. He'd be the first to know, she promised. Hannah and Tom were patient with Jeremiah, far more than Stuart would be. The demarcations of favoritism in the family had always been clear to Stuart: his father adored Hannah, who could do no wrong in his eyes, whereas Jeremiah saw his son as one big disappointment. His mother was usually the one to intercede on his behalf, to soften the punishments his father doled out: an occasional spanking or getting grounded for weeks on end. She'd taken Stuart into her realm, encouraging him to play an instrument, making him her chief helper in the kitchen. By the age of seven he knew how to make cookies and banana bread by himself. Stuart was thankful he took after his mother, artsy and fun-loving, not like his sister and father, both type A personalities.

The introduction of a new, quirky person into the family gave Stuart an opportunity to find common ground with his father. When, a few months, back the young couple mentioned their honeymoon would be "part camping trip to Acadia National Park, part pilgrimage to the White Mountains," Stuart and his father raised their eyebrows. They had never been an outdoorsy family, but Hannah seemed content with the arrangement. Tom explained that in the White Mountains they'd be recreating the trip Thoreau had taken with his brother, the basis for *A Week on the Concord and Merrimac Rivers*. "To be admitted to Nature's heath costs nothing," Tom said, quoting Thoreau. "None is excluded, but excludes himself. You have only to push aside the curtain."

"Do you think he whispers Thoreau or Whitman to her when they're doing it?" Stuart had asked when the lovebirds left to drive back to Penn. His father chuckled, but Molly looked dismayed.

"That's enough, Stuart."

"No, really, I should know, for my own edification. In case I need some good lines for the future, which one is more romantic?"

"Didn't you hear your mother? That's enough," Jeremiah barked. The reprimand was for Molly's benefit, though Stuart could see a glimmer of a smile underneath the gruffness. His father was not above laughing at crude innuendos. Soon after this exchange, Stuart and his father had started referring to Tom as Thoreau behind his back.

On Saturday afternoon, Stuart's parents floated among the wedding guests at the Prospero Inn, his father continuing to blow up balloons for anyone under ten, even those hotel guests not connected to the party, and his mother making sure everyone received their hospitality baskets.

Thursday night, Stuart had arrived at home in time to help stuff the baskets with fresh fruit, Molly's homemade scones and jam, and, at the request of the bridegroom, a copy of Walt Whitman's poem "To You."

Molly kept sending Stuart on useless errands—to the drugstore to buy matching, color-coordinated ribbon barrettes for the flower girls, shuttling people to Tanglewood for the afternoon matinee, and so on. "Go talk to my cousin Sylvia," she commanded, or, "Go see if Uncle Irv needs more aspirin."

"Maybe I should have gotten one of those portable helium tanks instead," Stuart heard his father say to no one in particular.

Just as Stuart was wishing he'd brought the pot with him to the hotel, a couple of the groomsmen—Tom's friends from high school? college?—came down in basketball shorts and asked Stuart where they could find a court. He hadn't pegged Tom to be the type who had basketball-playing friends. Stuart started directing them to the outdoor court at the junior high when the tallest one—holding the ball and looking, with his big hands, like he'd been born to rebound—invited him to play. "Okay, sure." Anything beat sitting around the hotel kissing elderly relatives and listening to Jeremiah make tired jokes about being the father of the bride.

As he was leaving, he passed his sister entering the lobby with her entourage of bridesmaids. "I see you've met the guys," she said, gesturing to Tom's friends. "By the way, what's with Dad? He's acting all weird."

Stuart shrugged. "And that's news to you?"

"He seems a little tense."

Stuart nodded. Despite the balloon façade, he knew this was not the good, wacky sort of weird, but the anxious kind, hinting at deeper emotions that threatened to erupt. With one Intro to Psych class this year, he'd gained volumes of insight into his parents' behaviors. "It's a defense mechanism. Just look at him with those stupid balloons," Stuart said. "He's clearly in denial that you're all grown up and getting married. Or maybe it's 'dissociation.' That's when you temporarily modify your personality to avoid emotional distress." He'd had to memorize all the defense mechanisms for his final exam.

Hannah looked at him curiously, and he silently congratulated himself for displaying academic prowess to his sister. "But why would he be in emotional distress? I mean, we're all kind of tense, but he's got to chill out."

Stuart nodded in agreement. Surely, he thought, his father was pleased for Hannah and wouldn't screw things up. He couldn't remember Jeremiah ever getting upset or exasperated by Hannah. "He'll be fine," Stuart said to her now. "Don't worry. What's the worst he can do? Make a few bad jokes in his speech? Get all the kids up on the dance floor and then beat them at the limbo?" At Stuart's bar mitzvah, Jeremiah had stayed in the limbo rotation until the last round, when one talented and wiry thirteen-year-old finally won.

She shook her head and sighed. "Just what I need right now. I'll have a talk with him. Maybe that will help."

Hannah saw Stuart glancing at the basketball players, who by now had given up waiting for him and were walking down the street. "Go. It's fine. See you at home later?"

"Yeah," he called, breaking into a trot to catch up. He'd play ball, then go home to shower and hopefully have a little down time before his mother called him back into service. Who knew what family duties she'd throw at him for tonight's rehearsal dinner?

Back at home, after the game, Stuart guzzled half a pitcher of cold lemonade, glad to be away from the hotel for a bit. He was still sitting in the kitchen, rethinking an easy layup he should have made, when Hannah entered, her eyes red, nose runny, with Molly just behind her. His mother looked exasperated and let out a loud groan.

"What's the matter?" he asked.

They relayed how Hannah had taken their father aside, trying to understand what was bothering him, and to ask him—please—to knock off his peculiar conduct. Jeremiah denied exhibiting any odd behavior, refusing to admit that anything was bothering him, and would everyone please just leave him alone? And then, out of nowhere, Jeremiah started muttering sarcastic, hurtful comments about her and Tom. "Don't tell me how to behave! I'm your father. I'm the one paying for all this! The least you can do is show me a little respect. I'm not acting peculiar. Why don't you ask your fiancé about peculiar? Always quoting someone or another. My god, how can you stand it?"

"It's like he doesn't want me getting married at all," Hannah cried. The more she'd pleaded with him, the louder he'd responded. Molly had hurried over, trying to intercede and shush him so the guests wouldn't hear, but that only served to further agitate him.

He'd started in on Molly too. "You! Who cares if the napkins match the tablecloths, and the tablecloths match the dresses? And your constant directives 'Run here,' 'Run there!'" Stuart could imagine his father gesturing wildly. "You're making me crazy with this wedding!"

Molly eventually succeeded in shooing him away and Jeremiah had stormed off, leaving his car in the hotel parking lot and heading on foot in the direction of the campus where he'd taught for nearly twenty years.

"Holy shit," was the only thing Stuart could think to say when they finished the story. For a brief moment he felt the gratification of hearing that someone else was the target of his father's invective, but then he thought, *Poor Hannah.* Why couldn't his father just behave himself for once?

"I'm sure he'll settle down," Molly said, trying to reassure Hannah. "He doesn't mean anything by these outbursts." Jeremiah didn't like the pressure of dealing with the extended family, and having Molly's mother around always made him uneasy, she explained. He obviously wasn't handling the fact that his little girl was about to get married. "Maybe you don't remember—it was already eight years ago—but when Poppy Abe died he had a similar reaction. Anger, lashing out at the people he loves the most."

Yes, Stuart thought, sometimes his father got thrown off-balance, even by small changes.

"But Grandpa dying and me getting married are two totally different things!" Hannah said. "That was a sad occasion; this is a happy one! That's no excuse. What if he doesn't come back before the rehearsal dinner?" She looked miserable and started crying again.

Molly rubbed her daughter's back and told her everything would be all right. Jeremiah would calm down; he wouldn't ruin the wedding. Stuart wasn't convinced. "Go get some rest," she ordered, back in drill sergeant mode. "He likes Tom. I promise. He'll come around. Now go." Hannah was too tired to argue. She wiped her eyes and headed to her childhood bedroom to lie down.

His mother spoke to him in hushed tones. "I need your help. You're the only one in the family he's not upset with at the moment, so I need you to find him and talk to him." Assuming Jeremiah had gone to campus, she said, he'd probably be in one of two places: either on the bench by the footbridge over the Housatonic or in the covered gazebo behind the main library.

Jesus, this was not what he had in mind when he left New York on Thursday. Talk his father down from some irrational place and convince him to act sensibly for the rest of the weekend? He was the last person in the family his father would confide in. But his mother was wringing her hands and rubbing her temples, exhaustion and anxiety coursing out of her, and Stuart understood that he had no choice.

In the three hours before they were scheduled to leave for the rehearsal dinner, Molly had to pick up more guests arriving via Amtrak in Pittsfield, plus shower and get ready. The dinner itself wasn't scheduled to begin until another hour after that, so they had a bit of leeway, she said. "Thank you, sweetheart," she added.

His mother went upstairs to retrieve one of her checklists, and when she came back down three minutes later, she seemed disappointed to find Stuart still sitting at the table. "What are you waiting for, Stu? You should get going!" She grabbed her car keys and as she headed back outside, she called out an idea. "Stuart? I think there are some extra scones. Take them with you—he's probably hungry, and food will help him relax."

Stuart had finished the last three scones in a fit of hunger after the game, but now was not the time to tell her. His mother was right: the way to his father's heart was through his stomach. Something sweet. He remembered that Molly kept some cake and brownie mixes in the second pantry downstairs. She preferred to bake from scratch, but when short on time or ingredients, she resorted to her emergency supply. Stuart wasn't sure if anyone else knew about the mixes, but as his mother's baking assistant, he'd been let in on the stash long ago.

"Holy shit," he blurted out to an empty room. He felt inspired, his mind hatching a beautiful plan. His sister would owe him one.

He showered while the brownies baked. Still no sign of his father. Less than an hour later, he walked out the door carrying the entire tray, wrapped in foil.

He found Jeremiah exactly where Molly said he might be: in the gazebo behind the library. His father was dozing, a *New York Times* magazine spread open on his lap. The balloon pump lay on the ground by his feet. Given such a setting, Stuart's plan suddenly seemed a little insane.

"Dad." He gave Jeremiah a gentle shake and he awoke, disoriented. His eyes seemed to widen as he remembered his whereabouts.

"You!" he said when he saw it was Stuart. "What are you doing here?"

"Looking for you. Is everything okay?"

"Yeah, yup." He yawned and rubbed his eyes. "Just dozed off for a bit."

His father appeared to be acting normal. "Here, brought you something," he said, unwrapping the tinfoil covering the tray.

"Mmmm. . .your mother's?" he asked.

"Yup," Stuart lied. "She thought you might be hungry. Fresh out of the oven." He took out a plastic knife and started slicing them.

"A good woman," Jeremiah said, biting into a brownie. "Sometimes I don't know why she puts up with me." He laughed at himself. "I'm a lucky guy."

Stuart watched his father finish the first brownie and reach for another. That was his cue to pop one into his own mouth. He wanted to stay a step ahead of Jeremiah. "These are good, aren't they?"

"The best." Jeremiah sighed. "This whole wedding business. I don't know why, but it hasn't been easy for me." In between mouthfuls, Jeremiah started reminiscing about his own wedding, back in '55. A grand affair, it was. Molly's mother knew how to put on a party. But Jeremiah and his parents had felt a little out of place, surrounded by all those *machers,* lawyer friends of Papa Mickey and their money and connections. His parents were simple people, immigrants. It wasn't that Molly's American-born parents made Jeremiah's parents feel inferior, but there was a sense that they were from another world. The Kellmans owned a private telephone line and a black-and-white television set long before his parents; as soon as color TVs became available, they bought one of those too.

His father started to guffaw as he reminisced about his in-laws and the early days of his marriage. "Would you believe I worried that your mother and her family would think I was no fun because I didn't smoke? Can you imagine?"

Stuart rolled his eyes; he'd heard the line before.

"I don't know why I'm finding this so funny! You know what, Stu? I'm feeling better already. By god, I'm starving. I could eat this whole tray."

"Better not, Dad."

"Have you seen your sister?"

Stuart shook his head no. Better to feign ignorance.

"She's probably not very happy with me," Jeremiah explained, his tone turning sober. He stopped, cutting himself another brownie. Apologies and admissions of guilt did not come easily to Jeremiah. "I probably said some things I shouldn't have. Thoreau's a decent fellow. Maybe a bit too transcendental for my taste, but I've got nothing against him. Even the religion thing—maybe it would have bothered me more if my parents were alive—but I'm not going to get all worked up about it." He paused to chew. "What it comes down to, I guess, is that marrying off Hannah. . .feels kind of like we're losing her."

"Why? She's not leaving the family, just bringing Tom in."

"I guess so. It's all a bit muddled in my head. When you have kids, don't have girls, okay? Boys are easier. There are these emotional ties with a daughter. . ."

"That you don't have with a son?"

"Exactly."

"Bullshit," he said, annoyed that just when he was starting to feel a buzz, he felt the familiar anger at his father pushing through. "I know plenty of guys who are close to their fathers. Did you ever think that maybe it's you? Why is it that *you* don't feel any emotional ties with me?" Stuart felt his voice breaking. Damn it, it was a question he thought about often, and now they were both going to be too stoned for a reasonable discussion. Or maybe it was better this way.

"That's not fair. Of course I do. Maybe there's more inherent worry with having a son, so there's a distance."

"You're not making any sense," he said, pointing his finger at his father.

Jeremiah closed his eyes, threw his arm around his son, and let out a sigh. "I mean, if you had been born ten years earlier, there's a good chance you would have had to go to Vietnam."

It was very fuzzy, this logic, but if he stretched his brain, maybe Stuart could see his father's point. All of a sudden he felt like a character in a comic strip, light bulb over his head. "Is that what this is about? All these years you allowed yourself to feel close to Hannah, to shut me out, or at least make me feel like I was never good enough, because one day—*if* I had been born ten years earlier—I might have come home in a body bag, like Uncle Lenny? That's messed up." A concept from his class floated into his head, though it was still a bit hazy.

"Actually you're nothing like Lenny. If anyone is, it's Hannah."

"You're missing my point." The concept came into focus. "I learned in my psych class, there's this thing called 'displacement.' It means you're separating emotion from its real object—the loss of your brother, which, I guess, you've never really come to terms with—by redirecting this intense emotion towards me." Stuart hoped he sounded erudite; his father should be impressed.

Jeremiah considered this for a moment. "Maybe you're not so far off. Who knows? Sometimes your mother likes to point out that I'm not always fair in the way I treat you versus your sister." He rested his head on Stuart's shoulder. "I'm sorry."

"That's bullshit. You could if you tried harder."

His father looked up and pointed his finger at Stuart. "You said 'bullshit' again," he said, starting to chuckle. "Good thing your mother's not here."

Oh, his father was definitely a head case. With Hannah too, displacement was at work, his father lashing out in anger at her when what he was really feeling was sadness or loss. Or was there a different name for that neurosis, because the object was still the same? He thought if he learned a bit more psychology, he could be a sounding board for his father. He could heal him, and in doing so, get him to admit he'd been wrong about Stuart all these years. Today was a start. Another idea started forming in his brain, inflating in slow-motion, something foggy about transferring out of the film school and becoming a shrink. He'd aced his psych final, after all.

Suddenly Stuart felt tired. He wasn't listening completely, but he encouraged his father to keep talking. He was starting to feel relaxed, a rising, out-of-body sensation, glad the pot was finally kicking in. Let his father prattle on about marriage and kids, responsibility and life's imbalances. It made no difference to him. What an excellent, superb idea this had been.

"Yup, boys are easier," Jeremiah said again, skittering back to the earlier topic and throwing his arm back around Stuart, which caused him to wake up a bit. "You've turned into a good boy. After all that mischief you used to cause. Remember when you toilet-papered the Kravitzes' house on Halloween and then bragged about it the next day?" Jeremiah started guffawing as he reminisced about his son's antics. "Mrs. Kravitz invited you over for a clean-up party, a stroke of genius! Ha! I don't know what made me think of that." Stuart recalled his father taking the punishment further, offering the Kravitzes his son's leaf-raking services every Saturday for two months. "I'm glad you've gotten those pranks out of your system."

"Yup, no more pranks for me." Stuart was trying very hard not to snicker.

"We should have these talks more often. I haven't laughed this hard in a long time," Jeremiah chortled. He started jabbering about all the mischief he'd caused as a youngster: "fixing" the radiators in his sixth-grade classroom making it too hot to sit inside, releasing the frogs at his mother's seder, a story Stuart had heard dozens of times. Again, Stuart started tuning out, but soon he became aware that his father was addressing a question to him.

"Do you want to get married, Stu?"

"I'm only eighteen!"

"I don't mean now, schmoey, I mean when you're older."

Why *schmoey*; why did his father always have to call him that? He'd try to remember to bring that up in one of their future "sessions." "I can't really see the benefits, to be honest with you."

"There are plenty of benefits, especially for men. I've come to the conclusion that men are much more dependent on their wives than vice versa. I know, this goes against all sorts of economic realities, but women, they've got this inner strength. In the first few years of a relationship, maybe we men have it okay. But a word of warning: once the children come along, it's like, 'see you later.' I could be trying to tell your mother something, but if one of you kids came in and needed her for something, she would just tune me out and only listen to you. See?"

Not really, Stuart thought. "So what, you're saying you regret having us?"

"Don't twist my words! I guess it's just a piece of advice I wish I had been aware of. For a long time I thought maybe your mother had grown sick of me, but then I looked around and saw a lot of other men in the same boat. After the children come, men are second fiddle. Period. But once the kids are grown and out of the house, if you've treated your wife okay all those years, she'll come back. It's all a bit of a power game. But you've got to let them think they've got all the power, see? Shhh. . ." he put his finger to his lips and started giggling again. "Don't tell the women we're on to them, okay?"

Stuart would need to mull over this new piece of wisdom, if that's what it was. He considered the possibility that the old man could teach him a thing or two. Share some of his life experience, and talk on a man-to-man level. As he contemplated this, he remembered the real reason he was here and reminded Jeremiah it was time to leave. A quarter of the tray of brownies remained, and Stuart wrapped them up; if need be he'd give his father the rest of them before the ceremony tomorrow.

Now that Jeremiah had shed his earlier, cantankerous mood and become jovial, Stuart made a suggestion he never would have made if either one of them had been sober. "Maybe you should apologize to Hannah, so she doesn't think you don't want her to get married."

"Sure, sure," he replied. "I'm happy for her. Thoreau's a good man. You're a good boy, Stuart." He kissed him on the forehead. Stuart let the words float in the air, but wondered why Tom was a man, and he was just a boy. Why couldn't his father have told him this more often? A topic for another future session, but for now Stuart tried to concentrate on his feelings of triumph. He knew his father would give Hannah a big bear hug and find a way to smooth things over. His mother would be relieved and grateful and say, *Let's move on*. His sister would forgive. That's the way things worked with Jeremiah: a never-ending cycle of blowups and forgiveness. Perhaps with Stuart's involvement, that could change.

"Do you think they're going to move to Walden Pond?" Stuart asked.

"I'm feeling a bit transcendental myself," Jeremiah said, bursting with giggles.

In one last stroke of genius before they made their way back to the wedding weekend, Stuart kicked the balloon pump off to the side. Jeremiah didn't notice a thing. He helped his father up and they left the gazebo, holding their sides, hooting like maniacs.

TOUGH DAY FOR LBJ

(1964)

Jeremiah checks his watch, trying not to rush Molly, but she can't stop fussing with her outfit and hairdo. The cocktail party is supposed to be a relaxed affair—a summer get-together for the political science faculty—but when spouses are invited, it's never informal. With his D.C. experience, Jeremiah expects a warm welcome from his new colleagues. If someone asks if he's rubbed elbows with LBJ and JFK, he'll nod and say, "Sure, sure. And don't forget Ike! What's he, chopped liver?"

Through the window a cricket chirps at regular intervals, a singular tune he'd never have distinguished in the city, but here in their quiet new Berkshires home it could be the only sound for miles. Their seven-year-old daughter is asleep upstairs. Outside, dusk has given way to a starry night, and Jeremiah feels his patience slipping away. He's been paying for the babysitter to watch *The Red Skelton Hour* for twenty-five minutes already.

"Mol! You okay in there?" The cocktail party feels like the official start to this chapter in their lives; making a good first impression is a crucial test. "Let's go!"

Molly emerges in a black and burgundy ensemble he's never seen before, her belly the size of a small basketball. Her eyes are puffy and raw and she grabs tissues to bring in her handbag. Her complexion looks washed out, no trace of her usual gusto. She's overwrought by the day's news, an FBI report that three bodies, thought to be the missing civil rights workers, have been discovered in a Mississippi dam. Of course every well-meaning person has been troubled by their disappearance, all the way up to the Attorney General and the President, but Molly is particularly distraught. Or it could be the pregnancy hormones.

"You look terrific. Is that new?" Anything to cheer her up so they can leave. All that crying can't be good for the baby, but he knows enough not to say anything on this sensitive topic—two miscarriages in the last three years. He plants a kiss on her cheek, salty from a stray tear, and waits a beat. "Okay now? Can we go? Can we put poor Goodman, Chaney, and Schwerner out of our minds for a few hours?"

"I'll try," she says, wiping her eyes again and whispering *sorry*. Molly's family vaguely knows the Goodmans from summers in the Adirondacks. She may have babysat once or twice for young Andy and his brothers, though she'd told him she can't recall with certainty. It's not a stretch to imagine that if the voter registration drive was going on a decade ago, when Molly was twenty-two, she'd have wanted to join the efforts. Jeremiah admires the fresh-faced, idealistic Mississippi Summer Project workers but wonders about the sensibility of going deep into Klan territory.

The main priority now was to get to the party and apologize for their tardiness.

In the car, Molly lists the tasks for the week ahead: find a pediatrician, join a synagogue, put the word out that she would be offering private piano lessons.

Jeremiah drums his fingers on the steering wheel.

"You're nervous." Molly reaches over to give his leg a squeeze.

"Me? No, I just don't like being late!" Sure, he's a greenhorn in the world of publishing and tenure battles, not to mention teaching, but with almost a decade of government experience and a Ph.D. from Columbia he ought to be fine.

He flicks the radio on. After a few moments of static, the announcer's voice comes alive, talking about some aggression in the Gulf of Tonkin,

the second time this week. "Jesus. Tough day for LBJ." Jeremiah
envisages the Sit Room, his former colleagues debating a course of
action in Southeast Asia. The President would be leaning forward
asking pointed questions while staffers reviewed the dispatches from
the *USS Maddox*. LBJ tended to become volatile when forced to make
a decision without all the facts, so Bundy would be trying to give him
clear and concise information. There will be a response, of that Jeremiah
is certain.

Two weeks have passed since Jeremiah's last day at the National
Security Council, and for the first time he is nostalgic. He misses the
meetings in Bundy's damp basement office, the breeze of staffers
rushing through narrow corridors with urgent telexes, the feeling of
doing something important. Eight years in D.C. working for
Eisenhower, Kennedy, and Johnson, and boy does he have stories!
Nervous to meet a bunch of political scientists? Ha! He's never been
more confident, certain his experience will give him instant credibility
with these guys. He'll be loyal to his oath of confidentiality, of course;
though he can't disclose the exact debate over, say, air strike vs. naval
blockade during the Cuban Missile Crisis, he *can* mention he was
privy to the discussions.

When they arrive, chatter echoes from the Daltons' backyard.
From the driveway they follow a lit brick path past evergreens and
sculpted shrubbery until a small crowd comes into view. Bill Dalton,
the department chairman, tends bar on a bluestone patio. Dalton is
broad-shouldered but not portly, with a head of gray hair that curls
at the back of his neck and gentle eyes of a kind pastor. His wife
Marion looks equally clerical, stalwart in her short-sleeved blazer
and matching skirt.

"We're so sorry we're late," Molly says to Marion, who motions to
the waitress, an older black woman in a white apron, to bring over a
tray of hors d'oeuvres.

"Well hello," Bill calls. "You're finally here!"

Jeremiah winces and forces a smile as two dozen pairs of eyes turn
towards them. He removes his hand from Molly's back and waves to
the group.

"Hello!" Molly's tone is cheerful. "Jeremiah was ready ages ago," she says. "I'm the reason we're late!" She indicates her pregnant stomach. Jeremiah knows Molly is saying this to make it clear that he is punctual, dependable, but he wishes she wouldn't make such a show of it.

The women in the crowd coo and immediately gather around Molly while Jeremiah is introduced to his new colleagues. They seem an impressive bunch, with doctorates from Yale, Berkeley, Minnesota, and Notre Dame. That the department includes one female professor (Joy McGratten, international relations) and one Negro (Nathaniel Williams, political communications) speaks well of his new institution, he thinks. The faculty members pepper Jeremiah with questions about his experience in Washington. *What's the mood been like since the assassination? What's the gossip on the election?*

Jeremiah has a lot to say and he might as well admit it: he enjoys the attention. They're gathered around him like he's some kind of superstar. And when has that happened before? Certainly not at the NSC where—if he's honest with himself—he was an assistant to the assistant of the man in charge and his colleagues never gave enough credence to his position papers. Even after so many years, he never felt like a Washington insider. He left in search of a place that he might make his intellectual home. A small university would give him the leeway to dig deeper into his research and the potential to be recognized for it.

Jeremiah swallows the last of his beer, and Dalton immediately replaces it with a gin and tonic. He's not a heavy drinker and he knows he should get more food in his system. With perfect timing, a waiter emerges holding an assortment of Melba toasts, deviled eggs, and cheese straws. Jeremiah would love to take a few of each but he doesn't want to appear piggish, so he selects two. He gives a friendly nod to the waiter, hoping he'll return soon.

The circle disperses into smaller side conversations, and when he finds himself alone for a moment he scopes the scene, trying to keep track of who's who. The colleague wearing a U.S. Navy Veteran pin on his lapel is an expert in European politics. The two standing to the side are engaged in an animated discussion on Khrushchev's reforms, but he can't recall their names. Nathaniel Williams mentions working on the Stevenson and Kennedy campaigns as a minority liaison. Someone else is talking about his year at Oxford.

Jeremiah is overwhelmed. Molly is far better at socializing than he is. Nearby, the ladies are asking about her due date, other children, and how she's finding the Berkshires so far. "It's so quiet here at night! I'm a city gal, so it's taking some getting used to," he hears her say. In her voice there is no trace of the grief from earlier in the evening. "But yes, all of the cultural things were a big selling point for me. . . A subscription to Tanglewood? We'd love to!"

Jeremiah catches Molly's eye for a moment and winks.

Joy McGratten seeks him out to quiz him on the need for the NSC. "But don't you agree with Kennedy's assessment—that there's no need to have a little state department in the White House?" she asks.

"I don't know about that," he says. "Just look at the Bay of Pigs—State did a terrible job of coordinating the response. So that's why Kennedy gave back some review powers to the NSC."

"Seems like a lot of extra bureaucracy to me," says another colleague, who shrugs, downs his whiskey, and then saunters away before Jeremiah can reply.

There is a bit of truth to this assertion, but despite its problems, Jeremiah is proud of his former agency. He can't help making snap judgements about his new colleagues, certain they are appraising him as well. The guy in the corner, a lush. Williams, quiet. McGratten, sharp but something irritating about her laugh. Bill Dalton is paternal, nodding with approval as Jeremiah describes the syllabi he's planned. His new boss moves through the crowd, refilling drinks and prodding people to the dessert table.

Jeremiah takes a few sugar cookies, passing over the runny Jello mold. He is moving off to the side when he catches someone doing a poor imitation of a Yiddish accent. *Vell, I can't complain: my oldest at Harvard and my youngest at Yale. Better boys, I couldn't ask!*

"What's that all about?" Jeremiah asks the guy standing next to him.

"Some guy in the math department," comes the response. "Never shuts up about how his boys are his own private victory over Hitler."

Jeremiah closes his slack jaw and presses his lips together, stung, but at that moment Bill clinks his fork on a glass. The department head wishes everyone a year of fruitful research, approved grant proposals, committed students, and success in publication. He thanks the wives for supporting their men (ignoring McGratten's poor sod of a husband), and welcomes Jeremiah and the other new members of the department.

Jeremiah smiles and nods, though he's a bit pickled from the drinks and his mind is awhirl. *What the heck? Are they making fun of a Holocaust survivor?* What lies under the surface never ceases to shake him. It dawns on Jeremiah that there are no Levines or Goldbergs in the political science department, no Rubins or Roths. The word "token" pops into his mind, unbidden.

Marion Dalton emerges from the kitchen with the news that the President will be holding a live press conference soon. Anyone who'd like to watch is invited into the parlor.

"That'll be an announcement about the Gulf of Tonkin," Jeremiah says. "Two attacks in one week. There'll be a response. Limited. But something."

The party gathers inside, crowding the small television, but there's a delay with the press conference. Side conversations continue, and footage from Mississippi rolls across the screen. How strange that no one's mentioned this news at the party. Because Williams is here? Or are civil rights not something on the minds of his new colleagues?

"Remind me again what you're teaching?" Jeremiah says to Williams, small talk his method to segue into what he really wants to ask. "I'm sure you said earlier but I haven't gotten everyone's fields sorted out yet."

Williams is younger than Jeremiah, thin-faced with a pointy goatee and ebony browline glasses. His voice is even, a bit cool and reserved, but not rude. "I've got one course on mass media and democracy, and another on campaigns, voting, and the press."

"Right, right! Political communications. I've got a friend who teaches a course at GW on the tension between a free press and national security decision-making. Fascinating subject. If you'd ever like to develop something similar, I'd be happy to collaborate."

Williams is thoughtful for a second. "Sure." There's a twinge of a Southern accent, and Jeremiah remembers that Williams is from Alabama.

"What do you make of all this news today?" Jeremiah motions towards the television. "My wife is pretty broken up over it, and I can't get those boys out of my head either." The three young men on the FBI's missing poster, a black face flanked by two white ones, will be seared in the collective memory of the nation, he's sure.

"Tragic," Williams says, and then after a pause: "but hardly surprising."

Jeremiah creases his brow, astonished at Williams' nonchalance. Before he can reply, Williams shakes his head and purses his lips. "I'm not sure you want to hear what I think."

"Sure I do. That's why I asked!" Jeremiah emits a nervous laugh, trying to sound congenial, though Williams' tone puts him on edge. Had he mistakenly assumed a certain sense of solidarity between them, as representatives of two oppressed people? Their rabbi in D.C. had marched with Dr. King in Birmingham, and had encouraged the Gerstlers—indeed their entire synagogue—to get out and show their support by attending the March on Washington last August.

"Quite frankly this whole media circus makes me a bit sick." The veins on Williams' neck contract as he takes a swallow of beer. His voice rises in disgust.

"But—"

"Do you know that in the six weeks the FBI's been searching for those workers, they found nine—*nine!*—bodies of black men and boys? Henry Dee, Charles Moore, Herbert Oarsby! A fourteen-year-old boy. I'd like to know where the outrage is over that. The coverage in *The New York Times?* It's only because *this time* two of them were white."

"Oh!" Jeremiah's eyes widen in surprise; he hadn't heard about the other bodies. "That's terrible." He desperately wants Williams to know that he's on his side. "We've got a friend of the family who went down there with the Lawyers' Committee for Civil Rights, filing briefs and affidavits for some of the people getting arrested at the voting rights marches."

"Yeah?"

"He said the whites down there were accusing him and all the other civil rights workers of being agitators. This guy told him—his quote—that before 'all the Jews and Communists from New York' got involved, they'd always had congenial relations with the local Negros."

"Oh sure, centuries of congenial relations." Williams spits the words, his voice bitter. "Don't get me wrong: the volunteers are fine, but it's the local Negros who're on the front lines."

"Right." Jeremiah nods. He cups his chin and moves his fist to cover his mouth, lips puckered as he considers what to say next. "I was very impressed with Dr. King's speech last August. He's a great leader for your people."

"Were you at the March?" There's a note of curiosity.

Now he'd done it, backed himself into a corner with his own fumbling stupidity. "Well, no, not exactly. . ." This is the last thing Jeremiah wants to admit, after making such a show of it.

Williams gives him a pitying look. "Right."

"I couldn't get off work, but I read the transcripts of the speeches in the paper," he says.

"I was there," Molly says. As if he's waved a magic wand, his wife has appeared at his side. "I'll never forget it."

Williams seems to consider this information with a nod to Molly. In the background, the network broadcasts images of the civil rights workers from different stages of their lives. Andy Goodman as a young boy in a pirate costume. Chaney's baby daughter, born eleven days before her father was murdered. Schwerner's college graduation picture.

Molly blinks back tears and bites her lip. "It's just awful." She tells Williams of her tenuous babysitting connection to the victim.

"We've got a handful of students down there volunteering right now," Williams says.

"Very good!" Jeremiah says. "And how are they?"

"Shaken up. But determined."

Marion Dalton is listening in earnest to their conversation. She frowns. "Our son wanted to volunteer in Selma last summer, but I told him in no uncertain terms that we wouldn't support it. Too dangerous."

Jeremiah starts—the Daltons struck him as liberal-minded people, though perhaps Marion is employing a mother's caution. Molly puckers her brow, causing his own neck to pulse with tension. Aside from a flicker of irritation in his eyes, Williams' face stays passive, as if he's heard this reasoning a million times.

"I can understand your concern, as a mother," Molly says. "But don't you think the volunteers are doing important work down there?"

"To tell you the truth, I don't understand what's so hard about registering to vote," Marion says.

Oh, for crying out loud. Doesn't the woman know that Negros in the South could lose their jobs—or worse—by registering to vote? Jeremiah turns, expecting Williams to expound upon the threats of violence his people face, but he's already spun around and walked away. "Wait!" Williams ignores him and heads out to the garden.

Molly launches into an explanation, but Marion is focused on her guest's abrupt departure. "Honestly, I don't know why he needs to be so uppity."

Molly wrinkles her nose and Jeremiah feels the prick of Marion's words. He's been on the receiving end of slurs—rebuffed for jobs due to questions over his "antecedents," denied guest entry to a country club in Bethesda, and what was that business a few minutes ago, making fun of a European refugee? But he's never considered what it would be like to face such ignorance and bigotry everywhere, at every turn.

The TV flashes to Rita Schwerner, the twenty-two-year-old widow, a rebroadcast of her statement from earlier today. She is pencil-thin, a mound of sandy-brown hair piled high on her head, her collared shirtdress belted severely at the waist. At the microphone, she removes oversized sunglasses and looks into the cameras, palpable grief rippling over her gaunt face. Through the White House grapevine, Jeremiah has heard how she faced down the President, dismissing LBJ's niceties and demanding he commit federal troops for the search. "Remarkable young woman," Jeremiah says.

"My husband, Michael Schwerner, did not die in vain," says Mrs. Schwerner. "If he and Andrew Goodman had been Negroes, the world would have taken little notice of their deaths. After all, the slaying of a Negro in Mississippi is not news." She repeats the same point Williams made ten minutes ago. "It is only because my husband and Andrew Goodman were white that the national alarm has been sounded."

Rita Schwerner says she wants her husband to be buried next to James Chaney, but even in death the State of Mississippi will not allow a white man and a black man to be next to each other. Why this fact should be harder to swallow than all the others Jeremiah doesn't know, but he feels a grinding sense of frustration. Will America ever be free of the scourge of slavery? Something tells him no. Erasing hatred from people's hearts is damn near impossible. Ignorance, perhaps. The key is to catch the ignorance before it turned to bigotry and hatred.

At last, the press conference begins and there is quiet in the Daltons' parlor. LBJ is solemn as he assails the torpedo attacks on the high seas. In his familiar Texas twang, the President says the United States will react with force and take all necessary measures against aggression in Southeast Asia. Limited air action against North Vietnamese gunboats is already underway, he says. Now Jeremiah understands why the press conference has been called for such a late hour; the President wanted to get word that the operation had started.

When the broadcast is over, side conversations resume. Though the president's announcement is exactly as Jeremiah predicted, he doesn't feel like standing around and discussing it. Tomorrow, he'll parse through the transcript and try to understand if this constitutes a change in the Johnson doctrine in Southeast Asia.

Williams is in the garden, steering his wife towards the exit, when Jeremiah finds him.

"You missed the press conference!" Jeremiah realizes he doesn't have the foggiest idea of what to say. He wants to demonstrate some outrage over Marion's narrow-mindedness, or show that he's not prejudiced himself. "I. . .uh. . .I'm sorry if I said something in there to make you feel uncomfortable." As the words come out he knows it's not a true apology—he doesn't know what he's done wrong, and his phrasing, *sorry. . . if,* puts the onus on Williams.

"Sometimes I don't know why I bother," Williams says. "I'm just sick and tired of it all. The lynchings. The government playing around with black lives. Do you really think the people responsible are going to sit in prison, even for a day?"

Again, Jeremiah is taken aback by Williams' tone. He shifts from foot to foot. "Well, if they make some arrests."

"Make arrests?" Williams' voice brims with frustration. "Are you kidding me? Do you know a thing about the way things work down there? The sheriffs *are* the goddam Klan!"

"Yes, but the Feds are on the case."

Williams shakes his head in disgust. "Even if they make arrests, a Mississippi jury's not going to convict anyone. But you know what? It wouldn't happen with a Massachusetts jury either. Northerners think they're so superior to the good ol' boys down South! Please. There's plenty of racism to go around up here."

Williams' wife is tugging on his arm; *let's go,* she seems to be saying.

"But surely here in New England. . ." Jeremiah protests.

"Surely nothing," Williams says. "Boston's one of the most segregated cities in the country! Never mind. I don't expect white people to do the battle for us. What I want is for black people to stand up."

"I can understand that," Jeremiah says. A feeble effort.

"Your President in there," Williams says, gesturing towards the parlor. "He doesn't represent me."

"And Goldwater does?" He doesn't get it, after all LBJ had accomplished this summer for civil rights.

Williams opens his mouth as if he's about to come out with more fighting words, to tell Jeremiah that he's no less of an imbecile than Marion. And maybe he isn't. Jeremiah's stomach clenches. Williams shakes his head and takes a step back. His derision turns into an appraisal, as if he's not quite sure whether Jeremiah is worth hearing what he thinks. He sighs and puts out his hand to shake Jeremiah's. "See you around."

Jeremiah watches Williams and his wife make their retreat, the heels of her shoes slapping against the stone walk. He replays the conversations in his head. Had he touched some nerve or did the man always sound so radical? He's at once offended and intrigued. It is time to find Molly and say their goodbyes.

The room is half full with Jeremiah's new colleagues discussing the press conference. But Jeremiah doesn't jump into the conversation, and no one asks his opinion. *Your President,* Williams had called LBJ. But did he represent Jeremiah? Was there any politician in Washington who truly did?

The interaction with Williams has shaken his confidence. Perhaps he'd been searching for an ally and Williams was the other natural outsider, but whatever bond he assumed they shared existed in his mind alone. Or was his discomfort an internal reckoning over his reaction—or lack thereof—to past slights? Has he been too quick to squirrel them away, pretend as though they were nothing?

"I think you'll do fine here," Molly says as they're walking out.

"I don't know, honestly." Was a true sense of belonging attainable? Now that he's met everyone it seems more out of reach, but he reminds himself it is the beginning. The party was not a smashing success but nor was it an abysmal failure. His head pounds. And what to say to the young minds who will fill his classroom one month from now, when he's still got so much to learn? He's got nothing to offer them. No guidance, no wisdom. Only the world's sorrow and anger, without a recipe for a cure.

He reaches for his wife—Molly is his rock, his grounding. She places his hand on her midriff. "Feel." Their unborn child is kicking.

EMERITUS

(2004)

A student sprang into Jeremiah's path as he strode down College Lane, nearly knocking him over. "Sorry, excuse me," the student said, holding up a Frisbee as an explanation. Jeremiah wanted to say, *Shouldn't you be in class?* Or *Get your eyesight checked, young man!* Instead, he glowered, jaw set under his gray goatee. The boy's face was familiar; Jeremiah had seen him in Franklin Hall waiting for office hours. Used to be, eager students would stop Jeremiah all the time as he walked the cobblestone corridors of campus, asking him to consult on research papers or clarify points made in class. Nowadays, most political science majors didn't know Professor Emeritus Jeremiah Gerstler, even when they tripped over him.

The crisp autumn air snapped at Jeremiah's fingertips. The campus was awash in campaign banners and students pushing Kerry/Edwards buttons. A lone Young Republican stood over a folding table, talking into his cell phone, asking if he could close for the day. The oaks and maples dotting the pathways painted a picturesque postcard of New England—melded hues of crimson, gold, and fiery orange. Jeremiah missed roaming the grounds daily, missed having to show up more than once a week for his graduate-level seminar, but Molly and the children said he'd get used to it. They'd encouraged him to reduce his teaching load. The title "Emeritus," conferred over the summer, a week or so after he turned seventy-eight, was starting to take on a bitter aftertaste: he now had to share his office with two adjuncts due to space limitations, and there'd been other slights, though he couldn't be sure if they were intentional. If the Frisbee player portended things to come, Jeremiah would soon become unseen, an obstacle in some younger person's way.

His purpose today was to find Jim Blackwell, the department chair, to discuss a ridiculous notion being promoted by the provost: mandatory coaching for all instructors in certain departments, newbies and tenured professors alike. The email had arrived in his inbox this morning and Jeremiah had almost deleted it, certain it wasn't meant for him. But no, political science was one of three "lucky" departments selected for this "exciting opportunity." A teaching coach would assess classes and make suggestions on teaching style, how to engage the students, etcetera, etcetera. Someone was going to come into *his* classroom and tell *him* how to teach after forty years at this place? Ha! Thanks, but no thanks. Anyone with the title "Emeritus" ought to be exempt.

Jeremiah arrived at Franklin as Jim's Wednesday afternoon class ended. A swarm of students spilled out of the lecture hall. The air was abuzz with utterances like "blown away by the lecture" and "that guy is freakin' brilliant." Inside, at the podium, several fawning undergrads surrounded Jim like he was a celebrity. Damn. Jeremiah'd always done okay with his students, but he'd never heard effusive praise like this. He'd been Jim's mentor when the younger man arrived on campus, twenty-something years ago, and he was proud of him, but damn. He felt a sudden, stabbing sense of dejection: delivering lectures and leading a room full of seventy or eighty students in stimulating discussions had given him immense satisfaction. Teaching a small seminar couldn't compare. At least he had the teach-in on the election to look forward to in a few weeks: his session on the candidates' positions on global trade was typed and waiting to be delivered. Perhaps, if the session went well, he'd develop a syllabus for a new course. He had ideas.

When he caught Jim's attention, he noted a slight crease in his colleague's forehead. As Jim spoke to the students, he massaged his jaw, a look of consternation on his face. "I'll be with you in a minute."

"I'll wait."

He had to hand it to Jim: the man looked much younger than his sixty-three years. The gray in his full head of hair gave him a distinguished look. The type ladies fell for, tall and lean, a runner's physique. Perhaps that was his secret to looking swell: Jim ran marathons and worked out at the gym. Twice a week Jeremiah swam some laps, more soothing than aerobic, good for relieving the tightness in his knees.

"I wanted to talk to you, too," Jim said when he emerged. He confessed to feeling a little lightheaded and in need of caffeine. Would Jeremiah join him for a coffee? He wasn't headed in the direction Jim meant, towards the student-run café, but he agreed. Anything to make the coaching thing go away.

Jeremiah gestured with his arm. "All right. You first."

"About the election teach-in a few weeks, I've got great news," Jim said. "I was able to get Richard Bass of the *Times* and Brenda Warren from the 9/11 Commission to come and give talks. I think they'll be a big draw for the students, don't you?"

"Sure," Jeremiah replied.

"The thing is, we've got to cancel one or two of the scheduled teach-in sessions."

Jeremiah halted. "You're cancelling my session?"

"Look, our goal is to get as many students as possible to this thing. And let's be honest. What's going to draw more of a crowd—a session on global trade or an expert on terrorism and a White House correspondent?"

Jeremiah was stunned. "You think the candidates' positions on global trade don't matter? Are you nuts?"

"Of course they matter. But we've got to create a program that the students can relate to."

"You want sexy topics? Fine. But these kids are going to be voting for the first time in their lives. Don't you think we owe it to them to talk about issues that'll have a hell of a lot more impact on the future of the country?"

"I'm not disagreeing with you," Jim said, stopping to take a deep breath. "What if we make it a separate session altogether? You can give the talk at the department's brown bag in two weeks."

Jeremiah snorted, resentment growing in his chest like a glowing spark. If they were lucky, ten students attended the department's bi-weekly lunches. But he could see Jim's mind was made up. A jerkish move. No doubt Jim had already asked the department assistant to delete the session from the teach-in fliers.

"I think it's a big mistake," Jeremiah said, "but fine." He cast a sideways glance at Jim, whose gait had slowed. "Okay, my turn now. Tell me, what's all this coaching nonsense? Seems like another one of these cockamamie ideas the development office dreamed up."

"Weren't you paying attention in the department meeting?"

Jeremiah had been physically present for the meeting the prior week, but he'd been pissed off. He'd volunteered to cover a colleague's class during her maternity leave and Jim had callously rebuffed his offer, giving the class to a new hire who wasn't even close to having tenure. He'd tuned out after that.

"We've been chosen for the pilot program because some of our student assessments from the last few semesters were…shall we say, less than complimentary."

"What are you talking about?" Jeremiah didn't read those silly student evaluation forms. "Anyway, I just heard your students coming out of there." He gestured back to the lecture hall. "They love you."

"I didn't say *all* the courses." Jim gave a knowing smile. "Just some. But that's not really the point."

"So, what is? A couple of guys in our department aren't the most exciting lecturers, and we all have to suffer?"

Jim rolled his eyes. "Jesus, Jeremiah. It's not about suffering. It's about helping us to become better teachers. To deliver the knowledge in a more accessible way."

"Bullcrap! You sound like you're reading from a brochure. Are you really going to have a 'coach' come in and watch you teach? It's absurd."

Jim shrugged. They reached the student lounge and got in line for coffee. "Really, it's not so bad."

"Well, I refuse. Plain and simple. It's ridiculous."

"You know, this coaching stuff is getting more popular, and in all different fields. My wife's company used a coach for motivating the salespeople. And my daughter-in-law is training to be a coach for kids with ADD."

"But teaching is different. Either you have it or you don't."

Jim lowered his voice. "People get tenure at this university for all sorts of reasons, mostly their ability to publish and do research. Teaching ability has nothing to do with it." Jim looked at him squarely and shifted to an audible mutter. "As you well know."

Jeremiah's stomach tightened. "What's that supposed to mean?"

"Nothing." Jim sniggered and raised his eyes to the ceiling, like Jeremiah was an exasperating burden.

"What's so funny?"

"I was thinking of this phrase the students say. 'Suck it up.' You're just going to have to suck it up. Deal with it."

"Suck it up? Suck it *up*?" Jeremiah said, his voice rising. "I'll be damned if I suck it up. This is just more university bureaucracy bullshit! How can you go along with it?"

Students around them were starting to stare. They moved forward in line and Jim leaned back on the guard rails, his face wan.

"Keep your voice down," Jim said, leaning in.

"Don't tell me to calm down!"

Jim closed his eyes as if Jeremiah's mere physical presence was painful. He let out a huff. "Damn it, Gerstler, you're being completely irrational about this. Do you realize that?"

"I realize no such thing." He seethed. "You can tell the provost: Gerstler refuses."

"You know what? Fine. I'll tell him." Jim studied him for a second. "But here's another thing: I wasn't going to mention it, but do you even read the student evaluations? Any idea how your courses measure up to anyone else's? Not favorably, let me tell you!" he hissed. "Your ratings have consistently been going down over the last decade, which is why—even when you volunteer for more teaching—I scramble to get someone else!"

The words were a thousand tiny daggers piercing his skin. He didn't believe it. How pathetic he must look in Jim's eyes. For years, decades, they'd worked together and had a warm relationship. Philosophical differences, yes. Discussions in which voices got raised when debating whether a post-Saddam Iraq would lead to a more stable Middle East or whether a unified European currency was a good idea, but such debates had been friendly and respectful. But now, the countless snubs struck Jeremiah's consciousness with a force akin to the smacks his mother used to give him when he misbehaved. The smug look on Jim's face was too much. The whole department was probably laughing behind his back: a conspiracy to drive him crazy.

Suck it up, Jim said, but he'd show the world he was no laughingstock. His hands flew up and grabbed Jim by the collar, their faces a few inches apart. Jeremiah's breath smelled of the tuna sandwich he'd eaten for lunch, but he didn't care. "What are you saying? Hmm? Just come on out and say it!" The look of surprise on Jim's face was exquisite. He seemed almost frightened.

Jim started to cough. The students' din grounded to a halt. Everyone was staring. "Get your hands off me," Jim commanded through clenched teeth. "Before they have to call security." His breathing was strained and his eyelids fluttered. Jim's eyes flashed panic; he'd broken into a sweat.

Jeremiah released him with a shove. Jim bumped into the counter, toppling plastic cups everywhere. The students in line and the servers behind the counter stood motionless, dumbfounded.

"You're losing it, Gerstler," Jim spat.

Jeremiah backed away, glaring, aware that people were watching him. A sinking feeling in his gut: he'd gone too far. He *was* losing it.

He stumbled back up the stairs, emerging from the building into the glaring sunlight. His knee was throbbing now, and he hobbled over to a bench around the corner. He hung his head low, rocking back and forth, rubbing his knees. What a fool he was! His mind was blank of all thoughts except: *Shit, shit, shit!*

At first, he didn't register the three students in white EMT shirts rushing by him with a stretcher, perhaps ten minutes later. When he hoisted himself off the bench, he saw a large crowd outside the building, a buzz in the air.

"It's Professor Blackwell," he heard. "He's collapsed."

◆ ◆ ◆

He confessed the whole story to Molly as soon as he arrived home. When he got to the worst part, his words came out as a whimper. "I really lost it," he moaned, holding his head in his hands. "I could have killed him." The black pit of guilt in his stomach doubled in size when he saw Molly's disappointed, uneasy expression: *What's the matter with you?*

An update from the department assistant later in the day assured Jeremiah and his colleagues that Jim was out of danger, thank god. Jim's wife and grown son were at his bedside. The doctors were calling it a mild heart attack, but no other visitors would be allowed for some time.

Art Brenner, Jeremiah's own cardiologist, whom he cornered at the Jewish Community Center gym the following day, assured him that one didn't get a sudden coronary from getting in a scuffle; most likely Jim had been experiencing mild symptoms for a few days and hadn't heeded the warning signs.

Jeremiah assumed everyone on campus knew about the Incident-of-Which-He-Was-Ashamed, and he kept waiting for someone—the dean, the provost, his colleagues in the department, campus security—to call him in for questioning. But no one did. In the department, there was shock that this could happen to a fit guy like Jim. Wasn't marathon running supposed to be good for your heart?

He scanned the student newspaper every day, certain some small news item would appear about the incident precipitating Jim's collapse. But maybe none of the students in the café knew who Jeremiah was, or maybe they *hadn't* seen anything.

The days crept by, and Jeremiah heard Jim was improving, slowly and steadily. They'd need to put in a couple of stents, followed by a recovery period of a month or two.

Molly's advice was simple. "You don't have a choice. You've just got to apologize. End of story." Easy for her to say. Beloved, retired piano teachers didn't have to contend with the passive-aggressive world of academia, where doctoral candidates could be blocked for promotions because of petty politics on the Appointments Committee.

Conference panelists disparaging others' research to make themselves look smart. No, her world was entirely rooted in the Berkshires cultural scene, in her hobbies, in their children and grandchildren.

Jeremiah wasn't sure he could face the man. If Jim had showed him the proper respect, a little deference to the senior member of the department, the whole thing could have been avoided.

But none of that mattered, Molly said. Even if Jim was acting like a jerk, he now held the moral high ground because Jeremiah was the one who'd lost his temper.

Word filtered out that Jim was being allowed visitors, but Jeremiah waited, sure now that Jim would speak up; what a crazy bastard Gerstler had become. The university administrators would come for him now. Press charges, or at the very least, force him into full retirement.

He knew he should prostrate himself by Jim's bedside, begging forgiveness. And yet he hesitated. Finally, he could no longer bear the disheartened look on Molly's face, waiting for him to act. "I'll go this afternoon, okay? Will you come with me?"

"Of course. Thank you." He wasn't sure why she was thanking him, but she busied herself with making a pie to bring to the hospital.

"Jeremiah, Molly! How good of you to come!" Jim's wife Patricia greeted them at the elevator on the cardiac floor. "He's resting now, but he'll be happy to see you."

Jeremiah flushed. "I don't want to bother him. Upset him, you know?"

"Don't be silly. I'm sure he'd be happy to have someone to talk shop with once he wakes up." She noticed Molly's pie. "Oh, you shouldn't have. Your cupcakes were delicious. I'm going to get fat."

Was it possible Jim hadn't told his wife? He exchanged a glance with Molly, who gave a slight shrug of the shoulders. Perhaps it was one of those memory lapse things, a kind of post-trauma amnesia. Was that common?

A nurse emerged from Jim's room. "He's awake," she said.

Molly suggested Jeremiah enter alone. "I'll take Patty down to the cafeteria for a coffee." His wife spoke in an evenhanded manner, her tone telling him not to refuse.

He took a deep breath and pushed open the door to the room. Jim raised his left hand in a weak greeting. In the space of a week and a half, more of his hair had turned silver; he'd lost weight and his skin seemed sallow. He strained to sit up but didn't get very far. Jeremiah hadn't known what to expect, but this was a very different man from the one whose collar he'd grabbed. "Jesus, Jim. You look like crap." As soon as he'd spoken he felt Molly's virtual presence, kicking him in the shins. "I mean. Sorry."

Jim raised his eyebrows. "Nice to see you, too."

Jeremiah pulled up the chair close to Jim's bed. He studied the man's face for a supercilious expression, or the patronizing look he sometimes gave Jeremiah, but saw none. "Jim, I. . ." He didn't know how to say it. Instead he reached into the shopping bag he was holding and pulled out a few journals. "I brought you some reading material."

"Thanks."

He was doing this all wrong. He hadn't even asked after Jim's well-being yet. What a moron he could be sometimes! "How are you feeling? Patty says they might let you out next week."

Jim nodded, yes. "But I'll have a bit of a recovery period at home. Truth is, you're right. I feel like crap. Can't really think about going back to work now. Hopefully in a couple months."

"I'm sure your students are disappointed."

Jim gave a weak shrug. "What can you do?"

Jeremiah cleared his throat. He was awful at this. "You'll get through this, Jimmy." Suddenly he felt paternal towards the younger man. He wasn't sure where "Jimmy" had come from—he'd never heard anyone other than Jim's departed mother call him by this name. "I feel terrible," he finally blurted. "I can't tell you how sorry I am. The other week. . .my behavior was unacceptable." There, he'd said it, addressed the incident head-on. "I keep thinking if we hadn't gotten in that scuffle you wouldn't be here right now." He felt his voice on the verge of breaking.

Jim's expression was unreadable. He closed his eyes for a long beat and didn't say anything.

"Do you remember what happened in the student lounge, right before you collapsed?" Jeremiah asked.

Jim nodded and directed his gaze at Jeremiah. "Listen, Jeremiah. Two things. One—if it hadn't happened then, maybe I would have had the heart attack later, as I was driving home, or somewhere else. Maybe you were the catalyst, I don't know. But we've got heart disease in the family, and apparently I'd been having symptoms before you lost your cool."

"Jesus." Jim being gracious and forgiving was the last thing Jeremiah expected. "Did you tell Patty? Or anyone else?"

He gave a shrug as if to say, who can remember? "Another thing." Jim's voice was low, and Jeremiah leaned in to hear. Jim pointed his finger in Jeremiah's direction. "You seem angry, or grumpy, a lot of the time. You've always been a little off your rocker. But—and I'll be frank—over the years, and especially lately, you've gotten worse."

Jeremiah pursed his lips, and looked down at the linoleum floor. The criticism was consistent with comments he'd heard from his children and Molly. But he hadn't been able to get his mind around a solution. "It's been tough to get used to my new schedule of not having to come in every day. I haven't been myself."

"No, Jeremiah. You've been exactly yourself. Just your worst self."

"Now you're going to suggest that I go see some kind of life coach." He glanced back at Jim, a thin smile at his own joke.

Jim raised his eyebrows. "You know the funny thing about you? You give off this gruff manner, and say, 'Don't make a fuss over me.' But in reality, that's exactly what you want. People to fuss over the great Professor Gerstler."

"Are you finished?" Jeremiah knew he'd brought this castigation on himself. Better here, in a private hospital room, then in a department meeting or in the provost's office.

"Jeremiah, all I'm trying to say is: get over yourself. I'm not angry at you. I was, right then, when we were getting coffee. And I probably said some awful things because you can be so damn exasperating. But now, I've got other things on my mind."

Was this an admission from Jim that he'd lied about the teaching evaluations? He didn't want to ask. It would have been simple for Jeremiah to check them himself, of course, but he was too ashamed to ask for help with the online system.

"You've got to take care of yourself," Jim said.

"Ha. Look who's talking."

Jim tapped his finger on his head. "I mean here."

He winced. "I know." It was the closest he'd come to acknowledging that working less—this terrifying idea that he was becoming archaic, obsolete—wasn't simple.

"Damn it, Gerstler. You've had a full career. Books published. Hundreds of students. A lot of people would give an eyetooth for a career like yours."

"I know. It's just that. . ." He wondered how to phrase it. "I don't do so well when I'm not busy. It was a mistake to reduce my teaching load. And it seems like there are all these signs lately that I'm not. . ." he swallowed. *Not wanted.* "That people are trying to push me out. That the things I have to say aren't relevant. Which is bullcrap. Because they are."

He hadn't intended to unburden himself to Jim, of all people. Since getting tenure decades ago, Jeremiah never had to worry about job security. If he was to get back in the game, he'd have to get creative. Perhaps show more flexibility towards change.

"Sure they are. Did they contact you yet?" Jim asked.

"Did who contact me?"

"I guess you're going to have your teach in-session after all," Jim said, "since obviously I'm not doing mine. So make it worth their while, yeah?"

"What's that supposed to mean?"

"See, there you go again, too touchy. All I meant is to make it a good session. Jesus."

"Obviously. Why wouldn't I?" If it was touchy to detest people talking down to him, he was guilty. Of course he'd try to make it the best goddamn session he'd ever given.

"I won't be there, but I'll get a report, I'm sure."

"I thought you said you couldn't think about work."

"True, but, well, I have my sources." He pointed to a large fruit basket on the window ledge. "Some of the students collected money and sent that."

"Nice." He wished he hadn't taken so long to visit.

Jim looked sleepy. "I'm beat. I've got to rest. You always manage to tire me out."

Jeremiah got up to leave and cupped Jim twice on the shoulder. "Take care now." His throat constricted. "And thank you," he whispered.

Jeremiah placed his handouts on the front table and reviewed his notes. An AV guy came in. He was there to set up a video camera in the back of the room—the sessions were being taped and would later be uploaded to the university website for alumni and the wider community. "You won't even know it's here," the guy said. "I'll just press record and then I've got to slip out."

Jeremiah shrugged. "Makes no difference to me."

At seven minutes after the hour, only ten or so students had taken seats, but Jeremiah felt he should begin. He passed out the candidates' positions on global trade, a few op-ed pieces on outsourcing and energy policy. By twenty minutes after the hour, the crowd had more than doubled. He played short video clips of the candidates and had the students dissect the speeches. A few of them seemed to be getting into the discussion, debating in loud voices. More stragglers came in, a goth girl, a boy in a rugby sweatshirt with a bandage over his nose, another one with shaggy red hair tossing a hacky-sack. Jeremiah summoned every particle of his patience to forgive their tardiness. When it came to split them into small groups, he counted thirty-four students. Not bad at all. He was exhausted, but he couldn't wait to tell Jim.

For the final ten minutes, he called the groups back together. The shaggy redhead who'd come in a half an hour late raised his hand to represent the global trade group. He stood to give his conclusion: NAFTA was the culprit for U.S. job losses.

A groan escaped Jeremiah's lips. "That's it? That's your conclusion? Nothing more nuanced, perhaps?" He was met by silence. "I note that many of you, including Mr. . ."

"Mayhew."

The name rang familiar but he couldn't place it.

"Mr. Mayhew missed my introduction because he arrived a tad bit—no, quite a bit—late. If this were a regular class I wouldn't stand for such tardiness. Let me remind the latecomers of the core tenets of international political economy." He waxed lyrical on the beauty of the field, the interrelation and complexities of political and economic power.

"As for Mr. Mayhew's conclusion on NAFTA: that's the position of some liberal-leaning, big labor-funded think tanks like the Economic Policy Group. However—as I've tried to explain here—that's a simplistic theory that doesn't factor in a whole host of other drivers. Currency manipulation, technology, China in ascendency."

Mayhew sat up straighter in his chair. "I think it's a well-established position, actually."

"And what I am trying to convey is that *your* position is simply incorrect. A very, very narrow explanation that serves the purpose of one interest group and isn't looking at the big picture. Most mainstream economists would agree with me."

"You see? 'Most'—it's a matter of opinion, not fact."

"No, sir!" Jeremiah felt his temperature rising at this verbal sparring. These impudent underclassmen, coming late without apology, trying to show how smart they were but spewing nonsense. "Mr. Mayhew, if you'd take a few more classes in economics or international political economy, maybe you'll get it." Jeremiah was sick to death of these types. "What's your major? Leisure arts?" He nodded at the hacky-sack, which Mayhew was jiggling on his knee.

A few of the students were smirking now, surely because they were sick to death of Mayhew types as well. "History," the boy said, without looking up. He stopped fiddling with the hacky-sack and began scribbling something in a long notepad. His hair fell over his eyes.

"Ah, a worthy subject," Jeremiah said, acceding. "Then you should know what happened in the Industrial Revolution. Refer to page four of the source sheets, at the bottom. If Mr. Mayhew here would get a haircut perhaps he'd see more clearly the point the author is trying to make."

Mayhew's cheeks turned crimson. One of his friends whispered something in his ear and the boy nodded and gave him a thumbs up. He whispered something in turn to the goth girl to his right and she grinned. Mayhew brushed his hair behind his ears and said, "Please, go on. Do enlighten us." His tone was smarmy. "I want to get it all down."

"I shall try to explain this point again. For the third time." Jeremiah turned to the rest of the room and asked if anyone would like to offer a different explanation. No one did. He was failing. What had happened to him that he couldn't get simple concepts across to the students? Jeremiah recalled the Frisbee player who'd knocked into him a few weeks ago, the feeling he was invisible. Were his words, too, evaporating before students could grasp their meaning, or was it a conscious tuning out on their part?

Afterwards, he couldn't say why he was picking on this Mayhew, but the smug tone didn't help. "Mr. Mayhew, have you been following the campaign at *all*? I would hope, that if you've been accepted at this university, you do know how to read a newspaper."

The students sniggered.

Mayhew leaned back with his arms crossed behind his head, a position of triumph. He held up a thin reporter's notebook. "Actually, I'm supposed to be writing an article on the teach-in for the *Daily*. I was covering another session, which is why I was late."

The goth girl next to Mayhew pulled something out of her bag. A camera. "Kathy here is the junior photo editor," Mayhew said, as she snapped several pictures of Jeremiah and the room.

Jeremiah was flabbergasted. "I see." He opened his mouth to say something and then closed it again. "You're going to write an article about the candidates and their positions on trade?" An article in the student newspaper could be an opportunity to generate awareness about a new class. He stood up a bit straighter and took on a more conciliatory tone. "Well, that's just terrific. Would you like me to review it?"

"I don't think that will be necessary," Mayhew said.

He took a deep breath. "My source sheets and expertise are at your disposal. You have my office hours and phone number on the top of the first page."

Mayhew smirked. "Got it."

"I may be teaching a new course on this topic in the spring—you can put that in your article."

"Sure," he said, though he was no longer scribbling in his notebook.

"Shall I go over that point again, so you're sure you've got it right?"

Now the air was abuzz with audible titters and a few groans. Jeremiah refused to acknowledge that he'd messed the opportunity up, that he was a laughingstock in their eyes. A couple of students wore expressions of pity.

"I think I'll manage," Mayhew said. "I don't know how much space we'll have for the article anyway."

"I see." A few students filed out, and when Jeremiah checked his watch he saw that the session was supposed to be over. "We have about fifteen minutes before the room is needed for the next lecture, so even though time is up, let's hear from the other two groups. Representatives?"

No one stood up. Two more students slithered out from the back exit.

"Where is the energy policy group?" A few students raised their hands. "Well come on, who would like to summarize the issues?"

"Our speaker had to leave," said a girl in the third row.

"Someone else then?"

He was met with silence.

"What about the outsourcing group? Any takers?"

He sighed, defeated. At last he waved them off. "All right, thanks for coming. Sorry for keeping you over time. And don't forget to vote."

A few students gave Jeremiah sympathetic smiles as they exited the classroom, as if to say: pity the poor has-been. And one, under his breath: "Jesus. What an asshole."

He locked the door after the last student left and sat puzzling over what had happened. Why had he lost his cool? Why did he bungle all attempts to get the concepts across to these students?

But who had changed here, him or the students? So apathetic and childish, students today. Wrapped up in their cell phones and then running to health services for therapy appointments. The university now offered massage chairs and dogs to cuddle with during exam season!

The knock on the door startled him out of his stupor: the AV guy coming to turn off the tape. "Oh shit," Jeremiah said. "Goddamn it. You're right. I forgot all about it."

Molly asked how the session went, and he gave her a curt, "Fine." He hadn't meant to sound snappy but he'd never been very good at moderating his mood, at compartmentalizing the crap in his career so that it didn't spill over to other parts of his life. But this time Molly didn't even look up from her book or raise her eyebrows at his tone. Had she, too, become inured to him? A terrifying thought; he almost teared up with relief a little while later when he understood she was simply engrossed in her novel. He knew what Jim would say: *Man, you're a paranoid pain in the ass!*

The following day, though he had no meetings, classes, or office hours, Jeremiah headed to campus. The *Daily* was on offer at dozens of places and he picked one up at the entrance to the library. He needn't have bothered: the article on the teach-in was relegated to page three, nary a mention of the global trade session. The accompanying photo showed the filled-to-capacity 150-person lecture hall from the session with the White House correspondent and the representative from the 9/11 Commission.

Why had they bothered to take notes and photograph his session if they weren't going to write about it? When he looked at the byline and photo credit he understood: no Mayhew or Kathy. He flipped to the masthead and did see a Brian Mayhew listed as managing editor and a Kathy Hardt listed as a junior photo editor. In retrospect, it made sense—their snickers, grins, little looks of glee—those damn kids had been toying with him. And yet a small part of him still held out hope: perhaps there'd be a follow-up article that discussed the issues in an in-depth manner.

Time went by and nothing more was written or said about the teach-in. But one person had seen the tape.

"What happened to you in there?" Jim barked over the phone.

"What do you mean?"

"I watched all the sessions. Why did you pick on that student?"

"I did no such thing," Jeremiah said, though an *oh crap* feeling was floating into his consciousness.

"Did you hear me? I watched. I heard and saw you with my own eyes."

"Then you also probably heard his poor explanations, that he wasn't getting the point."

"So the hell what? Harping and carrying on like a whiny widow isn't going to get you anywhere."

"A whiny widow?" Jeremiah couldn't help but laugh.

"It's just an expression. Maybe the wrong one, okay? How about windbag? Or elite asshole? Now do you get it?"

Jeremiah sobered up. "All right, you've made your point. I suppose I was a little harsh on that one kid. What did you think of the rest of it?"

"It was fine. We'll see what the feedback forms say. But those sessions are going up on the website. And guess what? We're not putting yours up!"

He made a semi-wheezing sound in disbelief. "Seriously?"

"Seriously. We don't want alumni seeing that little meltdown of yours."

"Meltdown?" Jeremiah felt he might melt down now. "I think that's a bit of an overstatement."

"Not really. You should thank me. Anyway, I doubt anyone will miss it."

"So you're just going to erase my session from the program, as if it never existed?"

"No, if anyone asks—which I seriously doubt—we'll just say something went wrong with the recording."

Some notion of self-preservation kicked in and Jeremiah knew to drop the topic. He said a hasty goodbye and hung up.

Within a half hour, he picked up the phone again and dialed Jim's number.

"You!"

Jim sounded sleepy. "Now what?"

"One: I forgot to ask how you're feeling."

"At the moment? Tired." He was sure Jim's eyes were rolling at the other end of the line. "But getting stronger, day by day."

"Good. Your health, that's the most important thing," Jeremiah said. "Are they letting you exercise?" Running was an important part of Jim's identity, his mental health, like swimming was for Jeremiah.

"Not yet, but thanks for bringing up a sore topic."

"Jeez. Sorry."

There was silence for a moment. Jim cleared his throat as if to end the conversation.

"Wait. There's a two." Jeremiah took a deep breath.

"Yes?"

"I'll work with the damn teaching coach."

"Good. I knew you'd come around."

"I'm not convinced, but Molly's of the opinion it's never too late to learn something new." A year ago, she'd joined a local investment club, of all things, and now studied the business section every day. She'd been encouraging him to show flexibility, to accept new ways of doing things.

"That's the spirit. Listen to your wife. She's usually right."

"I'm a pretty old dog, I suppose."

"Yeah, well, none of us are getting any younger."

"Except the students, ha ha. They seem to get younger every year."

Jim chuckled. "True. Just keep an open mind with the coach and you'll be fine. Do you think you can do that?"

"Do you still have the tape?

"Tape?"

"Of my session. Maybe I should watch it."

Jim paused, perhaps stunned, before replying. "I think that's an excellent idea, actually. Yes, it should be with the AV department."

"All right, then. Take care of yourself, Jim." He replaced the receiver on the cradle and was overwhelmed with a sense of gratitude toward Jim. He couldn't explain why.

◆ ◆ ◆

From a strict numbers standpoint, the student survey scores were better than expected. For "conveying the material in a compelling manner," his mean score was 3.5 on a scale of one to five. Not bad. The students indicated they'd had a weak grasp of the subject material prior to the session—score of 2.2—but following the session, this score jumped to 3.9. Some had been paying attention after all. Only three students had answered the open-ended question. "Kind of rude when someone didn't get the right answer," read one. "The first part was pretty interesting but then it dissolved towards the end." "Prof was offensive when he picked on one student" and "I thought 'Emeritus' meant retired?"

Well. Surely Jim would agree the numbers were more important than a few less-than-complimentary comments. The results gave him the first reprieve he'd felt in a long while. Around campus, his step was lighter, though he continued to avoid the café in the student lounge.

Election Day came and went, and by the time the coach arrived, Jeremiah had developed a forceful, ardent attitude, though the old combativeness remained. The coach used terms like "differentiated instruction" and "culturally responsive pedagogy" as if she'd invented them. He tried to listen without rolling his eyes. But his sporadic sleep told the true story: he'd been lucky, a cat with nine lives. How many times could he emerge relatively unscathed from his own senseless shortcomings?

Every day, real newspapers like the *Times* and the *Journal* ran stories on China "on the rise" and questions surrounding the Euro. The syllabus for his new course was coming along nicely. Molly squeezed his hand when he told her. He didn't mention that approval for the class had not yet been granted. And perhaps he'd offer some pro bono tutoring to undergraduates, one-on-ones with interested students, as the teaching coach had advised. He recognized that the coach had insights into today's students that might be worth listening to, though he always stood ready with his own terms to throw around: "national priorities" and "trans-border issues," together with "Emeritus" and "forty years of teaching experience."

The first snowfall of the season came one evening in mid-December, covering the campus in a magical, powdery white. It was finals season, but at 8:00 p.m. when Jeremiah headed home, dozens of students were outside frolicking, lobbing lightly-packed snowballs at each other. He took careful steps, relishing the crunching sound his boots made on the snow.

Snowballs flew through the air. Had they seen him? He didn't want to be walloped by a whizzing white orb, though a small part of him would welcome it. "Halt your fire!" he called, shielding his face with his briefcase. There was a polite pause in the pelting, he hoped because they'd heard him. As he stooped to scoop up an errant ball, the wind carried chatter and laughter, opposing groups planning their maneuvers. Jeremiah thought about pitching the snowball playfully in their direction but instead continued on his path. He tossed the snowball in the air twice before letting it fall to the ground with a small thud. He raised his hand high in the air and gave a backwards wave. "Goodnight, gentlemen!" he called. He didn't wait for a response.

THE DUTIFUL DAUGHTER

(1999)

Hannah's father spoke in a low voice, as if conveying a sensitive piece of intelligence, but her attention was on the view. They sat in the hotel lobby, where floor-to-ceiling windows offered a dazzling panorama of the Old City, its ancient limestone walls shimmering with the last orange and pink hues of Mediterranean sun. In the square outside Jaffa Gate, street vendors hawked elongated rings of bread coated in sesame seeds and *za'atar*. Hannah sipped lemonade with *nana*, the local version of spearmint. The tangy mix of sweet and sour joggled her taste buds, not unlike the entire sensory experience of being in Jerusalem this last week.

Hannah longed to relax after a long day of sightseeing, but Jeremiah, with his one-track mind, insisted on talking about work, rambling on about some colleague's research on labor economics. They shared genes and a profession, but their similarities ended there.

He leaned over and tapped her knee, snapping her to attention. "I don't want to worry her, see?"

Her could only mean one person—Hannah's mother, napping upstairs before dinner. "Sorry, what?"

Jeremiah shook his finger, reprimanding her like a schoolgirl. "You! Stop daydreaming!"

"I wasn't," Hannah said, insistent. She hadn't been thinking of anything in particular, taking in the scene outside Jaffa Gate with a mild sense of wonder and surprise. Surprise that at the age of forty-two, in the course of one week, she could develop feelings of attachment to a place she'd never been to before. She wasn't a spiritual person or religious in the least—the choice of her non-Jewish spouse no better evidence—but the term that kept flipping over in her mind was metaphysical. Or maybe transcendental?

A shame she hadn't pushed Tom harder to come. Though her parents had generously offered to bring the whole family to Israel, her husband said he couldn't get out of teaching his summer session. Her kids cried when she told them that the trip would mean they'd have to miss wilderness camp in Maine, the highlight of their year, so she'd come alone.

"Listen up. She might come down any minute. This is important." Her father repeated himself: the professor about whom he'd been speaking, a Palestinian political economist, had invited Jeremiah to come to Ramallah while he was here. "Your mother's against it, but she's not being rational." His plan was to play sick on the day they were supposed to visit Molly's cousins in Haifa later in the week; he'd abscond to Ramallah and then be back in Jerusalem before they were. His wife would be none the wiser. All Hannah had to do, he said, was make sure Molly didn't cancel the visit on his account. One of the bellhops from East Jerusalem could help him find an Arab taxi to take him the thirty-minute drive to Ramallah; he'd already researched the whole thing.

Hannah was stunned. "Are you crazy?" She sat up, back rigid, and glared. "So not only are you going to lie to Mom, but you want me to lie as well?" Her seventy-two-year-old father could be infuriating, but she'd never thought of him as crafty. Wait until her brother heard this one.

He shrugged. "You don't have to lie. Just don't make a face when I mention my sciatica. Reassure her that you should go to Haifa anyway, how much she's been looking forward to visiting with her cousins, yada, yada, yada."

"Yada, yada, whatever! You're crazy!" True, there'd been a few years of relative calm since the Oslo Accords, but tensions were always simmering in the West Bank, with individual stabbings and shootings on occasion. The latest analyses were predicting a second *intifada* if progress on the peace talks didn't come soon.

"Listen, I researched it. Since I'm a tourist, I can enter Area A without a problem."

"That's supposed to make me feel better? That if you were Israeli, it would be illegal, but since you're a tourist, it's fine?"

"Come on!" he argued. "Of all people, I thought you'd understand." Some years ago, her father had been supportive when *she'd* contemplated traveling to the Somali border for her own research on nation-building. When the UN pulled out, making the interviews she'd planned impossible, she'd been awash with a shameful relief that the decision had been made for her.

"From an academic point of view, of course I get it. It's just. . ."

"If I thought it was dangerous, I wouldn't be going. You know as well as I do that the media at home makes things out to be much worse here then they really are."

The thought of her father traveling alone to the West Bank, with no security, filled her with anxiety. *What if. . .?* But on the heels of this: a strong dose of liberal guilt at her gut reaction.

"You know your mother. She gets anxious for nothing. Remember how frantic she was when I was visiting Grandma during Hurricane Andrew and she couldn't reach me because the phone lines were down?"

"I was worried too," Hannah said, countering. She was like her mother in this way—like all mothers, everywhere?—her mind galloping to all the dangerous, worst-case scenarios whenever there was the slightest cause for concern.

"Look outside," he said, arguing. "That's normal, daily life here." At dusk the street lights below Jaffa Gate appeared as little glowing orbs. Young tourists with oversized backpacks rested against storefronts advertising money changing. Locals with every manner of head covering interacted in the plaza: *kippahs* and *khaffiyehs*, Jewish and Arab women in headscarves, Armenian priests in square hats.

"I know. I get it." She took a deep breath and tried to let her anxiety abate. Wasn't the scene outside proof that 99% of the time, there was coexistence?

"Be reasonable, Hannah." He looked away, tapping his foot and scrunching his cheek to one side. Her father's persistence, his sheer will to get things done, had served him well in his career. An admirable quality, but there was a fine line between persistence and pigheaded stubbornness. When he got on his soapbox—whether the topic was personal (his mistreatment at the hand of his mother-in-law), communal (the PC police at his university), or political (campaign reform)—they had to endure a tiresome verbal barrage that made her want to shoot him.

"*Nu*, can I count on your help?"

"I'll think about it." He could be such baby at times; if he didn't get to go to Ramallah, she'd never hear the end of it. She sighed. Why had she come on this trip again? Because living on two meager academic salaries didn't allow for trips like this? Because she hadn't explored her Jewish roots since the last time she stepped foot in Hebrew school, back in 8th grade? Nothing was free. Her father seemed to have no problem asking for her help with his scheme.

"Help you with what?" They hadn't seen Molly emerge from the elevator and cross the lobby, but here she was.

"Oh, just talking shop. I was asking Hannah to help with a little research problem," Jeremiah said. The deception sounded so natural, Hannah wondered how many other times he'd lied like this to her mother, or to her. His shoulders and hands flinched and his face jutted forward, imploring. *Come on Hannah, play along.* "Ready? I'm starving," Jeremiah said.

"Why don't you go to dinner without me?" Hannah said. She *was* hungry but said she wasn't. "I'm just going to curl up with a book in my room. I'll see you at breakfast." Before her mother could protest, Hannah gave her a peck on the cheek and started for the elevator.

"What am I, chopped liver?" Jeremiah called.

She flicked a wave in his direction but didn't glance back. "*Laila tov*!" The words sounded funny as they left her mouth. She was sure the pronunciation wasn't quite right, but she was proud of herself for picking up this little bit of basic Hebrew. "See you in the morning."

The next day Molly was on edge due to the heat; no one had cautioned them that a walking tour of the Western Wall excavations in July might be too much for her sixty-seven-year-old mother, who wore no sun hat. Hannah hailed a taxi, intending to ship her parents back to the hotel and carry on sightseeing, but her mother's peaked face and her father's crooked gait weighed on her. Filial duty called. With a sigh, she hopped into the front seat.

While her parents rested, she phoned Tom. "A bit exhausting, chaperoning my parents around the country," she said. She couldn't reasonably whine too much about her paid-for vacation when he was at home, teaching English composition to a cadre of summer students.

"I'm sure you can handle it." When she asked him what he thought of her father's scheme, Tom chuckled. "He's a grown man, Han. Let him be."

"God, sorry I asked!"

Dinner that night, at a Persian restaurant downtown, put everyone in better moods. They stuffed themselves with delicious flatbreads and salads, and Jeremiah couldn't finish his generous portion of schnitzel, fried to golden perfection. They took their time meandering back to the hotel in the balmy night air. Jerusalem swarmed with groups of teenagers on trips from America. Halter-topped girls, shoulders brown from the Mediterranean sun, hugged friends and flirted with Modern Orthodox boys, fringes peeking out from under their Mets and Rangers T-shirts. A Russian émigré earned shekels from the crowd playing klezmer tunes on his violin, while down the block vendors of cheap jewelry and hair weaves competed for the teenagers' attention. Years ago, Hannah's parents had tried to interest her in one of these Israel summer tours, but they'd held no appeal then.

Jerusalem pulsed with energy, a vitality she'd never felt within the staid boundaries of her American Jewish experience. In college, Hannah had met students who talked about their Jewish summer camps as if they were holy places, the shining light of their lives. Would her life have followed a different trajectory if she'd been one of those campers? Being Jewish to her meant holiday family gatherings, chicken soup, and chopped liver on Manischewitz crackers. A predilection for liberal politics and causes. She'd never felt the richness that others seemed to attribute to their heritage: Judaism as a religion, as a tradition of learning, as a tether to something larger than oneself.

They passed groups of Israeli soldiers waiting in line for shwarma or pizza and young ultra-Orthodox couples with five, six, seven children in tow. "If you had to describe Jerusalem in one word, what would it be?" Hannah asked her parents. It was a game she and Tom played when they traveled: D.C. was "power," New York was "energy," New Orleans was "festive."

"One word?" Jeremiah repeated. "Ooh, I don't know. Divided? Traditional?"

"Timeless?" Molly suggested. They nodded: yes, that was the perfect word!

"This trip has been great," Hannah said. "Thank you again." Even the controversial parts of Israel were refreshing in the way they challenged and stimulated her brain. She reserved her highest praise for things—books, concepts, places, and people—that caused her to wonder, to lie in bed at night and really *think*. While many of the places they'd visited offered the melded charm of ancient and modern, the real highlights were the meetings set up for them by their tour guide with representatives of a Jewish and Palestinian women's dialogue group, a young army spokesman, a settler. In this small country, everyone seemed to exude real warmth; everyone had a fascinating story.

Her parents smiled. "Our pleasure," Molly said, for once refraining from putting on her it's-too-bad-Tom-and-the-kids-didn't-come face.

"Let me ask you something," Hannah said. "Why didn't you give us more of a religious education? I mean, your mothers always lit candles on Friday nights. Your fathers went to temple most Saturdays. Why didn't you?"

"First of all," her father said, "temple is a Reform Movement construct. Your grandfathers, when they went, went to *shul*."

"Okay, semantics! Whatever!" She waited for his second-of-all but it didn't come.

"Oh Han," Molly said. "I did light candles sometimes. . ."

"Only when they came to visit."

"I'm sure that's not true." Her mother's defenses were up. "We were busy. We always had cultural engagements and concerts and such on Friday nights. I don't seem to recall you ever having a problem with it."

"I was a kid!" It bothered her, though she couldn't say why. Her life was full: a solid marriage, a fulfilling career, and two kids who were developing into fine human beings. "I guess I'm just realizing how much I don't know."

"Never too late to learn," her father said.

Her paternal grandparents—quintessential immigrants—had been gone for many years, but Hannah felt a sudden longing for the warmth of Grandma Rikki's embrace and the smell of her kitchen. For Papa Abe's hopelessly incorrect English spellings and the resonance of his voice. Despite sixty years in America her grandfather never lost his thick Galician accent. Her parents seemed so different.

"By the way, are you going to do a bat mitzvah for Pam?" her father asked.

The question caught her off-guard. Her daughter would be thirteen in less than a year. "I don't know." If Pam wanted one, Tom would probably go along. But in contrast to her parents, Hannah hadn't even invested in the most basic of watered-down Hebrew school educations. A speck of guilt began to sprout. "Maybe it's time."

Her mother clasped her hand, reading her mind. "It would be our pleasure to help. I mean if the tuition is too steep."

"They'll be starting from zero."

"Nonsense." Molly was an expert optimist. "They know a thing or two from us. They come to our seder every year and celebrate Chanukah and Rosh Hashana."

Hannah nodded in appreciation. Well. Something to think about. "Maybe. Thanks. I'll have to speak to Tom about it."

"Of course." To Molly, it was obvious that such a decision should be discussed with one's spouse. If Hannah was more of her father's daughter, she might act unilaterally. Jeremiah walked along, seemingly oblivious, whistling and upbeat—his thoughts already on something else?—and Hannah wasn't about to jinx it by asking him more challenging questions.

Despite the heat, they enjoyed excursions to Masada and the Dead Sea. At Latrun, Molly displayed an impressive command of pre-State history and the 1948 siege of Jerusalem. Every so often, Jeremiah would bring up his colleague in Ramallah: "Listen Mol, I don't think you realize the contributions Fuad's made to the debate on transculturalism and the Palestinian political economy."

Molly would reply that she didn't care if he was the world's expert, she didn't want him going. Jeremiah was incapable of easing up and a while later he might say, "Han, tell her how well-respected he is in our field. The man might be the first Palestinian to win the Nobel in economics!"

"You can go visit him in Stockholm, then."

These were little blips in their conversations, which would always end with Jeremiah saying, "Okay, okay, forget I said anything!"

Thursday morning, Molly appeared at Hannah's hotel room door looking concerned. "Dad had a bad night. Sciatica. He doesn't think he should sit in the car so long today."

Hannah wrinkled her forehead. She resented her father's audacity, doing what he pleased without guilt. But revealing his plan would cause strife, and she didn't want to ruin the last few days of the trip.

"We should still go," Hannah heard herself saying. "You haven't seen these people in, what, at least a decade?" She had a vague memory of her mother's older cousin Yitz.

Molly was hesitant. "I don't know. Of course I want to see Yitz, but I'm not sure I should leave Dad in this state. He's my first priority."

Hannah closed her eyes to roll them without her mother seeing. "It's not like he hasn't had bouts of sciatica before. He just needs to rest."

Her mother reluctantly agreed. Hannah peeked into her parents' room where her father lay in bed. He gave her a wink—infuriating!—and she hurried out of the room without saying anything.

Once they were on the road, Hannah driving the rental car and Molly navigating, her mother relaxed, talking with excitement about seeing her cousins. At various stops over the course of the last week, Molly and Jeremiah had revealed bits and pieces of family history, ties to this country that Hannah had never considered: a cousin who'd helped the fledgling Israeli Air Force in 1948, grandparents active in fundraising for the nascent Jewish State, a meeting with Golda Meir on their first trip to Israel in the '70s. "Yitz has some stories," Molly said now. "You should ask him. But I guess anyone his age has stories from that period."

Hannah nodded. On the coastal road north of Tel Aviv, the Mediterranean Sea danced in and out of view, faraway swirls of bluish-black waves surging towards the shore. Against the backdrop of a cerulean sky, about halfway through the two-and-a-half-hour drive, Hannah felt the weight of her father's deception lifting.

Yitz's wife Shula, a sturdy, compact woman who'd once helped to found a *kibbutz*, brought out endless new dishes—little salads, olives, and pickled cabbage, flaky pastries filled with spiced meat, humus, and more.

"Shula, it's too much," Molly said each time Shula set out a new dish. "Please stop fussing over us and sit! Jeremiah's going to be so upset when he hears he's missed such a feast!"

Hannah tried not to let an irrational panic rise up in her every time her father's name was mentioned. The smell of tuna salad with pickles made her nauseous. She sipped her water and took polite bites whenever Shula glanced in her direction. She chided herself that she hadn't thought to work out a signal, a contact plan with Jeremiah ahead of time. He didn't want Molly to worry, but the fact that *Hannah* might be worried hadn't occurred to him, the inconsiderate bum. No, not a bum. He was out there exploring, doing exactly what he desired. She couldn't decide if she was furious with her father or impressed by his fearlessness. Not too many American Jews made side trips to Ramallah.

Yitz brought out the photo albums, a dozen at least, and Molly oohed and aahed over every picture from family celebrations and trips abroad. Hannah tried to occupy her mind by reading the Hebrew words on the spines of the books in Yitz's living room, but her rudimentary command of the language, acquired at their temple's once-a-week religious school, was not up to the task. Was it too late to try again? Her undergraduates would get a kick out of her sitting in on an introductory Hebrew class.

She leaned over to get a closer look when Yitz brought out the album from his army days as a medic in '48, his unit having secured Eilat. A dozen or so pictures of Yitz posing with Egyptian troops, everyone smiling. "Looks to me like you were having a good time," Hannah said. As soon as the words left her mouth she winced; it had been wartime, how could anyone be enjoying themselves?

"Actually you're right," Yitz said, reassuring. "The Egyptians had given up by then, and I treated a few of them. We traded food and cigarettes."

Molly asked Hannah to phone the hotel to check on Jeremiah, and like a dutiful daughter she went through the motions, dialing the number, asking for room 324, hearing the phone ring and ring until she could think of what to report back to her mother. "No answer. I guess he went out."

"Well," her mother said, unconcerned, "I'm sorry he missed this, but I'm relieved he's feeling better."

Yitz assured her not to worry and kept saying how wonderful it was that they'd made the trip. These older cousins, with their creased faces and capable hands, seemed to represent every Israeli of their generation. In 1939, Yitz's *shtetl* ended up on the Soviet side of divided Poland, allowing the intrepid teenager to make a two-year journey to pre-State Palestine via Moscow, Riga, and Istanbul, forging documents and bribing or begging officials as necessary. His story was so different from the relative comfort of her parents' youth in America. Yitz and Shula were dreamers. Pioneers. Proud of the roles they'd played in building a modern state. Gratified by its successes, frustrated by its failures. "A work-in-progress," Yitz said of the tiny country, "but I wouldn't live anywhere else."

When the afternoon turned to evening, Shula made a care package of almond and halva cookies for Jeremiah and insisted that Hannah accept a few gifts for Pam and Ben: a pen from a bank, a tiny book written in microscopic Hebrew. Yitz gave them a photocopied version of the family tree his granddaughter had prepared for her bat mitzvah; some branches came to a stark end in Europe, a few continued in America, and Yitz's own—three children, ten grandchildren, and counting—flourishing here. It was a beautiful thing to see.

Again, a stirring in Hannah's bones: she was part of this. Connected to her people, to the generations of Jews who'd come before her. Her parents felt it, she was sure, and now she needed to teach her children. A Mediterranean breeze rustled through an open window as they said their goodbyes. Their ancestors had prayed for a return to this land for 2,000 years; for the first time, she could understand why.

Jeremiah was waiting for them in the lobby, his face rosy and tanned. Hannah's relief that he was back on the "safe side" of Jerusalem was so intense she worried Molly would notice the deep gasp she took when she spotted him. Again, this instinctive reaction shamed her. Emotions overpowered intellect on this trip. Her father stood, kissed his wife and then her, and professed that he felt "much better, much better!"

"We tried to call a couple times to check on you," Molly said.

"I don't need checking on!" Jeremiah's mood was boisterous, his voice ringing through the lobby. "Once I felt okay, I wasn't going to stick around in the hotel all day."

Hannah glowered, trying to suggest with her eyes that now was the time to confess. She flinched her hands and eyebrows to convey, *Well?*

This caught his attention; his ruddy complexion seemed to lighten for a second, as if he was considering what to say, but then Molly launched into a description of the visit, Shula's hospitality, and Yitz's stories about her grandparents.

"*Nu,* did you learn something, Hannah? How was Haifa?"

"You missed out." She shook her head in consternation, bothered now not only by his deception but because he, too, would have been touched by Yitz's stories. She didn't feel any obligation to answer his attempts to draw her out. "I see you've made a miraculous recovery," she said.

On their floor, Molly let herself into her room and Hannah hung back in the hallway, beckoning to her father. "How was it?" she whispered.

"Fantastic. We had a great meeting. We're going to co-author an article."

She pushed aside the pang of envy in her gut and pursed her lips. "When are you going to tell Mom?"

"When the timing is right." He paused. "Sometimes you've just got to do what you need to do. Not listen to what anybody else thinks. Take risks. In life, in testing your research theories. Don't I tell you this all the time?"

"Whatever." She had no desire to hear a lecture; she slid the electronic key into the lock of her room, waited a beat for the green light.

"Just because you're jealous doesn't mean you need to be huffy," he said, a bit indignant.

His words stung; she let herself in and left him standing in the hallway, mouth open, ready to say more.

The final morning of the trip was reserved for last-minute gift shopping. The ceramics store downtown—a co-op of eight local artists, each with his or her own style and colors and designs—featured beautifully crafted bowls and vases as well as seder plates, menorahs, and other ritual items. Hannah and Molly admired the different sets and chatted with the artist on duty while Jeremiah paced. "I'll leave the shopping to you ladies," he said, fidgety. "I'll get the paper and wait outside."

"Mr. Patience, as usual," Hannah said.

She helped her mother select apple and honey dishes as gifts for her friends, and then deliberated over whether to purchase a pair of pomegranate-shaped candlesticks. In this small way, she would start to reconnect to the tradition of her grandmothers.

Hannah handed the candlesticks to the saleswoman to bubble-wrap, and Molly murmured her approval. To her mother's credit, she'd never given her a hard time for marrying a (lapsed) Catholic or raising Pam and Ben without much of any religion, but now Molly seemed pleased. Molly selected two more similar sets—one for her and one for Pam— and then insisted on paying for all of them. For a moment, Hannah hesitated—would this upset the balance she'd created with Tom?— but then she rationalized: *it's a five-minute ritual, once a week. Take the risk.*

"I read two entire newspapers while you were in one store!" Jeremiah said when they emerged. "Listen. There's something I need to start working on. An article. Fuad told me I could get into the National Library. How about I go over there while you ladies keep shopping?"

"Fuad!" Molly said. "When did you talk to him?"

"Yesterday." He paused for a beat. "While you were in Haifa."

"Oh! You didn't mention it!"

Now, Hannah thought. *Now.*

Jeremiah bent over, possessed by a sudden need to retie his shoelaces. "I met him," he said, addressing his ankles.

"What?" Molly said, as the meaning of his words sunk in. Her expression went from ungrasping to furious in ten seconds. "Look at me if you have something to say!"

"I went to Ramallah," Jeremiah said, peering up at his wife.

Molly steadied herself on Hannah's arm, almost dropping the ceramics. "You didn't!"

Jeremiah hung his head. "I'm sorry. I do feel bad about not seeing your relatives. But this way you didn't have to worry about me all day, see?"

Molly's eyes widened and she sucked in her cheeks. Her face turned scarlet. "So you lied to me for my own benefit. Is that it?"

"I figured I'd tell you once I was back. You know I can't keep a secret! And you see? I'm fine. I survived. I saw the guy. It was fascinating. We're going to write an article together."

Hannah held her breath, waiting to see if he'd implicate her.

"Wait 'til you see what I got you," he said, patting Molly's hand, as if a gift could make up for his behavior.

"Oh. My. God. I'd like to wring your neck right now!" She sat down on the bench where Jeremiah had been sitting. He took her hands in his and tried to bend over to kiss them, but she pulled away. She turned her face skyward, as if God himself would reward such fortitude.

Her father shrugged. He wouldn't admit it, but the slight blush that crept over his cheeks meant a small part of him felt remorse.

"Shameless." Hannah shook her head.

"We didn't have to tell you, you know," Jeremiah said.

In an instant her mother turned on her. "You knew about this? Hannah!"

Hannah pursed her lips and looked down.

"Leave her out of this. It's my fault."

Molly jabbed her thumb in Jeremiah's direction. "From him, I'm sorry to say, I'm not surprised. But Hannah, from you? I'm just. . .speechless!" Her voice caught, and Hannah sensed her mother's exasperation swelling to full-fledged ire. Perfect.

"Happy now?" Hannah asked her father. She was livid he'd put her in the middle, but she didn't want to hang around to get a lecture or a guilt trip from Molly either. As maddening as Jeremiah could be, it was equally maddening that her mother put up with his shenanigans. But, incredibly, she'd been doing it for forty-five years. Hannah vacillated between thinking of her mother as someone with tremendous inner strength and someone who was inherently weak. Was this what psychologists called co-dependent?

Stop! The voice in her head roared. Sometimes it was better not to know.

"Go on, get yourself to the library. Go do your important research," Hannah heard herself saying. "I'll see you later. Maybe." She started walking at a brisk pace in the direction of Jaffa Gate. She wanted to lose herself, if only for a few hours, in this vibrant place, in the narrow, windy corridors of the Old City, its pale limestone buildings and walkways beckoning to her.

"Wait!" they called after her. They could find their way back to the hotel without her. And if they were going to work out their issues right there on the pedestrian mall, she wanted no part. "Where are you going?" she heard Molly call, but Hannah ignored her. She didn't dare turn around but she could picture her mother frantic, wanting to follow her while Jeremiah held her back.

She could make out a dim plea on the part of her father—"for God's sake, would everyone calm down?"—but by then she was close to the main road, where the rumble of cars and tourists and accordion-players drowned out his calls.

Hannah quickened her stride. She'd been an obedient child, an overachieving teenager, and now a devoted adult daughter who rarely did anything that upset or disappointed her parents. Darting away like this was instinctive, something her father, with his lack of impulse control, might do, but she couldn't take another minute with them right now.

At Jaffa Gate she bought lemonade with *nana* from a juice vendor and paused to decide what to do. Straight ahead was the Arab *souk*, colorful garments hanging high on display and shops filled with olivewood backgammon sets and other wooden trinkets. To the right was a narrow passageway that led past the Armenian compound and eventually to Zion Gate and into the Jewish Quarter, and she turned in this direction, hugging the gray stone wall to avoid the cars going through the tunnel. In the main square of the Jewish Quarter, she sat to rest, hoping to shake the annoyance with her parents out of her mind.

She couldn't imagine blatantly lying to get around something her husband had vetoed, yet complicity carried its own share of blameworthiness. *Was* she like her father? On occasion, Tom accused her of getting up on a soapbox, or being oversensitive to the littlest slights. And among students, her candor was interpreted by some as rude, though she wasn't a quarter as brusque as her father. One thing was certain: her marriage was nothing like her parents', thank goodness.

In front of her lay the ruins of a synagogue, constructed and destroyed many times over. Despite the rehabilitation of neighboring buildings, the huge, empty arch served as a reminder of the destruction, though—if she recalled correctly—their guide had said something about a proposal being discussed for rejuvenating the structure. Behind it stood the Cardo, a main thoroughfare of ancient Jerusalem, now restored, home to artist galleries and shops with luxury goods. A restaurant in the complex offered an "authentic" Roman culinary experience but the night they'd tried to go it had been fully booked. Next time, they'd said. Much as she longed to get home—ten days away from Tom was wearing on her—she hoped there would be a next time. Hannah knew words and pictures wouldn't be enough to convey everything she'd seen and felt on this vacation. She'd start saving for a family trip now. Perhaps in a few years, in time for Ben's bar mitzvah. But she was getting ahead of herself.

Now it came to her, how to describe the country in one word: resilient. Despite wars and destruction, the people here continually moved forward, rebuilding and innovating. Resilience might also be the quality needed for a lasting marriage, the ability to sort through problems and come out stronger. Her parents would be all right.

She consulted her map. Emboldened, she decided she would weave her way back through the Arab *souk*. But first, she headed towards a narrow corridor that led down to the Western Wall, a few hundred feet away. Facing the holy site, Hannah ignored the tiny voice in her head questioning her sudden desire to pray. She closed her eyes and offered a silent entreaty. For peace. For strength. For resilience.

AWAKENING

(1961)

The old Buick Special clawed its way north in the stifling July heat, and Jeremiah swore his next car would be one with air conditioning. Damn government salary. He blinked past mirages of water pooling on the New Jersey Turnpike. Molly dozed in the passenger seat, a look of lovely innocence on her face. She wore the Mexican peasant dress she'd received from her girlfriends for her birthday; he didn't care for its colorful cross-striping and purple and red zigzag design, but it was one of the few things his wife seemed enthusiastic about in the last few months, so he kept his mouth shut. Now, in the steaming car, she'd hitched it up over her knees, and he fought off an urge to stroke her bare thigh.

In the backseat, Hannah began to hum, spirited away into the musical, carefree world of a four-year-old. *Yankee Doodle Dandy*. "That's a good one for this weekend, Han, but Mommy's resting. Let's let her sleep, okay?" She nodded, her eyes wide and comprehending.

The doctor said: give her time. Molly had lost the baby early on—week nine or ten—but that had been four months ago, and Jeremiah was wondering, how much time, exactly? These last few months she'd turned inward, away from him, away from her girlfriends, her interests in poetry, psychology, and music abandoned.

When would Molly awaken, return to being the bubbly, adventurous woman he married, and not some distant mannequin with dark, hollow eyes and an untouchable body covered by a shapeless peasant dress? *Why is Mommy sad?* Hannah had never asked directly but Jeremiah could see that she'd sensed a change, too. The only real cure would be a new pregnancy, a healthy baby at the end of nine months, but that wasn't going to happen unless she let him back onto her side of the bed.

"It's nothing to be ashamed of Molly," he said, more times than he could count. "Stop punishing yourself."

This kind of thing occurred all the time, the doctor had said. In the days and weeks after, Molly's friend Diana had popped in with an assortment of muffins and casseroles. Diana and her beatnik husband, an anthropologist who studied the mystical life of the Mazatecs, tried to convince Molly to attend one of their retreats—she'd gone to one, pre-miscarriage, and loved it—but after losing the baby even this spiritual *narishkeit* couldn't lift her sadness.

Now they were headed to Molly's parents in Queens for July 4th weekend, and Jeremiah hoped that a few days away and her mother's pampering would do his wife some good.

"Are we going on the big bridge?" Hannah asked. "The one with the song?"

What a memory his daughter had! Once, on a trip to see *his* parents in Bridgeport, Molly'd taught her the words to "George Washington Bridge." They'd been in jolly moods on that trip.

Molly stirred and turned to give Hannah a warm smile. "Not this time, sweetheart, but we can sing it anyway." Both wife and daughter started singing, and within a bar or two, Jeremiah joined in, crooning the "peanuts, popcorn, and crackerjack" melody. He couldn't remember the last time he'd heard Molly sing with their daughter or even hum a tune to herself. She caught his eye and brought her hand to rest on his shoulder. He tapped the steering wheel all the way into New York with a flutter of hope: maybe, just maybe, his wife was starting to heal.

◆ ◆ ◆

Molly's childhood bedroom now contained a double bed with a solid wood, ash-colored headboard, and after setting down their valise Jeremiah stretched out on the mattress. On previous visits, despite the close proximity of her parents' bedroom, two doors away, Molly had welcomed some amour. He hoped he'd read that light touch in the car correctly, though it wasn't just the sex. So much of their relationship felt reversed. She had been the social one, dragging him to classical music concerts or Hadassah benefits and pulling him onto the dance floor when he'd rather be home watching Perry Mason or the Yanks. He indulged her, usually, because he felt lucky that she'd chosen *him*, even after all these years. *Give her time*, they all said, but for crying out loud, he needed her back now.

Molly called for him to join them in the kitchen. He stretched his legs, rolled his neck a few times to get the kinks out, and yelled, "Coming!"

Her mother stood at the stovetop, ladling tomato soup from a pot. "Sit down Jeremiah, I'll get you some soup," Sarah said.

He declined; it was too hot for soup. Sarah frowned, rummaging in her refrigerator for other options. Deli sandwich? Tuna? Piece of fruit? He settled on an apple.

Leaning against her counter, Sarah seemed to be surveying her daughter, granddaughter, and son in law. A slender woman, his mother-in-law wore her hair in a backcombed bouffant, her pointy glasses with the red trim meant to complement her lipstick. Unlike her mother, Molly didn't go in for big hairstyles and never overdid it with makeup.

Molly and Hannah swallowed spoonfuls of soup, though Hannah's bowl had turned into a red mush with crumbled up crackers. "You're too skinny," Sarah said to her daughter, wrinkling her face into a scowl.

"Ma, I'm fine," Molly said.

"You've lost weight since my visit. I can see it in your face. Your cheeks are too thin."

Sarah had stayed with them in D.C. for a week after the miscarriage, taking charge, cooking and cleaning and puttering around the house.

"I'm fine, Ma."

"Well, you look too thin to me. Doesn't she, Jeremiah?"

He took a bite of the apple and chewed slowly, putting a finger up to signal his mouth was full. Sarah was right, obviously. Molly had lost weight, Molly wasn't herself, Molly was still a wreck. But if his wife was trying to put on her best face for her mother it was his job to support her. "She's doing okay, Sarah. Really."

His mother-in-law arched her eyebrows at him, disappointed. When Molly whisked Hannah off to the bathroom to wash her face, Sarah pulled back the chair next to him and leaned in close enough that he could smell her lilac face cream. "She looks terrible, Jeremiah! How can you say everything is okay?"

He lowered his voice. "She's still a bit down."

"You've got to do something about it. Take her out. Make her feel special. Be extra sensitive."

"You think I'm not trying? Jesus Christ!" He'd gotten tickets to the philharmonic and Molly had insisted he take his sister instead. He brought home flowers every Friday evening, just as his father had always done. Not to mention the extra parenting duties: getting up with Hannah in the middle of the night when she needed help in the bathroom, sitting on the floor doing puzzles. "Give me a little credit. I'm not a complete *putz*!"

"I didn't say you were."

He didn't need this baloney. He scraped the back of his chair, tossed the apple core in the trash, and walked off.

Back in the bedroom, he paced, picking up old framed photographs of Molly and her friends and siblings. College graduation, family weddings, and one picture with Molly and a bunch of other teenagers in swimsuits—the famous lake crowd the Kellmans summered with in the Adirondacks. There'd been an older, wild gal Sarah had warned Molly away from, who'd convinced his wife to go skinny dipping— skinny dipping!—while the boys in their group had taken a rowboat to the far side of the lake. "They didn't see anything, don't worry," Molly had said when she told him the story, years ago. She'd given him a playful swat. "But it was fun."

Where was that Molly now?

◆ ◆ ◆

On their second night in Queens, Sarah insisted that he and Molly go out; she and Mickey would be happy to babysit. Though he didn't agree with her tactics and took umbrage at her insinuations, a small part of Jeremiah admired Sarah's unrelenting nature. Pre-miscarriage, Molly would, on occasion, stand up to her mother and refuse to be bulldozed. But now she was pliant, more mature than her younger self, who'd sometimes do outrageous things for the sole purpose of feeling free of her mother. After some deliberation over where to go, Jeremiah finally said, "Look, let's just go into Manhattan for a nice dinner. No protests. I'm deciding." In the end, though, it wasn't his decision. Mickey and Sarah raved about a restaurant with outdoor seating in Central Park, and Molly's eyes sparkled at the prospect; he had no choice but to take her there. Without seeing the menu he was certain that anywhere his in-laws ate would not agree with his wallet.

Molly rummaged through her closet and found an old dress. "It's a bit out of fashion."

"Never mind that. You look beautiful. Let's just go." He tried to keep the urgency out of his voice; he didn't want her to change her mind. "You look ravishing." It was both true and a lie. She was beautiful, but he had to agree with Sarah: Molly looked too thin.

"Now let's have a helluva time tonight," he said when they left.

She gave him a weak smile that said she'd try. He took her hand and squeezed it.

"Sorry I've been so. . ." She searched for the word. "So blue lately."

He nodded, waiting to see if she would say more, but nothing else came out. He had many things he wanted to say, but he bit his lip. He'd try to be patient and see how the evening panned out.

"This *is* a treat," he said with false cheer when they were seated. One glance at the menu told him his gut had been correct. Nineteen dollars for a steak! Nuts! Even in their absence, her parents made him feel inferior. He was trying to be on his best behavior, which meant not saying everything as soon as it popped into his mind. Turning on his inner filter, Molly called it. "Dining with my beautiful wife, on fourth of July weekend, in Central Park. Remember when we were poor students?" *Remember,* screamed the voice inside his head, *that I am a government employee, Grade 2 pay scale, and you are a schoolteacher?*

"Oh Jer," she sighed. Growing up the daughter of a big shot lawyer, Molly was oblivious to monetary concerns, whereas he'd learned the value of a nickel from an early age, helping out in his parents' liquor store. "So much has happened in nine years."

"Most of it good, baby. Only the last few months have been difficult."

She screwed up her face for a moment, and looked away.

"C'mon Mol." He took her hand. "Don't cry. I really wish you would talk to me."

She shook her head. "I know. I'm sorry."

"Well?"

"I don't want to spoil our dinner, but sometimes I just feel so sad. Like maybe I don't deserve another child."

He lowered his voice. "I know you wanted that baby. I did too. But we'll have another chance. I promise you."

"No, you don't understand. . ."

He cut her off. "So help me understand." He closed his menu and took her hand, striving to be his most patient self, his neck tense from the effort. If Molly could observe him from an objective viewpoint right now, he was certain she'd praise his restraint.

She bit her lip, as if she wanted to say something, but then looked away, out into the park. He followed her gaze to a gray-haired woman walking arm-in-arm with a younger, curvaceous woman in a red dress and short black hair. Or perhaps she was staring at the little boy, just beyond the women, whose father was hoisting him up on his shoulders. He waited for her to say something, but seconds passed by, then a full minute or two.

"What is it, Molly? You can tell me."

She shook her head no. "It's nothing."

"You're so withdrawn!" he said, bursting. "It's not like you're the first woman to have a miscarriage!" As soon as the words flew out of his mouth he knew he'd said the wrong thing. "I'm sorry."

Her face appeared stung.

"Aw, jeez, Mol. I'm sorry." He palmed his forehead. "You know me, always putting my foot in my mouth. C'mon. Don't cry."

"I'll be okay," she sniffed, dabbing at her face with a napkin. She excused herself to freshen up.

He cursed inwardly: so much for his false cheer. Would she ever go back to attending poetry readings or playing piano for pleasure? To baking sugar cookies with Hannah or packing his lunches with peanut butter brownies? Pre-miscarriage, she'd ask about his day at the office, amuse him with stories of her work as an elementary school music teacher—the third grader who sang off-key, the sixth-grade flautist whose mother insisted he was a prodigy. She'd gone back to work but with zero enthusiasm, and he couldn't recall the last time she'd asked about *his* job. And what he wouldn't give to see her showing him sexy dance moves when "Hound Dog" and "All Shook Up" came on the AM-FM.

Molly returned, her cheeks dry. "I'm all right now."

"Good," he said, though he worried that she was becoming some kind of neurotic. God help them. Maybe he'd enlist Diana or the other girlfriends to convince Molly to see a specialist. At this, a twinge of resentment: why did Molly always seem to listen to advice from her friends and not from him? Last week he'd noticed a book called *The Second Son* lying around, with passages underlined. Molly had written *yes!!* and *to discuss with D.* in several sections. He'd attempted to read the book, to take an interest, but he couldn't get past the first few pages.

"I guess I'm no good at understanding these women things. So I'm glad you have your girlfriends."

"Funny, I dreamt about Diana last night. We were in an open field, filled with flowers. So pleasant, I didn't want to wake up."

"Maybe you could try to dream about me a little bit, you know? Tell old Mr. Sleep to dapple you with some spousal fairy dust." His eyebrows moved up and down, hubba-hubba style.

She blushed and took his hand across the table, bringing it up to her lips. She pecked at his knuckles with tender little kisses. He started to relax, feeling a trickle of assurance that everything would turn out all right. Her skin was warm and smooth, and he inched his chair closer to hers. He stroked her face, tracing her slender cheekbone. "God, Mol. I've missed you." Under the table he rested his hand on her knee, and it was almost too much for him to bear. The matronly woman at the next table cast a disapproving stare. He ignored her; all he wanted was to dart out of the restaurant and head for one of the hotels overlooking Central Park.

"How about we ditch this place and get a room? We could just tell the waiter we want our order to go."

"Shhh!" she whispered. "You're embarrassing me."

"I can't help it," he said. He kept his voice loud enough for the matron to hear. "I'm starving and it ain't for food."

"Shhh!" she giggled, a special smile meaning she was willing. Hot diggedy.

Back in Queens, they let themselves into the apartment. While Jeremiah undressed and slid into bed, Molly went to brush her teeth. His in-laws were asleep two doors away; they'd have to be very quiet.

At last Molly entered the room, her slim figure silhouetted through her nightgown. He beamed at her, raised his eyebrows, and pulled back the covers. In the dim light, despite her thinness, Molly looked more beautiful than she had when they'd first met as students. She hesitated for a moment, a twitch of nervousness in her cheeks, but then climbed in and turned out the light on the night table. He cradled her head in his arms—*gently, gently,* he cautioned himself—and kissed her on the forehead. Her body was tense, and he banished the thought that she was only doing this to fulfill some wifely duty.

He traced his fingers up her arm, his hand still on the outside of her nightgown, as if needing to re-familiarize himself with her contours. "I've missed you," he whispered. "And these." His hand moved gingerly to her breasts, cupping first the right one, then the left. "I'm going to make you feel so good, Mol." She stiffened but a groan of pleasure escaped her lips. "Shhh. . ." He let his fingers drift downward,

downward, slow circular motions, trying to relax her, until he reached the bottom of her nightgown and lifted it up above her head. She complied and stretched to remove it completely.

He propped himself up on one arm—enough moonlight filtered in through the window so he could watch her, see the tension draining out of her face, her expression turning sensuous. And though her body coiled with bliss, when she opened her eyes he was surprised to recognize the same look of pain that had accompanied her for four months. But she was trying, he could tell. He'd have to be patient. When she fondled him, every nerve ending in his body felt electrified. He had to muffle his moans. A slight smile formed on her lips and he kissed her with the hunger of a nineteen-year-old. He slid his briefs off and with one hand reached for the lotion he'd placed next to the bed, moistening his own hand with it and squirting some on his penis. *God, he'd missed this.* Never mind that his wife did not seem to be kissing him back with the same level of passion, that her stroking seemed mechanical. "Don't stop," he whispered. Molly was on her back, and he massaged her, fingers dipping in and out, as she keened with desire. Just a little longer and he could bring her to orgasm. He loved the way her shallow panting took on a different, more urgent pitch as he brought her closer and closer to climax. He thirsted to be inside of her already. *C'mon, c'mon.* She'd stopped stroking him and her eyes were closed in concentration. His fingers were working at lightning speed. Faster and faster. She was almost there. *Almost, almost.*

"Stop!" It was so sudden he didn't register until she pushed his hand away.

He was bewildered. "What's wrong?"

"You're hurting me."

"What?"

"It's just that. . .you've rubbed me raw." She moved his hand away and clamped her legs shut. The look of pain was back in her eyes and she folded her elbow across her face.

"You were enjoying it. Just let yourself relax." He tried to keep his voice gentle.

"Was. But it's too late now."

He felt dizzy, like he'd just been punched. The color drained from his face, and the blood in his erection retreated. He fell back on his pillow and let out a low groan.

After a minute or two, he heard her say they could keep going. "Just because it's not going to happen for me tonight doesn't mean we have to stop," she said. He didn't believe for a minute she wanted to continue, but with one hand she took up his now-limp penis and started caressing it again. He felt the blood returning, and within seconds he was hard. He tried to shut out every thought, concentrating only on the sensations. She spread her legs, but just as he was about to enter, he noticed her shoulders were shaking. She was weeping silently. Her eyes scrunched shut, tears trickling down her cheeks.

"For god's sake, Mol. I can't do this if you're crying."

She opened her eyes but made no response. Her lips were pressed together. A tear spilled onto the pillow.

"Jesus Christ!" He rolled off the bed, wrapped a towel around his torso, and stormed out to the bathroom in the hall where he finished the job himself, utterly unsatisfying. He felt punished.

Molly seemed composed when he returned. She'd put her nightgown on and was huddled under the covers, the sheets and summer blanket pulled up to her neck.

"I'm sorry," she started.

He was sick of her apologies. He didn't trust himself to speak without raising his voice.

"It's just that. . ." she stopped. He knew what she was going to say. That in his haste and hunger, he'd gone too fast.

"Never mind." He stopped her. "Forget it."

"If you were a woman you'd understand."

"What kind of a stupid statement is that? Obviously I'm not a woman."

"Diana says. . ."

"'Diana says, Diana says,'" he said, mimicking her. "I don't give a goddamn what Diana says."

"I guess I'm still not ready. I'm sorry, sweetheart. I really am. You'll just have to bear with me a little longer."

"Molly, you could be pregnant already by now, if we could just. . . do it! But you keep getting all weepy on me! How do you think that makes me feel, seeing you cry, knowing that I'm causing you pain, when I just want to make you feel good? When all I want is for you to be happy again?"

He had a vision of his wife, starry-eyed, just home from a girls' night out or one of those ridiculous meditation meetings she attended with Diana, her face glowing with contentment. Pictures of their outings, with Molly relaxed and gleeful, leaning in close to the other girls. When was the last time he'd made her feel like that? Like pieces of a puzzle coming into focus, he began to see the situation clearly: his wife had become a homosexual. She'd admitted to dreaming about Diana, hadn't she? Diana was the type to experiment. He'd wring her neck when he got back to Washington for drawing his wife into it.

Could someone just "turn" like that? He sat down on a chair facing the bed as the thought spun and twisted in his mind. The notes from Diana. The book he'd found. Were there other clues? Molly was always going on about Jackie Kennedy, how beautiful and classy she was, but unlike other women, she'd never swooned over the President himself. It was a crazy notion, and one he wasn't sure about. Hadn't they just rolled around in bed, even if it had ended badly? A sinking sensation told him he'd done something to repel her, to turn her off from men.

"Okay, then at least tell me this. is it me? Are you upset with me for something?"

She insisted she wasn't, but when he pressed her for answers she wouldn't budge. They went around in circles, and when he was too tired to continue, he climbed into bed and turned away from her.

The next few days passed in a blur, both preferring to focus their energies on Hannah. Jeremiah stewed. What else had Diana exposed her to? At one time, Molly had liked men. Liked him. He tried to swallow back the fear that their entire future was uncertain. When it was time to pack up the Buick and drive home, he envisioned Molly announcing that she and Hannah would be staying in Queens.

On July 4th, Jeremiah declined an offer by his father-in-law to play tennis. He avoided the kitchen, where Molly and Sarah prepared potato salad and desserts for a neighborhood barbeque. Molly's parents' friends always wanted to talk politics with him, and at the barbeque everyone wanted to know about the Bay of Pigs debacle: whose heads were going to roll? "Not mine," was all he said. Molly cast him a warning look—his answers were getting too curt—but he scowled and went inside to find the room where Hannah was napping. He lay down on the floor next to her, trying to nap, to no avail.

Later, he trudged behind his wife, daughter, and in-laws towards Astoria Park, where the Kellmans watched the fireworks. He was ready to leave New York; the coolness of his in-laws' apartment felt artificial, stifling; he itched to get back to his office. Work was the only thing that felt secure.

As they waited for the fireworks to begin, Molly and her parents chatted with friends on neighboring blankets. They were an educated bunch—doctors, lawyers, psychologists, professors—and normally he could hold amiable conversations with them, but now he felt tired. He rested his head on the pillow they'd brought for Hannah. Molly squeezed his hand and offered a sad smile. He wondered if the gesture signified the end of something or if she was merely trying to convey that she regretted the way things were.

He caught snippets of the conversations going on around him: a local theater struggling for funds; a brain-modifying research project going on with convicts in Boston to reduce recidivism. In a similar mind-altering project, the person said, divinity students were being given psilocybin—"magic mushrooms"—to see if they'd experience a profound religious or mystical encounter. Molly shook her head and said something under her breath that Jeremiah didn't catch.

"I've read about them," the psychologist said. "*Life* magazine had a piece, a few years back, about this banker from JP Morgan. He and his wife go all over the world collecting these magic mushrooms. Made them sound pretty enticing."

"Strange hobby," Sarah said, a thin line of distaste spreading over her face.

Molly wrapped her summer sweater tightly around her arms; she was shivering.

"Are you okay?" Jeremiah asked in a quiet voice. Sarah glanced over and frowned.

Molly nodded though her teeth were chattering and she looked like she might be ill.

When the first sparks of red, white, and blue flashes appeared in the sky, Hannah jumped into Jeremiah's arms and buried her head in his chest. The sounds were too loud for her and she started crying, "Take me home! Now!" No amount of hugging her to his chest or shushing succeeded in pacifying her, and after a few minutes he scooped her up to carry her the four long blocks back to the apartment. Molly stayed planted on the blanket, looking up at the bursts of color, saying she'd come soon.

Once inside, Jeremiah gave Hannah warm milk and read *Madeline and the Gypsies* until her eyes closed. As he shut her door, loud voices came from the entryway.

"Don't you think I know that, Mother?" He understood from Molly's tone that she was annoyed. "Don't you realize that all I've been thinking is how stupid I was?"

"It's just disgraceful, Molly," he heard his mother-in-law say. He started down the hall towards them, and Sarah thrust an accusing finger at him. "How could you let her go!"

"What are you talking about?"

"I'm talking about the fact that you let Molly go to these spiritual awakening things!"

He took a deep breath, trying to stave off his contempt. "She's a grown woman, Sarah. I might not like them myself but she can do what she pleases."

"You've let her get involved with all sorts of people. Can't you see what's going on in your own home?"

"Stop it! Stop it!" Tears streamed down Molly's face and she moved toward him. "It's not his fault! Don't blame him, Mother! He doesn't know anything about it." He pulled her into his shoulder and ran his fingers through her fine hair, glaring at his mother-in-law. After a moment, Molly led him to into the bedroom. "I need to speak with my husband in private."

"She hasn't even told him," he heard Sarah say. "My god!"

Jeremiah's stomach clutched, a mixture of anger, fear, and confusion. Whatever she was about to tell him, the fact that she was only saying it now after a fight with her parents made it worse. He squeezed his eyes shut trying to contain his indignation until he'd shut the door. "What in god's name is going on?" The words came out muffled, through gritted teeth.

She took a deep breath. "I made a mistake. A huge mistake. When I went on that retreat with Diana, and then a couple of times afterwards. . ."

Jesus, here it comes.

"They wanted me to try stuff."

"Stuff?" He felt like he hadn't taken in oxygen in several minutes. "What stuff, Molly?"

"Those special mushrooms we were talking about."

He heard her words but they made no sense.

"From their trip to Mexico. Part of some rite they do down there. You chew the mushrooms, very slowly, and then you see these amazing visions."

"And?"

"I don't know if I can really explain it. I saw spectacular colors all in harmony, designs unfolding before me, like a kaleidoscope. Then they turned into other things—a palace with verdant lawns and intricate mazes." She cut herself off. "That was the first time. It was amazing. But now," here she started to cry again, "I think that's the reason I lost the baby. I'm sure of it."

"Why didn't you tell me any of this before?"

"I was ashamed." She wept, choking on her words. "I'd eaten these mushrooms with her once before I was pregnant, and then once or twice after."

He repeated his question: Why hadn't she told him?

"Because I knew you wouldn't approve! I guess I wanted to experiment a bit without anyone judging me. They claimed I'd have a religious awakening."

"And did you?"

She shook her head, tears running down her cheeks. "It was such a stupid mistake."

"But you kept doing it. How many times? That's what I don't get!"

"Each time was. . .revelatory."

"What the hell is that supposed to mean?"

"Eye-opening. . ."

"I *know* what the word means. What exactly did these visions reveal to you?"

"Things about my life. My decisions. What I want."

Springing up over his fury, a shiver of fear. He struggled to keep his voice level. "What is it that you want, Molly?"

She shook her head, as if to cut off that line of questioning. "Nothing. I don't know. The thing is, I didn't realize it was dangerous until I lost the baby. It took *that* to happen for me to admit—these Mexican mushrooms are like a drug." She collapsed on the bed, her voice high-pitched and desperate. "I'm a mess."

"You're telling me."

"I'm so stupid!"

He didn't respond; his brain was still processing the information. His wife, Molly Gerstler, nee Kellman, nice Jewish girl, mother to his child, street smart and sensible, had displayed an astounding lapse in judgment. It defied belief. "I'm trying to make sense of it." He sat down on the bed, holding his head in his hands.

"I'm so sorry," she said, her voice muffled. "My mother wouldn't let me alone on our way home from the fireworks, and somehow it came out."

His anger came hurtling back. "For four months you've been avoiding me like the plague. I've been trying to get you to talk to me. And *your mother*? Your goddamn mother gets you to talk? Unbelievable!" He was shouting now, not caring that his in-laws could hear. He felt like she'd punched him in the stomach. "Why would you do a thing like that?"

Her face stayed buried in the pillow. "I'm so ashamed and embarrassed. That's why I didn't want to tell you."

"That's it? That's what's been going on with you—guilt?

She nodded.

"You're sure? That's it?"

Another nod.

He didn't quite believe her. That word—revelatory—gnawed at him. What was it about their situation that she found lacking, needed an escape from? Christ, he was working his *tuchus* off to provide for his family, to navigate and rise up in government, the oldest boys' network of the nation. Didn't she realize the reason he'd been passed over twice for promotions had less to do with his abilities and more to do with his last name?

"And tell your mother to back off. All weekend, she's been treating me like it's my fault you're in this state."

"I will."

The rush of emotions that washed over him, one after another, were so quick he barely had time to register one before the next arrived. Astonishment. Anger. Shock. Relief. Back to anger. The humor of his previous assumption. Back to relief she hadn't "turned." But also: dread.

"Diana can go to hell for dragging you into this," he said finally. Molly uncovered her face and peered at him. He shook his head, still stunned. "For god's sake, I hope you can see that now!"

"I know. You're right," she said softly. "I've been so stupid."

"I hope you'll stay far away from her."

"Diana doesn't think that's what caused the miscarriage. She says it could have been any one of a number of factors."

That's what the doctor said, too: *any number of factors*. But it would serve Molly right to think that it did. "No more 'Diana this' and 'Diana that,' okay? You're done with Diana. Period."

"It was my mistake. Not hers. I take full responsibility."

"What else?"

"What do you mean, what else?" she asked.

He took a deep breath and tried to keep his voice steady. "While you're in confession mode, is there anything else you haven't told me?"

"No! I swear!" Her chin began to quiver and her eyes were about to spill over again. He wanted to believe her. "Please just—"

"Shh. . ." he said. "I need time to think."

Things about my life. My decisions. Could that mean him? He wasn't ready to ask the question. Tamped it down because he didn't think he'd ever be able to voice it. He raced through possible scenarios, and other, easier questions formed in rapid bursts, like fireworks. Would she need to go for some kind of testing now? Was his reaction too strong, or too weak? How was one was supposed to react to such a thing? If he'd stifled her creativity in some way, he couldn't see how.

He paced around the room and could see her studying him, waiting quietly. The expression on her face had turned to one of fear, the same white-knuckled terror he'd seen four months ago when they'd raced to the emergency room.

"Do you think. . .do you think you can just try to view this as a mistake?"

"A colossal one. Jesus Christ, Molly, I still can't believe it." He wasn't sure how to go on from here. He kept his back to her, wandering around the room. He picked up a photo of their wedding day, Molly looking so young, himself a nervous groom. God, he'd felt so lucky that day, and most days since, wondering how on earth Molly had chosen *him*. She was six years his junior, but when they'd first met she was a sophisticated city girl, schooling him in local politics, cultural trends and so much more. For almost a decade, he'd felt indebted to her for her affection, pinching himself at times, thinking he was unworthy. And now he saw that in his gratitude, he'd placed her on such a high pedestal he'd been blind to her faults. Number one among them her ability to communicate. Hadn't he proven that she could trust him? If he knew what she wanted, he'd do his damnedest to get it for her. "You. Need. To. Talk. To. Me. Okay? I know I can run my mouth off too much, but you don't need to be the opposite. God knows both our mothers don't hesitate to tell our fathers if something is bothering them."

"I'll try."

"Damn it, Molly. You're going to have to do more than try!"

"What do you want me to say? I swear on my life, okay? Is that good enough for you?"

Another burst came from outside and he looked out the window to see more fireworks coming from the direction of the Bronx. He jimmied up the window and stuck his head outside to gulp in the fresh air. Across the river was Manhattan, where they'd first met. Their time of magic, a long, transcendent honeymoon period, was over, and they'd entered a new phase of married life, fully awake. He closed his eyes, wishing he could deny the implications. He could have sworn he understood Molly better than anyone, but then this outrageous mistake kept coming back to him. He knew nothing, nothing at all about the world. Self-doubt, rationalizations seeped in already, because not forgiving her wasn't an option. In the deep reaches of his chest, he knew his forgiveness would come before she'd forgive herself. But, he wanted to ask, which decisions were haunting her? The unanswered question would prowl in the recesses of his mind.

He drew back inside and closed the window, blinking against the harsh, suffocating light of the bedroom. Molly was sitting up now, her slender arms hugging her knees. Her eyes were swollen, fixed on him, expectant. He swore under his breath but moved next to her, instinctively protective, reaching out to pull her towards him. Her head rested on his shoulder and felt oppressive in the summer heat.

MIXMASTER

(2009)

Jeremiah kept thinking the wet tea bag in his peripheral vision was a glazed donut hole, and each time he looked up and saw it wasn't, he felt a wave of disappointment. The gnawing for something sweet tugged at his stomach. He shifted his weight to his better leg, eased himself out of the desk chair, and made his way to the kitchen. He opened the cupboards and closed them, opened the refrigerator and shut it, and then the freezer. He knew exactly what was in each one, but he played the opening and closing game hoping there was some hidden-away treat he'd failed to see the first time. There were a thousand ways he missed Molly, but it was the lack of home-cooked food that upset him late at night, made him feel off-kilter. Sure, he was managing—at least that's what he told his daughter. He could now make himself eggs and pasta, and he kept a supply of deli meat in the fridge for sandwiches, but it wasn't the same. For a time, Clara Bernstein or Maude Freed or one of Molly's other widowed friends would stop by with a casserole or pie, but that had ended. And though he'd grumbled to Hannah that the ladies were far inferior to her mother in the cooking department, he missed those dishes now.

It was too late to call Hannah. Even if she was awake, she was not about to drive thirty minutes at this time of night to bring him donuts or cookies to satisfy his sweet tooth. Jeremiah wondered if the local Dunkin Donuts delivered, or if they would make an exception for a long-time customer who could no longer drive at night. He hung up after two rings, realizing it was a foolhardy idea. He tried phoning Stu out in LA to say hello, but a babysitter answered and informed him that his son and daughter-in-law were out.

He made himself a cup of tea and added an extra spoonful of sugar, but this was a poor substitute for baked goods. There was a dull ache at his core, a low-burning resentment against Molly for deserting him. For not foreseeing the massive heart attack ahead of time. There had never been any doubt in either of their minds, with his litany of recent health problems, and him six years her senior, that she would survive him. It had been over a year, and he was still surprised to come home and not find her in the kitchen, whipping up a batch of peanut butter chocolate chip cookies or rugelach. Arriving home from a long day at the university, he used to put his arms around her from behind and kiss the nape of her neck. "Mmmm, mmmm, delicious," he would say, meaning both her and whatever had just come out of the oven. She would giggle and slap away his hand when he reached for a third or fourth cookie. He missed her easy laugh, and how she would brush away the crumbs from his beard.

Thank goodness he still had his research, even though the teaching component had long ago been given over to younger and more energetic professors. At eighty-two, Jeremiah didn't plan to ever face the dreaded "R" word, and bristled to hear Hannah say he was semi-retired. He tried to push Molly out of his mind, ignore his craving for sweets, and focus on editing the article in front of him. Debt relief was not his field per se, but he had agreed to review the paper for the department's comparative politics journal. Gone were the days that he could stay up working until one or two in the morning, and just before midnight, he shuffled into bed, exhausted.

Jeremiah awoke to the sound of a vacuum cleaner. Every Tuesday he managed to forget the cleaning lady was coming. What had he been working on last night? Something he thought his daughter might find of interest. He tried to steer conversations with his children away from the state of his own health, or how he was "managing." He thought, all things considered, that he was doing well: swimming three days a week, still driving during the day, and shopping for himself. It frustrated him whenever Hannah brought up the idea of getting full-time help, someone to cook and clean and be around in case his angina flared up.

"Do you know what I had a craving for last night?" he said into the phone. "Remember those chocolate peanut butter bonbons mother used to make? Did she ever teach you how to make them?"

Hannah let out a sigh. He knew the answer without even asking, but he did it anyway as a means to talk about Molly. "No, I don't think so, Dad. I'll bring you some brownies this weekend. Okay?"

Brownies and more brownies. Was that all she knew how to make? His poor son-in-law. "All right. I'll take what I can get."

"How about a, 'Thanks Hannah'? God, you're impossible sometimes!"

"Okay, okay. Don't get all huffy on me. You know I love your brownies. And I appreciate you making them for me." He rolled his eyes but turned penitent. Easier to talk about work. "How's the nation building research going?" What a joy it had been, what a surge of pride he had felt, all those years ago when Hannah followed in his footsteps and completed her doctorate in political science. Now his grandchildren were in college, which made him feel ancient.

Both Ben and Pam were coming home for the weekend, Hannah said, so Jeremiah could expect all four of them for a visit on Saturday.

"Sounds grand," he said, then paused. "Are you bringing the mutt, too?"

"Cody's a purebred black lab. As you know. Do you have a problem with him?"

"No, no," he protested. "I was just wondering. Last time he dug up your mother's flower beds."

"That was four years ago, Dad."

"Oh. Right." They'd had the conversation a dozen times, and he knew it.

She asked again if he needed anything else, and he insisted he was fine. Perfectly self-sufficient. When *she* got to be *his* age, he hoped she'd be swimming daily at the JCC.

On Saturday, he spied the blue Honda pulling into the driveway and peered out through his office window to see who would emerge. Four people, no dog. Hannah was carrying the brownies and a few bags of groceries she had picked up for him. She was a dedicated daughter, no doubt about that, coming to see him at least once a week, despite her teaching load, research, and community involvements. At fifty-one, she looked more and more like Molly every time he saw her. Her hair was graying, closely-cropped, and today she wore khaki three-quarter length pants and comfortable walking shoes, just as Molly had. Tom lifted a wrapped package out of the trunk and Pam was holding what looked to be a Barnes & Noble bag. Books. Excellent! Perhaps Hannah had picked up the new Rynhold book on the Marshall Plan, or the Kissinger biography that had just come out.

Jeremiah opened the door for them and accepted the kiss from Hannah and hugs from his grandchildren. "What's all this?"

"You'll see," they replied. They dumped the bags in the kitchen and Hannah started unpacking. Jeremiah put on the kettle and started fussing with some apple cake he'd bought at the supermarket, but Hannah shooed him away to the living room. He sat down next to Ben on the faded sofa and started quizzing him on his classes, and then made a few jibes to Tom about how the Yankees had really stuck it to the Sox last night. The visit was his favorite time of the week.

Hannah emerged from the kitchen carrying the big wrapped box and the bag of books. "We had a little idea for you. Actually, it was Stuart's idea."

His children were conspiring against him. He groaned. "Another hobby you want me to try?"

"Consider it an early birthday present," his granddaughter said.

"Something more practical than a hobby," Hannah added. He noted something resembling mirth on all of their faces. A joke. He tore open the wrapping paper and was stunned to see a picture of a shiny white mixer, with a bowl and accessories on the box.

"Are you kidding me?"

Tom was trying not to laugh. "Oh, Jeremiah. I wish you could see the look on your face right now."

"Very funny."

"Seriously, Dad. We all know what a sweet tooth you have, and how you miss Mom's baking."

"And how," Ben chirped in, "you didn't really like those other ladies' cakes and stuff."

"So," Hannah continued, "here you go, Mr. 'Please-make-me-bonbons.' Now you can bake to your heart's content." She produced two cookbooks from the bag: *100 Sweet Treats in Less than 30 Minutes* and *Dreamy, Creamy Desserts for the Serious Sweet Tooth*.

"I don't know how to bake!" he exclaimed. "That was Molly's department."

"Come on, Grandpa," Pam said. "If you're smart enough to write about world politics, I think you can manage following a recipe."

"I don't have the touch. This is nuts."

"Have you ever tried?" She wouldn't back down, Pam. Just like her mother. He opened *Dreamy, Creamy* and studied the pages. He had to admit, the pictures were enough to make him want to run out and buy some basic ingredients. They had thought of that, apparently. Hannah led him into the kitchen and showed him where she had unpacked the eggs, butter, sugar, baking soda, baking powder, vanilla extract, and cocoa.

"Hmmph," was all he could say. He didn't know what to make of this, and wished, for the thousandth time, that Molly was there to explain it all.

The toffee fingers were a disaster. He should have started with something simpler, he realized. And then the chocolate mousse would not gel, no matter what he did. But he had moderate success with the oatmeal raisin cookies. They were chewy and soft, except for the batch he left in the oven a few minutes too long. When he spoke with Hannah on the phone, she would ask how the baking was going, but he still didn't want to give her the satisfaction of knowing that he was trying. He didn't put it past her to snoop around in his kitchen, so each time he used the mix-master, he was careful to clean it and put each part back in its plastic wrapper, and then back in the box. If he ever got it right, he thought, he would surprise them. Perhaps bake a cake for Pam's college graduation. The whole thing was preposterous—at his age, puttering around in the kitchen! His mother, Molly and all the women who had ever baked for him must be looking down and having a good laugh.

The idea to take the class came one day after his swim. He was planning on returning home to work on an article on the politics of immigration, but the smell of cinnamon buns beckoned from down the hall. Jeremiah knew the JCC offered classes for retirees, but never considering himself in that category, he hadn't looked into them. Peeking in, he saw five men and three women, all in their seventies and eighties, whipping up cream to go on top of the buns. He was surprised to see Maude Freed, one of the widows who had brought him food right after Molly died.

"Why, hello there, Jeremiah! Come in," she beckoned, and he had no choice but to enter the room. She introduced him to the instructor and the other members of the class. As he sank his teeth into a mouth-watering bun with just the right amount butter, cinnamon, and cream, Maude babbled on and on about the desserts they had made and how much fun they were having in the class. She put her mouth up close to his ear, and he could smell the cinnamon on her breath. "I'll tell you a secret. Before this class, I used to bake from mixes. I couldn't be bothered with all that patchkerying. Oh, I'm sure Molly never needed a class—she was a wonderful cook—but it never came easily to me. And now? I'm whipping up cakes and cookies like no tomorrow!"

She urged him to come to the next class—they would be attempting to make chocolate decadence—and he promised to think about it, as long as she swore she wouldn't mention it to his daughter. He had no idea what chocolate decadence was, but it sounded inspiring.

◆ ◆ ◆

It became part of his regular routine: on Mondays and Wednesdays, after his swim, he stayed for the baking class. And he kept practicing at home. He talked to Molly as he tinkered with the recipes. "I'm sure you're having a good laugh right now," he told her after the cookie batter splattered all over the kitchen wall. Or "What the heck is a pizzelle iron? Can you explain that to me, please?" She never answered, but he felt closer to her, working in her domain. Plus, now he had treats readily available to nosh on while doing his real work. He tried not to worry that he was keeping his belt on a looser notch, and told himself his doctor would be pleased with the weight gain.

For Pam's graduation party he decided he would make a double chocolate cake. It had been blistering hot at the graduation itself, and if Ben hadn't been there for him to lean on, he might have fainted. He was intensely proud of his granddaughter and her accomplishments, though he wondered out loud how the family, firmly grounded on both sides in the liberal arts, had managed to produce in Pam a pre-med student.

"Well, you know Mom thought about becoming a nurse at one point," Hannah said. No, he replied, he didn't recall that.

The party was a few days after the graduation. With the cake in the oven and the frosting chilling, he went downstairs to the second pantry to look for the cake platter he knew Molly had somewhere. He hadn't poked around in this pantry since her death. In fact, he didn't remember opening it much when she was alive. Wouldn't Hannah and Pam be surprised when he showed up with this cake!

He scanned the shelves but had to bring over a chair to sit on while he took the old cookware out. The light was dim, but he noticed a row of red boxes on the bottom shelf. Most of the pantry contained old baking tins, a double boiler, cookie sheets, and the like. Molly never got rid of anything. But the red boxes? Never seen them before. He pulled one out, blew off the dust, and was shocked to see a baking mix for peanut butter chocolate chip cookies. He didn't get it. He had seen Molly make things from scratch and assumed that was how she always baked. He pulled out the other boxes: more mixes. Banana bread. Brownies. Angel food cake. All of his favorite things. Jeremiah felt deflated, and sat on the chair trying to catch his breath. The air was dusty and his chest heaved. He wondered if Hannah knew, or if all of the other ladies knew. He didn't know if he should laugh or cry.

"What the hell are these, Molly?" he shouted to no one. "Is this a joke?" No, he couldn't ask her. He'd never be able to ask her, or know what other secrets she'd kept from him.

Questions swirled in his mind, but the timer went off on the oven, shaking him out of his daze. He extended his good leg first and got up from the chair to go take the cake out. He had half a mind to bring it to the party and feed it to the dog, but decided that would be a waste. He iced both layers and decorated the top. The chocolate cream frosting feathered in just the right places. It was a home run of a cake, one for a bakery window. He sat down to admire his work, and then thought: the heck with it. He'd show off his baking skills at a later date, once he'd sorted through this new piece of information about Molly, his muddled feelings. In the meantime, he cut himself a hefty slice and savored its velvety texture.

Readers' Group Guide to *The Book of Jeremiah*

1. Do you like Jeremiah as a person? With which of his traits do you identify, and conversely, which traits do you dislike?

2. How does Molly function as a foil to her husband? How does the marriage grow or shift over the course of their lives? Does the relationship remind you of any couples you know?

3. Which decisions or actions of Jeremiah as a husband, father, and professional can be traced to his earlier life experiences? What role do Rikki, Abe, and Lenny play in shaping Jeremiah's personality?

4. Discuss Jeremiah's approach to his children. How similar or different does he seem to his own mother and father?

5. How does Jeremiah change over the course of the book? Why do you think the author decided to structure the novel in a non-linear fashion?

6. Which cultural, political, religious, or ethnic forces shape the characters' lives? Do you know people who are similar to Jeremiah, Molly and their families? Do you identify with any of the characters?

7. Is Jeremiah satisfied with his choice of career? Why/why not? What does Jeremiah seek, and how do his desires change as he gets older?

8. Jeremiah deeply loves his wife yet does not always act in ways that are considerate of her. How do you reconcile his behavior and actions?

9. Discuss the themes of guilt and grief. Do you see parallels between any of the characters in the ways they handle traumas, crises, or mistakes?

10. How does Jeremiah's view of his brother change over the course of the book? What effect does Lenny's death have on Jeremiah?

11. What do you make of Jeremiah's public behavior versus his private behavior? Between Molly, Hannah and Stuart, who is most effective at handling him?

12. Hannah vacillates between thinking of her mother as having tremendous inner strength and someone who is inherently weak. Can a person be both at the same time? What do you think of Molly?

13. What role does Judaism play in Jeremiah and Molly's lives? How is their relationship to religion and culture similar/different to yours?

14. At the end of Signals, Jeremiah wonders, "Could you ever really know another person?" Where else does this theme play itself out in the book? Do any of the characters get closure to this question?

A note from the author

I am indebted to dozens of people for their support of my writing over the last decade.

My journey to publishing this volume began over eight years ago when I wrote about a crotchety widower named Jeremiah who found a way to deal with his grief by adopting one of his wife's hobbies. From "MixMaster," the final story in this book, I worked backwards (and, at times, forwards) to unravel Jeremiah's life.

Many teachers, workshops, and writing groups helped shape the characters and chapters in this volume. Evan Fallenberg is a wonderful teacher and mentor, and his early words of support and continued encouragement of my writing spurred me forward. Ellen Lesser at Vermont College of Fine Arts was instrumental in strategizing about the structure of the book and made vital suggestions to "A Strong Hand and an Outstretched Arm." Long before I began writing fiction, Bruce Lippman taught me valuable lessons on revision. My classmates at VCFA, Catapult Story, and Gotham Writers Workshop made numerous suggestions. Much love and gratitude to those in my local and virtual writing groups, including Rachel Karlin, Susan Cohen, Jennifer Lang, Ondine Sherman, Caroline Saul, Susan Becker, Jennifer Kircher Carr, Jan Elman Stout, Stacy Burns, Lisa Ferranti, Jolene McIlwain, Andrea Eberly, Donna Robertson Aderhold, Georgiana Nelson, Elizabeth Pettie, Buki Papillon, Claire Polders, Jacqueline Doyle, Lynn Mundell, Dorothy Rice, Judy Colp Rubin, Natalie Shell, Helen Schary Motro, and Michal O'Dwyer. Many thanks to Lisa Srisuro for her sharp edits in the final round.

I am grateful to the editors and readers who picked my stories out of the slush pile and gave many of these chapters their initial homes. Massive thanks to Kevin Morgan Watson for believing in these stories, sharing his generous wisdom, and bringing me into the Press 53 family.

Caitlin Hamilton Summie's publicity efforts have helped this book find its way into the hands of readers, and her calm, assuring demeanor was much appreciated.

Amy Ariel, Suzanne Kling, and Lisa Brezel were early supporters of Jeremiah, and Jonathan Rynhold added insights into Jeremiah's professional world.

Various bits of family lore made it into many of these stories, and I am grateful to the keepers of my family history, including my parents, Deborah Cohen Zuckerman and Wallace Zuckerman; my uncle, Joseph Zuckerman; and cousins Jerome Konsker, Wendy Glantz Swain and Carole Glantz Jaffe. My parents instilled in me an early love of reading, and I am fortunate to be their daughter (for this, and hundreds of other reasons). To my sisters, Rebecca and Aliza, my in-laws, Linda and Ed, and the entire Zuckerman and Kulp families: thank you for being stalwart supporters.

Finally, my deepest love and gratitude for the people who enrich my life every day: to Yadin, Zohar, Anan and Rakia, for making me proud, and to Josh, for your unwavering faith, honesty, support and love. I am very blessed.

Julie Zuckerman's fiction and nonfiction have appeared in a variety of publications, including *The SFWP Quarterly, The MacGuffin, Salt Hill, Sixfold, The Coil, Ellipsis, Crab Orchard Review* and others. A native of Connecticut, she now lives in Modiin, Israel, with her husband and four children. *The Book of Jeremiah* was runner-up for the 2018 Press 53 Award for Short Fiction and is her debut story collection.